Fitzwilliam Darcy

...in his own words

_____

SHANNON WINSLOW

~~*~~

Mr. Darcy soon drew the attention of the room by his fine, tall person, handsome features, noble mien, and the report which was in general circulation within five minutes after his entrance, of his having ten thousand a year.

The gentlemen pronounced him to be a fine figure of a man, the ladies declared he was much handsomer than Mr. Bingley, and he was looked at with great admiration for about half the evening, till his manners gave a disgust which turned the tide of his popularity;

for he was discovered to be proud; to be above his company and above being pleased; and not all his large estate in Derbyshire could then save him from having a most forbidding, disagreeable countenance, and being unworthy to be compared with his friend.

~~*~~

Pride and Prejudice

Prologue

I still occasionally suffer that recurrent dream – a nightmare, really. I awake at Darcy House in London. Morning light is filtering through the diaphanous draperies at the windows, painting ghostly shadow patterns across the opposite wall. I feel a great sense of wellbeing at the start of a new day. All is right with the world, or at least my portion of it.

Then I turn toward the other side of the bed and see… not Elizabeth, as I expect, but the Honorable Miss Amelia Lambright. Only of course she is no longer an honorable miss, not when she has spent the night in a man's bed. Then I suddenly remember why she is there. Her name is Miss Lambright no more; she is Mrs. Darcy now. My heart lurches and I break into a cold sweat, not because the former Miss Lambright is so horridly unappealing, but because she is not Elizabeth.

I tell myself it surely must be a hallucination or some trick of the light. So I shake my head to clear any cobwebs, rub my eyes, and blink. Still, the wrong woman is before me. *Please, God, let it be a dream!*

I fight to awaken, to claw my way back to the world where I belong, the world where Mrs. Darcy has not blonde but dark, satiny hair and sparkling eyes. My throat constricts; I cannot breathe. I cannot find my voice to call out. *Elizabeth, where are you?* I must find her! My life depends on it.

When on these disturbing occasions I at last come to myself, it is many minutes before my heart and breathing return to normal, and longer still until my mind can quiet itself. Even after I have verified that Elizabeth is indeed beside me where she belongs;

beheld her face, a peaceful portrait of repose in whatever meager light offers; pulled her warm, familiar form to fit close against mine; and heard her sleepy but unmistakable voice murmuring my name with affection…

Even then my soul quakes within me for how close the vision from which I have just awakened came to being true, how close I came to missing Elizabeth altogether. Then she and I would have been only two ships sailing the same stretch of sea, perhaps even passing within sight of each other occasionally but never happening to come into a common port together, at least not until it had been too late.

My happier outcome depended on the slimmest thread of unlikely circumstances being precariously strung together without error. At any one of a dozen junctures, the course of my life could have carried me in a completely different direction.

When I consider this, I shudder. Then I thank God for His providential care in guiding me safely through. I thank Bingley for Netherfield. And Wickham. Strangely enough, now, years later, I can think back with some philosophy, enough to acknowledge the part he unwittingly played. Were it not for Wickham and his nefarious but timely interventions, I would likely be married to Amelia Lambright today.

1
Expectations

I meant to do as my father directed. I meant to select a wife with an eye to duty and the honor of my family name, as he had raised me to do. By this reckoning, Miss Lambright was the perfect choice. Well, to be brutally honest, my cousin Anne de Bourgh would have been equally ideal, but that is a topic for another time.

"Choose wisely," my father told me a few months before he died.

It was not the first time he counselled me on the subject of selecting a wife, but as it turned out, it was the last. We had been making a tour of the estate together on horseback, as we so often did when I was at home, and we paused at a favorite prominence, a rocky outcrop which overlooked the house, the grounds, and the lake. Vast tracts of productive Pemberley farm and timber land lay beyond, nearly as far as the eye could see. Then in the distance, the quarry, from which another portion of the estate's income derived.

"As heir to all this," Father said, motioning to the expanse of open country before us, "you have a responsibility to please more than yourself when you marry. Pemberley is a living, breathing thing, with scores of souls dependent on its continuing to prosper. Every one of them – tenants, servants, laborers, villagers – takes a degree of pride in belonging to Pemberley and to the Darcy family. In some measure, your success and prestige are also theirs. Of course, by the same token, your failure and disgrace are theirs as well. You have a duty, therefore, to all these dependents, same as to all the family – that goes without saying, I trust – to marry very well."

"Of course, Father," I answered. "I perfectly understand."

"Good. I knew I could depend on you, Son. Follow my example, and do not sell yourself cheaply."

"Cheaply?" I inquired.

"Yes, you have much to offer. Although you have no title of your own – I wish I could have done that for you – still, you are the grandson of an earl, thanks to my marrying your mother. It is something to be proud of and that no one can take from you. Do the same for *your* children, if you can. Nobility often marries wealth, you know. Find yourself the daughter of an impoverished viscount or earl, and then make a good bargain for her. A woman like that will be grateful to be made mistress of Pemberley. And what's more, she will know what to do with the opportunity."

"Yes, I do understand what you mean, Father, but I had always hoped for somewhat more than a favorable business arrangement. I had hoped to find, not romantic love – I am not so fanciful as to expect that – but agreeable companionship, a woman who is not only capable and well-bred, but one I can hold in some little affection or at least regard."

"Naturally, naturally." He coughed before continuing. "Affection is desirable and will come in time. Well… it does in most cases, that is. But in the long course, it is of little matter. Affection, you can always find elsewhere, if necessary. In a wife, respect is the key thing, or regard as you have put it. Ask yourself, 'Is this a person I can be proud to present to others of rank as my partner in life? Will she be able to give my children every advantage in society?'"

I scoffed, boasting, "I care little enough for society!"

"Very well, Son. Very well. Be as independent as you choose. Just remember, though, to snub society entirely is to cut off your own nose to spite your face. You never know when you might need those connections to secure some important benefit to yourself or someone you care about. Only a fool would throw away such an advantage when the smallest exertion will keep you on good terms with everybody."

With a nudge of his boot, he set his horse into motion once again. I kept pace with him at a walk.

"Now, as I was saying," my father continued, "will your prospective wife add to the dignity of the Darcy name and manage Pemberley House with competence, stateliness, and refinement? In other words, will she carry on in your mother's footsteps, as she would have wished it? Perhaps these considerations are more to your taste."

It was true. I had little intention of marrying to please society. But for Pemberley and to honor my mother's memory… that was a different matter entirely.

"Perhaps you would even think of Miss Lambright," my father suggested. "Now, there is a young lady who would do you proud."

"But she is a child!"

"She is a bit young at present, I grant you, but all she wants is a few more years. And you are already somewhat acquainted. Excellent noble family. Just the kind of connection I have been recommending."

"Yes, Father, however…" Then he went on before I could finish.

"Oh, affection is all very well, but it will not make up for the rest. How long do you suppose your regard will survive if you are perpetually embarrassed by your wife, because she is forever mismanaging the servants or insulting your friends through her lack of understanding? Then when all esteem is at an end, you will be left with nothing but regrets and no way to remedy the situation. I have seen it happen. Believe me, an inappropriate wife will be a millstone about your neck for the rest of your life."

That made a charming picture: the deadweight of a burdensome female tightly bound about my neck and shoulders to where I could neither move nor breathe. And I was left to ponder it for several minutes.

We had come upon a section of the trail, both narrow and steep, where no further conversation was possible. Rocks jutted out on one side, and on the other, a good view of the abyss into which one might plunge with a single missed step. Much care was needed by man and beast to navigate it safely on horseback, to avoid disaster.

Was it a deliberate analogy for the point my father had been attempting to make? – the importance of staying on the straight and narrow? To choose the wrong path, to be careless of the way, to neglect minding every step, was to invite calamity of a kind most painful and permanent.

When the landscape broadened to allow riding two abreast again, my instruction continued.

"No, my boy, do not be taken in by a pretty face, a fine figure, and pleasing conversation. It is likely that many unworthy females – or their scheming mamas – will make your fortune their object, and they will use all their cunning arts to entrap you. Such a girl will draw you in with her smiles and make you fancy yourself in love… or at least in lust. You must be on your guard against that sort of thing, lest your baser desires betray you into making a very foolish match. The wise man chooses with his head instead of his…" He waved his hand dismissively. "Well, that is enough said on the subject, I trust. I did not raise a simpleton, and I know you are old enough now that you can apprehend the danger."

I have often wondered what my father would have said if he knew the choice I made in the end. Perhaps he would have been disappointed in me, at least at first. I like to think Elizabeth would have soon won him over and procured my full pardon. No man could object to her for long, surely.

But until I myself fell under her spell, I had every intention of abiding by paternal advice. I meant to choose a wife with all the qualities my father described for all the reasons he outlined. I had great respect for the man, and so his words were very persuasive. And yet I had an even more convincing teacher to warn me against the dangers of allowing the unreliable heart to lead: experience.

2
Early Instruction

My early years had taught me, again and again, that to love was to suffer pain. To love was to surrender a part of oneself, to give the object of that love power over one's life – power to wound or to destroy, either by accident or with intent.

As a boy, I watched my mother endure a series of failed lying-ins. With the anticipation of each one, she would smile cheerfully and make plans, hopeful of a better outcome than what had usually transpired before. She would allow herself to fall in love with the babe within, only to have her hopes dashed and the agony of loss repeated when the infant was either lifeless at birth or failed to long survive afterward.

Each dead child carried away another measure of my mother's youth and vigor to the grave. With each one was buried another piece of her heart. Months might go by, and she would recuperate tolerably well, only to begin the cycle once more. By the time Georgiana was born, I believe my mother was afraid to risk her heart again, afraid to give my sister the generous measure of affection she deserved, afraid this latest child would not tarry long on this earth either.

Naturally, I was shielded as well as possible from the harshest aspects of these events, especially when I was younger. But I was a serious boy, quiet and observant, and I would wager that less escaped my notice than anybody supposed.

Doubtless my father grieved these losses as well, but in a vastly different style. With his wife – whom I believe he did truly love, after a fashion – spent and unable to spare any comfort for him, he sought comfort and diversion elsewhere, only adding to my mother's pain. Thus, he was from home when my mother finally succumbed after being brought to bed of another dead child.

I was allowed by her attendants to see her for a few minutes, just before she slipped away. I recall the moment with preternatural clarity.

The room was hushed and dim, like a church in a state of disuse. Only instead of an altar at the center, a bed, and laid out on it was my mother. I still remember how abnormally white her face appeared. Already drained of all but the last ounce of blood, her skin had more the look of cold porcelain than living flesh.

A fresh counterpane had been carefully draped over her and drawn up just below her chin, as if she were a child tucked up and ready for a good night's sleep. But it was morning, and, as I considered much later, no doubt the true purpose of the added covering was to conceal from me the carnage from the recent struggle for life, now given up as lost.

She knew she was dying, and so did I.

She told me she loved me and that she was sorry to leave me. Then she said, "Look after your sister, William, and do not judge your father too severely. Even the strongest of men may have feet of clay." After this, and after one lingering last look, she closed her eyes, never to open them again. Georgiana was only six years of age at the time and I, seventeen.

According to my mother's dying wish, I did not blame my father, at least not as harshly as he blamed himself. In all other respects he had been a dutiful husband and father. But now it was his turn to suffer cruelly, both in heart and conscience, which he did for long duration. In truth, I am not convinced he ever fully recovered.

Every time death and loss visited Pemberley, I took the pain, held it inside, and learnt from it. My repeated lessons taught me to protect my heart, the last lesson coming when my father himself left us several years later.

Georgiana and I had been visiting our relations in Kent when I received the urgent summons home. It was worded in such a way as to leave no doubt as to the expected outcome of my father's sudden illness. The only question was whether or not it would all be over before we arrived.

We were in time, thank God. Father was very weak but still alive, we were told, and so we went directly to his bed chamber. Although I thought I had mentally prepared myself for the expected change in him, it still came as a shock. The vigorous man who had always taken me in hand, who had managed all Pemberley with such confidence – he was gone, replaced by a ghost of his former self, one so feeble he could no longer lift his head from the pillow, let alone impose his will over a small empire as before.

He called Georgiana, who was then twelve, to his side first, receiving her parting kiss, praising her character, and remanding her to my care. Then it was my turn. My heart quaking within me, I went to him. Kneeling beside the bed, I took my father's blue-veined hand, enclosing it within both of my own. It was a gesture of affection, certainly, but also one of weakness, for I could not bear to look at the thing – newly withered, shaking, feeble, and impotent.

"I am glad you have come in time, Son," he said in a half-whisper. "It is a heavy mantle I must now pass on to you, but one I am confident you are able to bear."

I was far less convinced of this. "Father, I am grieved, grieved and… and afraid," I confessed, my voice faltering.

"You mustn't fear for me or for yourself either," he said. "I am going to join your mother at last. And you… you are ready to come out from behind my shadow. I have taught you all that I know, so you are fully equipped to assume your place as master of Pemberley. Take as much care superintending it as I know you will with your sister."

These were some of my father's final words, and they hearkened back to our many earlier conversations.

When it was over, I remained at my father's bedside. How long, I do not know, but inside me a battle raged between fear and the claims of duty as I tried to come to terms with what had happened. Grief at my father's death gathered thick and bitter in my mouth, but it was not only that. Selfishly, I mourned for my own situation as well. I knew nothing would ever be the same for me again. At three-and-twenty, I was suddenly and unexpectedly charged with the care and keeping of a younger sister and of all Pemberley estates. As my father had said, it was a heavy mantle to bear, and a desperate part of me wanted to run from so much responsibility.

I could not, of course. Georgiana and so many others depended on me to do what was right. *My father* depended on me. It was the thing I had been trained up for – to carry on in his footsteps – and yet it had come far too soon.

For a time I mourned the loss of my father. I mourned the loss of my youth and of my freedom. Then I did my best to harden my heart and get on with the job before me.

To do all that was expected of me, I must be strong, I told myself. I could no longer afford the luxury of any weakness, sentiment, or the risk of further injury to heart or mind. So I erected a kind of mental fortress from which I could safely preside over my new life of duty, where I could not be touched by such suffering, grief, or loss again. And yes, that meant I could not afford the luxury of love either, Georgiana being the one exception. It was too late to guard my heart against her. I would not have chosen to do so in any case. Now, with both her parents gone, she needed the security of my unconditional affection more than ever, and I could not turn my back on her. Still, although my deep and genuine fondness for my sister was a source of great joy, it did make me vulnerable and would inevitably lead to more suffering in the years to come – one more proof of the wisdom of my resolve against falling victim to love in the future.

Of course I meant to marry eventually. A man must have a wife to answer his needs and for the purpose of procreation; that is the established order of things. Moreover, in addition to my other duties, it was my responsibility to raise up an heir for Pemberley and for the Darcy name.

I did not mean to surrender my heart to my wife, however. In the interest of self-preservation and out of respect for my father's wishes, I meant to choose a wife with my head. She would be some entirely appropriate young lady of impeccable character and breeding, perhaps even titled. She would be a woman who was my social equal or better, familiar with and comfortable in my sphere. So long as she had a congenial temperament, some reasonably intelligent conversation, and was not unpleasant to look at, I meant to be satisfied. I would ask for nothing more, especially not for love, but I would accept no less either.

These were my sanguine expectations – natural and just, as I had been taught to believe – and with Miss Amelia Lambright, now grown up, I was well on my way to meeting them.

3
Young Wickham

I am getting ahead of myself, however. No recitation of the difficult lessons of my early life would be complete without some mention of George Wickham. Although his was a very different case from the deaths of my parents, it was likewise instructive.

As I have said, to love is to give the object of that affection power to wound or destroy by accident or malice. And as a young boy, I did love George with that extravagantly loyal attachment children often feel for their closest playfellow. My Fitzwilliam cousins and I may have had the tie of blood to bind us together, but George Wickham had the advantage of proximity; he was ever present during my childhood.

As the son of my father's steward – a very respectable and honorable man – George Wickham grew up at Pemberley. Because of the disparity of our respective stations, however, we two, though of an age, might have rarely met. In most cases, the son and heir of a great estate will have little to do with the son of a man in its employ. It is still a matter of some amazement to me that my father allowed it to be otherwise, as attentive to the demands of rank as he was in most respects.

Perhaps it bespeaks a natural compassion for me on his part, procuring me a playmate where none other was available – no brothers, no appropriate near neighbors. However, I do not doubt that my father was most influenced by his sincere regard for his steward and for young George himself, whose highly engaging manners, I believe, so recommended him as to allay any anxiety that might otherwise have been excited by such an unequal friendship.

In any case, George Wickham was allowed, even encouraged, by my father to move freely about the estate, including in and out of Pemberley House and of my company.

Although our temperaments were very different from the start, it was a friendship that seemed to operate to our mutual benefit. It exposed George Wickham to society and education far better than what would otherwise have been within his reach, which must be considered a prime advantage for any ambitious young man. As for my part, with an enterprising friend close at hand to go adventuring with, I was more often drawn from my quiet, cerebral habits to livelier activity out of doors.

There were the usual boyhood entertainments, of course: riding, swimming, tree climbing, fishing, and endless explorations. But my friend never lacked schemes for more daring amusements, not all of them harmless. So occasionally I did have to refuse him, and then I might expect to take some abuse.

"Are you afraid?" I remember him asking in a taunting manner when I had denied his proposal of investigating an abandoned quarry on the estate. We must both have been eleven or twelve at the time.

"It is dangerous," I explained. "There are treacherous pits one can fall into and loose boulders that may come crashing down at any time."

"*I* am not afraid."

"It is not brave but foolish to do such things. Besides, my father has forbidden it."

"Oh, yes, of course, and you *always* do what the old pater says, don't you?"

"Generally, I do. What of it?"

George laughed. "It is just as I said."

"Laugh if you choose, but I am not ashamed of obeying my father. He is a great man. And you should speak of him with more respect, for he has been a tremendous friend and benefactor to you!"

"I am always careful to speak *to* him with the utmost respect; that is nearly the same thing. But it does not mean he is always right. The difference between you and me, Will, is that *I* choose to think for myself. I do not mean to let somebody else, even your high and mighty old man, spoil my fun. Now, are you coming with me or not?"

"No, and perhaps I will tell my father if you go."

"You will not, because I have a thing or two I can tell him about you too, you will recall. You are not really as perfect a son as you would have him believe."

Wickham was right, of course. He had been a party to – and often the instigator of – whatever acts of disobedience or indiscretion I had committed. He knew it all. And I knew, even then, that he was perfectly capable of betraying me. Such knowledge should rightly have made me cast Wickham off as an unfit companion. But it did not. I suppose I thought that if I proved my friendship, if I demonstrated dogged loyalty, I would inspire the same in him in return.

So another time I bore punishment and my father's disappointment, alone and in silence, when I was blamed in Wickham's place for one of his schemes gone wrong. The sacrifice was in vain, however. Wickham never thanked me for it. Indeed, as I found out later, it had been he himself who pointed the finger at me whilst swearing to his own innocence.

In any case, I went to the quarry with him that day. I did not enter it myself, but since I could not prevent my friend from tempting fate, I wished to be on hand to go for help should he get into any real trouble. But he seemed to live a charmed existence then, rarely suffering for his misdeeds. He dashed across hazardous ground without a care. He jumped jagged fissures and balanced on a knife edge between safety and disaster, coming away unscathed and more sure of himself than before. I was never to hear the end of it, of course – how he knew better than I and my father, how he had gone where I had not dared to go.

A part of me resented him for such perilous escapades, especially for the false position he often forced me into by them.

18

Yet another part of me admired him. My attachment of friendship persisted, and I was unwilling to give up his company. Such are the strange propensities of youth.

I was not completely unaware of the miscreant aspect of his character, and over time, the mounting evidence of it began to sway my opinion. It was not until we were away at Cambridge together, however, that my eyes were finally and irrefutably opened. Out from under my father's watchfulness, Wickham's natural inclinations no longer felt any restraint. Instead, they flourished, his profligacy redoubling. The extent and description of his bad behavior I should be ashamed to repeat. Suffice to say that it soon became clear that there could no longer be any true fellowship between Wickham and myself. It taught me that we were too different, the disparities between us growing wider by the day. So I at last abandoned our friendship and any hope of my influence working for his remediation.

My father, Wickham's steady benefactor, remained in ignorance of the vicious character of his godson and protégé to the end. Perhaps if I had been aware that he intended to provide for his favorite with a church living, I should have undeceived him. I discovered this recommendation in his will instead. Fortunately, Wickham preferred taking the money I offered to the taking of holy orders. The business was soon settled, and I hoped never to see my errant childhood companion again.

For three years, we heard little of him. Then one day, I received this letter. Recognizing the handwriting on the direction, I was immediately wary:

Dear old Friend,

I trust you are in good health, and Georgiana too. I often remember you both and think of my happy years at Pemberley. What glorious times we had together there as boys, you and I! A day rarely passes without one of our mad adventures coming to mind, and then I laugh heartily. Do you recall, Will?

Sadly, I have had little other occasion for laughter in recent months as my luck has run from bad to worse. I found the law an excessively tedious and unprofitable study, and it has left me in circumstances exceedingly bad. Indeed, I would be embarrassed to tell you how desperate is my current situation.

But now a way of escape from my difficulties is provided, surely by God himself.

The news has reached me of Doctor Wethersfield having passed on to his eternal reward. Although it is a sad loss to us all, it does open the way for what your revered father, my old benefactor, had intended all along – that the living at Kympton should be mine. As I am now firmly resolved on taking orders, and as I am well aware that you have no one else to provide for, I look forward to receiving the presentation of the living after all.

I am sure you will agree that is what your father would have wanted. How pleased he will be, looking down on us from heaven, when his cherished wish has been fulfilled. Do write soon, Will, and perhaps you would be so good as to advance me twenty or thirty pounds on account to see me through.

Your old friend,
George Wickham, Esq.

Only by idleness, dissipation, and gross mismanagement could Wickham, in the space of just three years, have frittered away such a sum as I had settled on him, but so it must have been. And from the tone of his letter, he apparently suffered no qualms over it, for there was no admission of error, no apology. Neither had he expressed any fear of failing in his application to me for some immediate relief as well as the presentment of the Kympton living.

If it had come from anybody other than Wickham, I should have been incredulous. But I knew my old friend too well to be amazed. He did not understand *my* character as fully, however, for he seemed to expect my direct accession to his request, despite all that had gone before. Instead, this is what he obtained:

Dear Sir,

Please be advised that I have received your letter. However, I have no intention whatsoever of acting as you have suggested therein. You seem to have forgotten (but I have not), that three years ago you unequivocally resigned all interest in the church and all claim to the Kympton living. You requested and received from me a substantial monetary compensation instead, with which you might have established yourself in a profession and been made comfortable for the rest of your life. I have thus already discharged my responsibility to my father and to you. Your current distress of circumstance is of your own making, sir. I take no share in it. Another man – one more suited to the office – will be given the living of Kympton, and there is an end to it.

Fitzwilliam Darcy

A man who is used to talking his way into what he wants does not give up so easily, however. And so I had several more repeats of his petition – ranging in tone from harsh to conciliatory – to listen to before the business was indeed at an end. Wickham had deceived and used my father. He had taken advantage of my friendship and betrayed my once-steadfast loyalty. I was determined that he would do so no longer. This is a faithful recitation of the pertinent facts involved in all my early dealings with Mr. George Wickham.

4

A Kindness to Georgiana

As a young man, I was in no particular hurry to acquire a wife. I had enough demands on my time and attention as it was without introducing another challenging project to the list. It was no small matter attempting to understand my new responsibilities and to, overnight, grow into my father's imposing shoes as master of Pemberley.

When other men speak of desiring the life of ease afforded by the wealth of a great estate, they speak in ignorance. Perhaps there are masters who leave their properties entirely to underlings to oversee or to nobody at all, but they will soon find their wealth and respectability sifting through their fingers like sand. Although no man can successfully govern an estate the size of Pemberley single-handedly – without the assistance of trustworthy managers and servants – no great estate will long prosper under the master's neglect.

Nevertheless, although I was steadily occupied with estate business, I did consider that taking a wife sooner rather than later might be a kindness to Georgiana, for she would then have the benefit of an older, experienced female to guide her more successfully than I could myself. My innate disadvantage in that role came home to me again and again, especially when we had moved beyond the relatively simple demands of childhood. After all, who was I to teach a girl coming of age how to be a woman?

Over the years, I consulted about various aspects of Georgiana's upbringing with Colonel Fitzwilliam (whom my father had named her co-guardian), but he was no better equipped for the job than I was. A wise and affectionate aunt might have filled in what we were both lacking, had Georgiana possessed one. As it was, however, I relied too heavily on her learning what was required at school. Unfortunately, I proved particularly unlucky – or particularly inept – at selecting an establishment of that kind for her.

In March of 1811, I received yet another melancholy letter from Georgiana, relating her profound disappointment with her current situation and her desperate desire for a change.

She had been several months at a private seminary in Staffordshire only to find, after preferring it herself at first, that it did not suit her at all. She had discovered the location to be too isolated and the headmistress too unyielding. And whether due to her natural reticence or otherwise, in all that time she had apparently failed to form any meaningful friendships among her fellows to make the situation more palatable.

I am lonely and desolate here, she wrote, *and if you do not take pity on me, Brother, I shall surely perish…*

She was a girl of barely fifteen, and though my own flesh and blood, she was also a foreign species to me. I had not the least idea what to make of her dire assertions, but I could hardly ignore such a plea for help, and only so much can be learnt through letters. Therefore, I determined to go to Staffordshire and evaluate the true state of affairs for myself. Perhaps I had overlooked something important when I had first been there to investigate the place, some inherent flaw or evil tendency. I meant to make no mistake about it this time, to view each detail with a critical and discerning eye, for Georgiana's sake.

When I arrived, however, I found the place just as pleasant as it had seemed before – hardly the secret chamber of horrors my mind had been constructing based on my sister's string of unhappy letters.

"Mr. Darcy, what a compliment you pay us by your presence," the headmistress said nervously when I was shown into her office immediately upon my arrival. "To what do we owe this unexpected honor? You will wish to see your sister, of course, and I will be only too happy to arrange it. Although we take our academic studies very seriously here at Ashcroft Seminary, in consideration of your coming, I will excuse Miss Darcy from the rest of her classes today, if you like."

"That is very good of you, Mrs. Davis," I returned. "I will wish to speak to my sister directly, but first, a moment of *your* time, if you please."

"Certainly, Mr. Darcy. Whatever I may do, I am completely at your service. Shall we be seated?"

I accepted the woman's invitation and then commenced. "Thank you. Now, to speak frankly, Mrs. Davis, Georgiana tells me she is unhappy here. Can you explain to me why that should be?"

"Unhappy? Oh, dear me, dear me. No, sir! There has been nothing amiss that I am aware of, and I keep a very close eye on every aspect of this school, I assure you. It is my life's work, you understand, and I take a good deal of pride in providing our young ladies the best possible education and preparation for their future lives. You will find no one but what will give Ashcroft a good name."

"I can appreciate that, Mrs. Davis. I am not looking to cast blame, only to discover what can be done to make my sister more content. So you have observed no problems yourself?"

"Well, Miss Darcy is not particularly fond of our most serious studies, preferring music and the arts. And her spirits have never been what you might call high. But I put that down to her native temperament and perhaps a spot of homesickness that would improve in time. Not every girl is the same."

This line of inquiry led no nearer to discovering the source of the problem or a solution. With Mrs. Davis being unable to shed any further light on the question, I asked to be shown a room where I might speak privately with the only person who could: Georgiana.

Like the sun coming out from behind a cloud, my sister's countenance lit when she saw me. And she had been on the point of breaking into a run to close the distance between us when Mrs. Davis loudly cleared her throat to remind her reluctant pupil to behave with proper decorum. Restraint held only until that lady closed the door, leaving Georgiana and myself alone in the small parlor given over for our use.

Georgiana then threw her arms about my neck, crying, "William, William, you have come for me at last!"

I could not help but be touched by this outburst, touched and moved, though I did my best not to betray it. I was not at liberty to act according to my own inclinations alone, to evince only the pure joy of a loving brother at seeing his affectionate sister again after a separation. Here, as in every other realm of my life, I was obliged to behave as duty dictated. In this case, I was required to conduct myself with more the demeanor of a father – a sagacious parent, come to direct what would happen next, whether firm discipline or the desired relief.

We sat, and what followed was a long and sometimes tearful (at least on Georgiana's side) conversation about what was best to be done.

"Clearly you are unhappy here," I said after she had enu-merated all the aspects of Ashcroft that disagreed with her constitution, tastes, and sensibilities. "But that in itself is no answer. Sometimes we are simply obliged to endure difficult circumstances for our ultimate good." Georgiana's face fell, and I found myself softening. "At the very least," I said, "a viable plan must be arrived at before a change can be seriously considered. What is it that you would propose?"

Georgiana sat up straighter and dried her eyes. "I have given that question a great deal of thought, William, for I knew you would require me to be rational in the end."

Encouraged by her perception, I nodded.

"Could not an establishment be made for me in town?" she asked. "That is what I believe will suit me best after all."

"Town? But you prefer the country! You always have. Why, I cannot count how many times I have heard you say so. If you do not like it here, there are other schools, or I could engage a private tutor for you at Pemberley."

She paused, taking a deep breath before continuing. "You know that I love Pemberley best of anyplace in the whole world,

William, and I shall always be pleased to spend my summers there with you and with our friends visiting. But you are so often away during the rest of the year, and then I would be alone, with no other young people about me. In town, at least I would have friends nearby, the best music masters available, and the great halls of culture to delight me. There are no concerts, theatres, or museums of art here in this rustic situation. Neither are there any within easy reach of Pemberley. You must admit that is true."

I could see I needed to be firm. "Your reasoning is faulty, Georgiana. School is not meant primarily to indulge your interests or as a means for your entertainment. No, it is for the purpose of acquiring a proper education, which must include serious subjects and decorum classes, whether you like such essentials or not."

Georgiana's gaze dropped to her folded hands, and for a moment I thought she was ready to submit to my better judgement on the subject. Then she looked up with wide-eyed innocence. "William," she said softly, "instruction such as you speak of – for the mind and in proper behavior – can be found anywhere. But music and the arts provide food for the soul. Would you deprive me of *that* essential?"

All my fine logic and sham parental authority were instantly undone, and I could not at that moment have denied her anything that was within my power to give.

Only much later did it occur to me that I had been outmaneuvered by my own adolescent sister. Georgiana had prepared her arguments well and skillfully applied the tools at her disposal to achieve her aim, that being her release from Ashcroft Seminary, though Mrs. Davis did protest most strenuously against the withdrawal of her "most distinguished and promising pupil."

Georgiana and I returned briefly to Pemberley, where subsequent inquiries soon brought forward a suitable London situation, an establishment recommended by a trusted colleague of mine, whose own daughter was contentedly settled there. It was another private seminary, this one managed by a woman by the name of Mrs. Younge.

5
A Past Encounter

With this latest trouble concerning Georgiana, with this most recent reminder of my inadequacy to serve as her sole parental figure, my mind turned once again to the need of finding assistance in the form of a suitable marriage partner. I had by this time got over the initial shock of having all Pemberley unexpectedly thrust into my hands. I was of a good age for getting on with what must come next: finding myself a wife. And with Georgiana settled in London, I was at liberty to undertake the project.

The customary way to proceed might have been to throw myself into the marriage market of a London season. I had seen enough to know that with noble connections, a generous income, and extensive properties belonging to me, I would not have long remained without companionship in that environment. However, it has always seemed a very vulgar business to me, what with all the extravagance, pomp and parade, deals to be struck, and prime goods going to the highest bidder. Although my father had advised not to sell myself cheaply, I could not believe *that* is what he had in mind. And personally, I had no desire to be made a party to such a coarse practice again. Besides, I lacked two of the essentials for enjoying a London season, those being a great appetite for dancing and a facility for conversing with strangers.

I chose a quieter, more dignified approach instead; I chose to look to established connections rather than attempting to forge new – and possibly questionable – ones beyond.

When I considered those established associations with my new object in view, two suitable candidates immediately suggested themselves. I could seek a wife in my cousin Anne de Bourgh – my mother's early design for me – or I could look to my father's more recent suggestion of Miss Lambright. I knew that with one I acquired an overbearing mother-in-law, a woman whom I was obliged to tolerate as my aunt but did not necessarily desire any nearer connection to. With the other I acquired no mother-in-law at all, for the viscount had lately lost his lady to illness. All other considerations being more or less equal in my mind, that seemed a good basis for deciding where to begin. Consequently, I made plans for visiting Viscount Harcourt at once.

The viscount and his family were not in our closest circle of acquaintances, but while my father lived, he had made a decided point of maintaining the connection. Although it was true that since then the association had suffered some neglect, I was quite certain I would be well received just as before, since several letters of ceremony had circulated between our two households in the interim. Georgiana and I had been favored with a very handsome letter of condolence from the viscount on the occasion of my father's death. And I had been careful to return the courtesy when the viscount's wife, who I believed to have held me in some affection, had herself died.

Therefore, I could come to them at Ravenshaw under the auspices of the past, not needing to reveal my more particular interest on this occasion unless or until the moment became right to do so. I could renew my acquaintance with Miss Lambright without being suspected of pretentions to marriage. I could dis-cover if she were still at liberty without making myself ridiculous. Then I might see if I could like her well enough to consider anything more – anything more than maintaining the longstanding friendship between our two families. Such was my strategy.

Although I could not recall having formed any notions of particular regard for Miss Lambright as a result of our prior encounters, neither had I any unfavorable ones. I remembered her as a somewhat plain-looking, even tempered girl several years my junior, neither overly shy nor inappropriately gregarious. When I had most recently seen her, she must have been fifteen or sixteen years of age. Though her figure was still somewhat unformed at that time, it was clear even then that she was built tall and spare like her father.

These lingering impressions of Miss Lambright were based on fairly limited – and now outdated – information, since the visits between our two households were infrequent and the fact that usually Georgiana, and not I myself, had been the young lady's chief companion on these prior occasions. The last time, however, Miss Lambright and I were necessarily thrust into closer company, my sister having stayed at home ill and Miss Lambright's brother Franklin being away when my father and I had made the yearly pilgrimage to Ravenshaw.

"The weather is particularly fine," my father observed after the five of us (for Lady Harcourt was also still living then) had been sitting in the drawing room together for about half an hour. "Miss Lambright, perhaps you would be so good as to give my son a walking tour of the park. I daresay there are many beauties to behold this time of year."

At nearly one-and-twenty and thinking myself quite grown, I remember I had much rather have stayed in the company of the adults that day. But it was not to be. Perhaps my father made his suggestion with an eye to a match between Miss Lambright and myself even then. Or perhaps he only wished me out of the way so he could speak to her parents on some private business. In any case, Miss Lambright and I had no choice but to obediently leave the room in order to seek the splendors of the open air together.

"What would you like to see first, Mr. Darcy?" the young Miss Lambright asked a bit nervously.

I am afraid I did little to conceal my discontent at my lot, saying with an unbecoming degree of hauteur, "It is of no consequence to me, Miss Lambright, I assure you. Please lead wherever you will."

"In that case, perhaps you would care to see the stables?" she tentatively proposed. "We could go there by way of the rose gar-den, if you like. When your father spoke of 'beauties,' it could be the rose garden he meant. Perhaps he remembers that it is my mother's favorite place. Would that be agreeable to you, Mr. Darcy?"

"By all means, Miss Lambright – the rose garden and then the stables."

In truth, I had little interest in roses, and I could no more tell one kind from another than I could fly. Miss Lambright was obviously far better educated on the subject, likely the result of her mother's tutelage. She took pains to tell me which was a China rose and which a Damask or some other sort, and she bade me to sample the fragrance of this one and that one of her favorites. Although I daresay I finished nearly as ignorant as I began, it was half an hour not altogether unpleasantly spent.

As the two of us proceeded from there down the long gravel walk that would take us to the stables, my companion and I lapsed into silence. Miss Lambright may have been worn out after her singular efforts in the rose garden, and I... well, I was still disconsolate at being dismissed by the adults and foisted outside with this mere girl instead. I had nothing to say to her and could not trouble myself to imagine what she might like to hear.

To her credit, Miss Lambright did not seem to be made unhappy by my stupidity. In fact she seemed to have a slight spring in her step, and I several times noticed her looking up at me, smiling a little. At last, this unsealed my lips.

"You smile, Miss Lambright," I said, stating the obvious. Not brilliant conversation, admittedly, but it was a start. "May I know the reason?"

"I like walking with you, Mr. Darcy," she replied.

I waited for more information. When none came, I was just curious enough to ask, "Why is that? I am certain a young lady such as yourself, who is used to the best of company, must know many others whom you would find more entertaining on a walk."

"Oh, yes, many," she said matter-of-factly.

I was a bit taken aback, I confess, more accustomed as I was to being flattered by females. Giving her a sharp look, however, I discovered her to be entirely in earnest, with no hint of coquetry about her. That was refreshing. And I could hardly dispute what had been my own words to begin with. So I soon recovered. "Very well, then why do you prefer walking with me?"

"It is because you are tall."

She said this in the same straightforward manner – no prevarication or coy smiles. Yet it was still a less than satisfactory answer, still less than a full disclosure. "Because I am tall? Come now, Miss Lambright, I cannot help thinking there must be more to it than that."

She sighed. "Really, Mr. Darcy, I probably should not have said anything, but you might be surprised to know how dreadfully prevalent men of short stature are amongst my acquaintance. It is a pure pleasure, therefore – a genuine luxury – for me to be able to walk naturally and not outpace you, to stand up straight and not feel as if I need to apologize for being too tall myself."

This seemed an odd sort of idea. "You need never apologize for such a thing as that, Miss Lambright," I said. "A person, lady or gentleman, can take neither credit nor blame for his height."

"I daresay that ought to be true, Mr. Darcy, and that you yourself have never felt the necessity of doing so. And yet honestly, you can have no idea how some gentlemen seem to take my height as a personal affront, as if I had set out on purpose to embarrass them by it. So I have learnt to… to make *accommodations* where I can in order to get on. But with you, happily there is no need."

What else we talked of that afternoon, I really cannot recall, but this one peculiar conversation remained in my mind. It was a new perspective, something I had never considered before. As I drove to Ravenshaw those years later, I thought of it again. I could not help wondering if Miss Lambright had grown many inches taller in the intervening years. I hoped for her sake that she had not.

6

Ravenshaw

Advised by return post, I knew the viscount was expecting me, so I suffered no apprehension of making the two-hour journey from Pemberley to Ravenshaw in vain. And indeed, arriving in a timely manner, I was shown into the library at once to find Lord Harcourt waiting for me there.

"Ah, young Mr. Darcy," he said, rising and coming towards me with his hand extended. "How very good it is to see you again."

I bowed first, somewhat awkwardly, and then took his proffered hand, saying. "The pleasure is all mine, my lord."

"Let us dispense with the formalities, shall we? We are old family friends, after all. If you have no objections, I will call you 'Darcy,' as I used to do your father, and you might try calling me simply 'Harcourt.' It will make things so much easier. Now, do come and sit. I will not embarrass you by telling you how much grown you are since last I saw you, but I cannot help observing that you are very much the fine young gentleman now. No doubt it is the years spent following your father's excellent example. How very strange it seems that you should be here without him. Are you getting on tolerably well at Pemberley?"

"Tolerably. It has been difficult, but everything was left to me in good order, and I am learning."

"I have no doubt but what you will fully rise to the occasion over time. I hope your father's managers – his land agent, his man of business, and so forth – have stayed on to assist you. That can make all the difference in the world to a young man like yourself, trying to get his feet under him."

"As you say, sir. I am very fortunate to still have Mrs. Reynolds to manage the household. My father's steward, old Mr. Wickham, only survived him by a year, however. But the new man, a Mr. Adams, is doing very well, I think. He has my complete confidence."

"Glad to hear it." After offering me one, which I declined, Lord Harcourt took a moment to light a cigar for himself, puffing contentedly at it before resuming our conversation. "And what of your sister, Darcy? How does Miss Georgiana do? Still fond of music, is she?"

"Yes, it is her one true passion."

"I remember how wonderfully she played last time, especially for one so young. What is she now – thirteen or fourteen?"

"She is fifteen."

"Can it be so? How time does march on, whether we wish it to or not."

"Quite so. I can scarce believe it myself that Georgiana is nearly grown. She is very well, though, I thank you. She is settled at a school in London, which seems to suit her, according to a letter I lately received."

"Good. Good. Perhaps I will have occasion to see her when next I am in the vicinity. Or Franklin may. He is much the eligible bachelor about town these days. Prefers London to the country, you know, as so many young people do. But Amelia is here. We will join her in a minute if you would care to renew your acquaintance."

"Of course. There is nothing I would like better," said I, without lending the words any special significance.

"Excellent. She has been curious to see you again. And it will be a welcome diversion for her to have someone other than a stodgy old man to talk to. Poor girl misses her mother, you know, and then... Well, I should not divulge all her secrets. It is just that your presence is sure to do her good. And as for me, having you here is the next best thing to a much-overdue conversation with your father, if you see what I mean."

"Yes, sir."

"The longer the gaps between our visits, the more we had to say to one another. So you must forgive me when I run on so. Now, shall we go to Amelia? I believe we will find her in the drawing room."

Not waiting for an answer, Lord Harcourt rose, and I followed him.

Miss Amelia Lambright looked much as I remembered her, only with a few more years of maturity to add elegance and a more womanly appearance. As for her height, it was difficult at first to judge, since she remained seated.

I crossed the room to her, bowed over her hand, and said, "Miss Lambright, how delightful it is to see you again. You look very well." And it was true; she was the picture of good posture, good grooming, and good health, if not true beauty. Her attire was tasteful, her complexion flawless, and her burnished blonde hair was done up in quite a pleasing arrangement.

"I am well, Mr. Darcy," she said. "Will not you sit down?"

"Thank you," I replied, taking the place near her that she had indicated.

Lord Harcourt sat as well, in the chair that was the mate to my own. "There now, is not this pleasant?" he said. Then his cheerful tone faded away. "We are only wanting a few absent friends to make our joy complete."

"Yes, Papa," said Miss Lambright, her eyes momentarily downcast. "But how can we be melancholy when Mr. Darcy is come to Ravenshaw? Now," she said turning to me, "do tell me all about Georgiana and the news from Pemberley."

It was gracefully done, I noticed – how Miss Lambright had sidestepped her father's mournful allusions to turn the conversation into a more serviceable avenue. As any skilled hostess would know to do, she set her guest at ease by inviting me to talk on comfortable topics – subjects sure to be near to my heart and about which I was most well informed.

It occurred to me then that Miss Lambright had recently been called on to fill her mother's shoes at Ravenshaw in much the same manner I had been abruptly required to fill my father's at

Pemberley. We had that much in common to begin with. This was exactly the sort of thing my father had been speaking of too – the reason Miss Lambright would be the kind of lady who would do me proud. She would know how to preside at Pemberley, to manage the household with refinement and efficiency, to entertain guests from the highest strata of society. She would know because she had been born to it. She had learnt the skills required in a house on a par with my own. She had studied her station from an early age and was already putting that knowledge to practical use.

I answered Miss Lambright's interest in my sister and then asked after her brother, his health and activities. This conversation, encompassing some fifteen or twenty minutes, was not particularly animated – no lively or daring opinions ventured on either side, and no ill-advised attempts at humor. Instead, it was everything that such an interaction should be: dignified and pleasantly sedate, with no awkward silences despite my lack of facility for talking. Miss Lambright adroitly saw to that.

Miss Lambright then stood, and so, naturally, I did as well. Only when I saw that Lord Harcourt's eyes were closed did I realize he had not spoken a word in some time. His daughter crept to his side and carefully eased the smoldering cigar from between his fingers, placing it safely on the side table in the metal tray designed for that purpose. Then motioning for me to follow, she noiselessly left the room.

I could see then that Miss Lambright was indeed tall and thin, just the same but not more so than I remembered from when I had seen her last. Now, however, she moved with the added polish and grace of a grown woman – a lady of quality.

Stopping when we had reached the hall, she said, "Since my mother died, my father has taken to indulging two habits that she could never abide: smoking and falling asleep at the most inopportune times. You must excuse him, Mr. Darcy. He means no insult by it."

"Of course," said I. "Perhaps I will do the same at his age."

"Kind of you to say so. Which do you mean, though? The smoking or the sleeping?"

I thought perhaps she was teasing me, but a look at her sober countenance convinced me she was not. So I answered accordingly. "Given the choice, I would prefer a restful nap. Like your mother, I never could abide smoking myself."

"Well said, Mr. Darcy. You have chosen the better part." She led the way into a small parlor decorated in a more feminine style – no doubt one set aside for her particular use – and we seated ourselves again. "Still, I am surprised that Papa should have fallen asleep today, so much as he has been anticipating your coming."

"Do you receive many visitors here at Ravenshaw, Miss Lambright?"

"Not so many as we could wish for. There are a few families we associate with in the local vicinity. Certain friends from the north stop whenever they pass by this way, coming to London or going home again. And lately there has been a gentleman or two calling. Do you know Mr. John Fairhaven, Lord Avery's second son?"

"No, I do not believe that I have had that pleasure, Miss Lambright."

"Ah, well, he is a very pleasant young man. Very amusing, I daresay. He has called on us several times in recent months, ever since our being introduced to him in town. I thought perhaps... But it is of no consequence. In any case, we are very glad that you have come to us today, Mr. Darcy."

She remained silent, and I felt the weight of finding a new topic. Not surprisingly, I made poor work of it. "Miss Lambright, allow me to say again how sorry Georgiana and I were to hear of your mother's passing. It must have been a grievous loss to you and your family."

Her countenance instantly fell, and she covered her mouth with one hand.

"Pardon me, Miss Lambright," I apologized at once. "That was unforgivably clumsy of me."

"Not at all, Mr. Darcy," she said when she presently regained her composure. "You are not to blame. It has been nearly a year, after all, and I myself mentioned my mother's death to you only a moment ago. I often think I am thoroughly inured to hearing it spoken of, and yet occasionally it still takes me by surprise. Although your losses are further behind you, perhaps you remember being similarly susceptible yourself."

"I remember, Miss Lambright. Believe me, I remember all too well."

Sometime later, after dining with Miss Lambright and her father, I drove away feeling quite satisfied with my visit to Ravenshaw. I had seen for myself how suitable a choice Miss Lambright must be considered. And from the viscount's friendly manner towards me – and from his encouragement when I left that I should repeat my visit "just as soon and as often as you like" – I had little doubt of a favorable reception if I should apply to him for his daughter's hand.

Miss Lambright herself was more difficult to judge. I had detected in her no symptoms of peculiar regard for me, not as I had imagined might have existed when she was a girl. But then perhaps she was more practiced in the art of concealment now, and, as I understood it, young ladies were schooled to steadfastly avoid betraying a preference until the gentleman had first declared himself. Nevertheless, she seemed a very sensible young woman who would know what was in her own best interest. Doubtless she would act accordingly when the time came and not refuse me if I asked.

Although it was too soon for deciding on such a definite course of action, I felt as if I had already gathered much of the information I would require to do so. There never was any question of Miss Lambright's being suitable. Beyond that, though, she was pleasant and well-spoken in all respects. I believed I could abide her composed, straight-forward manner very well. It was infinitely to be preferred to Miss Bingley's cloying obsequiousness or even my cousin Anne's timidity. I was sure she would be a sensible, steadying influence for Georgiana as well.

A life with Amelia Lambright as my wife would be calm and predictable. No surprises. No drama. No tears. Was not that what I had been asking for?

7
Pivotal Plans

A second visit to Ravenshaw a fortnight later confirmed my earlier impressions of Miss Lambright and my sanguine anticipation of receiving an affirmative answer to an offer of marriage. And so, I went home to Pemberley afterward to make up my mind on proposing the next time I saw her.

It would be good to have that aspect of my future life decided once and for all.

Some thought had to be given as to how best to go about it, though, since I had no experience. I had never proposed marriage to a woman before. Nor had any of my closest friends – not Bingley and not Colonel Fitzwilliam either. My other male Fitzwilliam cousin, the colonel's elder brother, must have done something correctly when he offered for the woman who later become his wife. He obviously succeeded in procuring that lady's favor. But then, there is never much doubt of a future earl's being able to carry his point with a marriageable lady, so perhaps very little of his success could be attributed to a winning technique.

In any case, I was on my own and would have to do the best I could by my own wits.

Since I abhorred pretense of any kind, I would use no elaborate verses or disingenuous words of love. That much was already decided. A simple avowal of my sincere esteem for Miss Lambright and for her family, and a brief recitation of the advantages to us both in the match: that should suffice. Unless her affections were otherwise engaged – something I had been given no reason to suppose – I expected to be solemnly engaged that same day and then married shortly thereafter. Perhaps it could even be accomplished, my bride and I returned from our wedding trip, in time to spend a portion of the summer at Pemberley with Georgiana.

All this made very pleasant fodder for my musings – Amelia and Georgiana renewing their acquaintance, now with the much nearer connection of sisterhood to bind them in affection. Perhaps some of our other friends would join us, paying the new Mrs. Darcy a bride visit and staying to enjoy our hospitality. I pictured the former Miss Lambright moving about Pemberley House and seamlessly directing matters for the comfort of her husband and her admiring guests.

"You have done yourself proud," Fitzwilliam might say, clapping me on the back. "Mrs. Darcy is a treasure."

My sister, overhearing this, would turn, smile contentedly, and give me a nod of assent. Bingley might be a bit disappointed for his sister's sake, but even he would come round to my way of thinking when all was explained. He always relied on my opinions for what was right, so there was no reason this should be any different.

While I was pondering when to act in order to make this agreeable vision a reality, I received a communication from Georgiana.

Dearest William,

I continue very well and very happy, which is in great part owing to your extraordinary kindness. The longer I am here, the more satisfied I am become with my new situation. The other young ladies are very friendly and obliging, much more so than the girls of Ashcroft, I assure you. But lest you think me too frivolous, I must tell you that I am industriously attending to my studies as well.

Mrs. Younge could not be more solicitous of my comfort and welfare. Already, she has arranged for me to attend a very fine concert and the opera twice, accompanying me herself on every occasion! Is not that kind of her? Now Mrs. Younge has bestowed on me an even more marked attention. At the end of our term here, which is coming soon, she is to go for a holiday to Ramsgate. And what do you think? She has invited me to accompany her as her very particular guest, with your permission of course.

That is why I am writing to you today, Brother. I would so very much like to go! May I? The shore must be exceedingly pleasant in summer, and Mrs. Younge has assured me that sea air is the healthiest thing in the world. You are not to worry about any question of propriety either, for I will always be properly attended.

Naturally, I will spend the rest of the summer at Pemberley, as always. Granting me leave to go to Ramsgate would only delay my coming to you for three or four weeks. Perhaps that would be just as convenient for you. In any case, I await your kind answer.

With prayers for your health and happiness, I remain your loving sister,

Georgiana

On the whole, the effect of this letter must be encouraging. Georgiana was well and happy; that was the material point. There was also some personal satisfaction in knowing I had played a role in procuring that happiness for her by placing her with Mrs. Younge. This time, it seemed, I had made a wise choice for my sister's education.

As for this proposed excursion to Ramsgate, that would require more thought. Despite what Georgiana had written – that I was not to worry – the fact was that I worried for her to some degree whenever she was out of my sight. But there was no reason this seaside scheme should be fraught with particular peril. Adequate measures for Georgiana's protection were easily within our reach. As for my own convenience, that was not worth considering where my sister's wellbeing was involved. However, it did occur to me that Georgiana's being occupied in Ramsgate until the end of June or beyond would afford me extra time to accomplish my plans with Miss Lambright.

In the end, I penned a note giving my permission to Georgiana, smiling to think of how happy receiving it would make her. Then I penned another of a more serious character to Mrs. Younge. I first thanked her for her kindness to my sister, and then I made very clear to her my requirements for how safety and decorum must be managed in order for Georgiana's accompanying her to Ramsgate to be allowed. Mrs. Younge immediately wrote back with the guarantee of all the safeguards I required, adding, *for I assure you that I know what is due to Miss Darcy of Pemberley.*

As this correspondence flew to and fro, the post brought another surprise to this effect. Lord Harcourt had decided to give a private ball at Ravenshaw *for the amusement of my children, now that our official year of mourning is over.* By such means, he apparently meant to tempt his son home from London as well as giving pleasure to his daughter.

In light of my rekindled intimacy with the family, it was no surprise that I should be invited, although I did wonder if the occasion was meant to further promote my attentions to Miss Lambright. Indeed, if I had come to the point before that date, which had been my intention, the ball would no doubt have served as the perfect opportunity for Harcourt to announce our engagement to the entire company.

The scene was before my mind's eye in a moment. Perhaps a hundred people or more, most of them strangers to me, would be dancing and making merry. Then at the supper, Harcourt would demand everybody's attention to, through tears and smiles, impart the important information.

"Ladies and gentlemen," he would begin. "I thank you all for coming tonight. As you know, my beloved wife left us one year ago, and we have mourned her loss – inwardly even more than outwardly – ever since. Now, however, I bring you happy tidings instead! Yes, after so much grief, this family at last has something to celebrate, something in which I know my late wife would have been very glad to join us." He would look at the two of us then, saying, "Do stand so that all may see you." Then continuing to the crowd, "It is my great pleasure to announce to you that my daughter, the Honorable Miss Amelia Lambright, is newly engaged to this fine and very worthy young man, who has long been a friend here at Ravenshaw. Her partner on the dance floor tonight and for the rest of her life is Mr. Fitzwilliam Darcy of Pemberley. Please raise your glasses in a toast to the happy couple!"

We would have our health drunk to. We would be looked at, teased, interrogated, and congratulated. There would be endless conjecture about which of us had made the better bargain by the match. And depending on the amount of wine already consumed, there might even be tasteless jokes, or at least innuendo, about the wedding night from some of the men present.

I shuddered at the thought. An engagement between a lady and a gentleman was an ordinary occurrence best celebrated in private; that was my view. And I would not willingly give cause for making a public spectacle of it.

So I postponed. Instead of visiting Ravenshaw again immediately to solicit Miss Lambright's hand in marriage, I simply responded to the invitation by post, accepting with thanks and begging the pleasure of Miss Lambright's hand for the first two dances of the evening. That would be attention enough for the time being, I decided. Sometime after the ball would do as well for the rest... or perhaps a good deal better.

8
The Ravenshaw Ball

I did not anticipate obtaining any great personal pleasure from the Ravenshaw ball, no more than with most other balls I had attended. The dancing itself would be agreeable exercise, but there would be too many persons unknown to me with whom I would be required to make polite conversation. This was not something I had ever enjoyed or achieved even an average facility for.

I was glad, however, that I could go in the safety of relative anonymity. Although there would be some who would undoubtedly speculate if Miss Lambright indeed awarded me the first two dances and especially if there were more, we would at least escape the special notoriety a definite engagement between ourselves would have created.

I would be pleased to renew my acquaintance with Franklin Lambright, Miss Lambright's elder brother, whom I had not seen in more than five years. And I was almost surprised to find, as the day drew near, how much I was looking forward to spending more time with Amelia herself. I only hoped that the genial mental images of her as mistress of Pemberley that I had lately been entertaining had not built her up too high in my imagination.

When I arrived, Lord Harcourt was there to receive me, as well as his other guests. "Darcy!" he said, wringing my hand enthusiastically. "So good of you to come, my boy!"

"Not at all," I replied. "The pleasure is mine, Lord Harcourt, and I thank you for inviting me."

"Of course, of course! And it is 'Harcourt' to you, remember? We are old friends, after all. Amelia is somewhere about," he said, craning his neck to see her without success. "She is circulating amongst her guests, I expect, but I know she has reserved the first two dances for you, as you kindly requested. And Franklin is just over there."

I looked in the direction Harcourt indicated. "Very good, sir," I said. "I will speak to him without delay."

"Oh, yes, do! And I hope you will have an exceedingly enjoyable evening."

I bowed, thanked Lord Harcourt again for his hospitality, and excused myself to greet his son. Although my old friend had changed in five years, as had I, he was still easily recognizable, and he looked as happy to see me as I was him. We exchanged the standard pleasantries in the relaxed style of old.

"Darcy, I cannot tell you how pleased I was," he said, "when my father wrote me that you had paid your respects to him and to my sister. And then to discover that you would actually be here tonight! It has been far too long, friend."

"I agree; far too long. And how much has changed since I saw you last."

"Yes, yes," he said soberly, "for us both. But now, tell me. How are you getting on at Pemberley? Have you mastered the art of being the master yet?"

"I would never presume to say so. I still have much to learn."

"You are too modest, I am sure. As serious and conscientious as you always were, I would wager you have things well in hand. You only want to find a wife to make the picture complete. But perhaps that is what you are come to Ravenshaw to do, eh Darcy? My father is very fond of you, you know. And I think you could have my sister for the asking!" he finished with a laugh and a slap on my back.

Momentarily stumbled by this, I recovered to answer calmly enough. "Your father is very kind, and your sister is everything charming, Lambright. But again, I would not presume any such thing."

"And I say again, you are much too modest. But have it your own way if you wish. I will leave off teasing you and Amelia for now, lest you both should begin on me. *I* certainly have no plans for matrimony at present… although there are some very pretty girls here tonight to tempt me," he added, his eyes following the progress of one such young lady crossing the hall. "You must excuse me now."

Franklin set off in hot pursuit of his quarry, and I proceeded in search of Amelia, feeling some misgivings about what had already passed. Franklin's allusions to his sister and myself may have been purely in jest, however they had not sprung from the air. It seemed likely the idea had been inspired by something his father – or his sister? – had dropped. I wondered which, and if my attentions, which I considered so circumspect, had already given rise to certain expectations. I hoped not. Although I had every intention of following through, I liked to think I had not yet committed myself.

Amelia's reception set me more at ease.

I found her in the ballroom, looking quite regal with her tall figure and upright bearing. She was wearing white. As to any details of her finery, I will not attempt a description. I can only say that the overall presentation was very pleasing. She smiled when she saw me coming over to her, but she made no special fuss that could draw attention. In fact, when I discovered her, she had been speaking very cordially to another young man.

A bow and a curtsey were exchanged between us.

"Mr. Darcy," she said, "I am very glad to see you."

"As am I you, Miss Lambright. I am looking forward to our dances. Thank you for reserving the first two for me."

"Of course. I was only too happy to do so." Then she turned to the young man she had been speaking to a moment before. "Mr. Fairhaven, I do not believe you know this gentleman. Allow me to introduce you. This is Mr. Fitzwilliam Darcy. And Mr. Darcy, this is Mr. John Fairhaven."

We eyed each other and bowed.

John Fairhaven. I remembered Amelia mentioning him before. Lord Avery's second son. He was well turned out, to be sure, but with something of the air of a dandy, I thought, and no taller than Miss Lambright herself, if that.

"Now," continued Amelia, "forgive me, gentlemen, but I really must see to our other guests. So until later, I bid you both adieu."

I bowed again and watched her go.

Then Mr. Fairhaven, also following her with his gaze, said testily, "So *you* are the gentleman who has secured the prize of the first two dances with Miss Lambright."

I nodded. "That is true; the honor seems to have fallen to me."

"I asked as well, only to be told I was too late."

Was I expected to apologize for this? His attitude implied it, but I would not. "There are other dances to be had, I am sure."

"Quite so. Miss Lambright has just consented to dance the last before the supper break with me," he said triumphantly.

Again, I searched for the appropriate response. "I suppose I must congratulate you on your success, Mr. Fairhaven. Here, you have anticipated *me*. I had hoped to share the supper with her. We have much to discuss. It seems instead she will be listening to you talking."

"Yes, and you can be sure that I will make the most of it. Good-evening to you, sir." And with a curt bow, he walked away.

This was an interesting development. It seemed I had at least one rival for Miss Lambright's favor. Although that was hardly surprising, when I stopped to think of it. Amelia was so very eligible a young lady, especially considering her family connections and, as I understood it, a tolerable fortune. It would have been astonishing if she had not attracted other suitors about her, as bees to a flower. Still, I had confidence in the strength of my position. Unlike some of the others, presumably, I had as much to offer as to gain by the match, and I could certainly not be suspected of being a fortune hunter.

Although I was not put off by the presence of Mr. John Fairhaven, I was disappointed that I would be unable to spend more time with Amelia because of him. What I had told him was true; I had indeed hoped to claim the dances before the supper break – and thus the supper break itself – with my intended bride.

But perhaps it was just as well I could not, for such repeated and prolonged attentions might indeed have drawn the undue interest of onlookers that I was so desirous to avoid.

After first Amelia and then Mr. Fairhaven left me, I glanced about for a familiar face amongst the collecting crowd, someone with whom I might converse in tolerable comfort. Seeing none, I made my way towards the perimeter of the room to stand unobtrusively until the ball should actually commence. It was a good location from which to observe without being observed, and yet nothing going forward in the ballroom particularly interested me. People I did not know were parading about, apparently to make a show of their finery. And I saw Franklin Lambert carrying on – talking and laughing gaily – with the attractive young woman who had caught his attention earlier.

At times like this, I envied that free and easy way some men possess of conversing with members of the opposite sex, for he really did seem to be enjoying himself immensely whilst I was not. In general, I cared nothing about such things, for I was not bent on impressing anybody or catering to the dictates of society. But neither did I wish to give offense where none was intended. That was the real danger.

That very night, for example, I knew that I should by rights ask some of the other ladies to dance when I was not occupied with Amelia. To do otherwise would be deemed unpardonably rude. But the thought was unpleasant, almost repugnant to me. What should I say to a woman I had never met before, with whom I had nothing in common, and whom I would likely never meet with again? And yet to dance without speaking at all might be judged more impolite than to decline to dance in the first place. I could see no graceful solution.

Then my eyes alit on fair Amelia again. At least I could begin with her. She was familiar to me and familiar with my ways. For her, I was prepared to make an effort, and she would not expect too much of me. Such reassuring knowledge gave me confidence.

9
Dancing

"How well you dance, Mr. Darcy!" Amelia said once we had got underway.

We separated for a moment, and then, when the movements of the dance brought us back together, I replied, "As do you, Miss Lambright, and yet you sounded surprised."

Again a parting and another reunion as we fitted in our bits of conversation where we could.

"I suppose I am, a little. I did not have you reckoned to be a fine dancer... In fact, I thought I remembered you once saying you disliked the amusement."

"Very likely you did hear me say something of the kind... but not liking a thing is different from being unable to do it, even well... Growing up, Miss Lambright, I had very regular sessions with the dancing master, the same as you, I would wager... And for the record, the dancing itself, I find rather invigorating; my disinclination is for all the rest."

"All the rest?"

"The social trappings that accompany the dancing... with whom one may and may not dance, how many times is acceptable and how many is too much... the gossiping speculation of the onlookers, the polite conversation that is expected to accompany the exercise, even if one's partner is a stranger."

"I had no idea. Well, we need not speak if you do not like it, Mr. Darcy."

It was her usual matter-of-fact tone, not the one of a person who has chosen to take offense. Nevertheless, I felt as if I had blundered. "Forgive me, Miss Lambright," I said. "I am very glad

to speak to *you*, even while dancing. That is always a pleasure…
I am simply hopeless when it comes to conversing with strangers.
I have no talent for it… I cannot seem to catch their tone quickly
enough or appear interested in their superficial concerns, as I have
seen others do."

"Men like my brother, do you mean?"

"Well, yes, according to my observations tonight. Whereas
some people are gifted with social grace, I am not. I am sorry to
confess it, but so it is."

"You need not apologize for what you cannot help. You once
gave me similar advice. Do you recall the occasion?"

"I believe you must be referring to a conversation, some years
ago, when I said you need not apologize for being tall. I have not
forgotten it."

She smiled, apparently pleased by this. "I have never forgotten
either, Mr. Darcy. It was good advice that I have attempted to put
into practice."

"I have noticed."

"Really? How so?"

"It is in the way you carry yourself. There is no stooping or
crouching. You stand upright, no matter who is beside you."

She sighed. "I suppose you are thinking of Mr. Fairhaven. Yes,
it is a shame he is not just a bit taller. It is not for my own
convenience I would wish it, you understand, but for his comfort… Ah, well, as you say, there is no use regretting what cannot
be helped."

I was glad I had attended well to my dancing lessons, as my
mother had insisted, for that is what made such a disjointed
conversation possible on top of the demands of the dance. If too
much concentration were required by one or the other, a man must
forever be tripping, either over his words or over his own feet.
Fortunately, since I was comfortable with both the moves of the
dance and my partner, I did not go too far wrong, at least not to
my own knowledge.

Miss Lambright danced very well; my telling her so was no
mere pleasantry. And she seemed to be enjoying herself, although,

once again, there was nothing in her manner that gave irrefutable evidence of any particular regard for me. It was all polite amiability and friendliness, at least on the surface. What might be her deeper sentiments, I had no true notion.

The first of our two dances came to an end, and as we began the second, I considered if there was anything in particular I should say to my fair partner before our time together was over. Now that I had been awakened to the idea that Miss Lambright might indeed have other suitors, I wanted to at least leave her with the assurance that I was serious in my attentions to her. Perhaps I should even look for an opportunity to propose marriage before the night was out – and before Mr. Fairhaven or one of the others could come in ahead of me. After all, my resolve on doing so had not altered since I had last seen her, only the timing. As long as we could avoid an actual announcement before the entire company, I did not mind that the business should be concluded that same night.

"Miss Lambright," I said while we danced.

She spun about, as the dance required, and came back to me. "Yes?"

"Miss Lambright, I wonder if you would do me the honor..."
Again my thought was interrupted by the demands of the dance. It really was a most maddening way to try to accomplish something as simple as asking a question and having it answered. I nearly gave up altogether. But then we arrived at the top of the set and were idle for half a minute together. This was my chance.

"You were saying, Mr. Darcy?"

"Yes, quite. Miss Lambright, I wondered if you would honor me with another dance later tonight. Perhaps the last, if it is not already spoken for."

"I am flattered, Mr. Darcy. But are not you afraid of those very things you spoke of before? – the social implications. To dance again with me might be considered a very marked attention. It might not be seen as quite proper between disinterested parties."

"I am hardly disinterested, Miss Lambright. I thought perhaps you knew that by now."

She studied me in silence as we rejoined the dance. Holding gloved hands, we stepped forward towards each other, stepped back, and then together again. "Very well, Mr. Darcy," she said evenly, showing no emotion, either positive or negative. "I will reserve the last for you, if you wish it."

"Thank you."

There. I had set things in motion, and I was in a fair train to accomplish my purpose. If all went well, I would receive a favorable answer from Amelia before the night was out. Then I could linger until the other guests were gone so that I might speak to her father. Or perhaps it would be better to put that part off. I could easily ride back over to Ravenshaw the next day instead to speak to the viscount. In any case, it would soon be settled.

~~*~~

At the conclusion of those first two dances, Amelia introduced me to two of her friends – a Miss Alexander and a Miss Harris – and before I could allow my natural tendencies to dissuade me, I had asked each of them to dance in turn. Miss Alexander was agreeable enough company, not seeming to expect much conversation from me, and Miss Harris only smiled knowingly and tittered with continual laughter as we danced. In any case, by the end of these exertions, I felt I had done my duty to the female portion of the population, at least for a time, and I retired to the card room until the supper break.

I had Franklin Lambright nearby during the supper itself, so there was at least one familiar person to talk to. And then during the second half of the ball, I danced as little as good manners would allow me to do, preferring to hover in the background the rest of the time.

Whenever I had leisure for private thoughts, however, I took the opportunity to contemplate my forthcoming rendezvous with Miss Lambright and how the business had best be managed.

One could not actually propose marriage while dancing. Well, I supposed one could, and no doubt it had been attempted before, but it seemed inadvisable to me. Surely a situation with increased privacy and decreased distraction would be rather more appropriate to the occasion and more conducive to a favorable outcome. My idea was to take Amelia aside at the conclusion of the last dance – perhaps a moonlight stroll in the garden. Yes, that would be just the thing.

And so, with this plan in mind, I stepped forward to claim my place across from her when the last dance was called.

As we stood in silence those few seconds, waiting for the music to begin, Amelia looked composedly at me. I returned her steady gaze, thinking, *This is the woman who will become my wife. This is the face I will see across the dinner table nearly every night of my life to come. I will soon promise to honor her – and only her – with my body, and she will be the mother of my children.*

The realization did not disturb me, for her person and visage were pleasant enough, and her conversation invariably agreeable. I was fully prepared to do my duty and enter into marriage.

We soon set off, and I commenced with a rather pedantic remark. "It has been a very fine ball, Miss Lambright. I hope you have enjoyed it."

"I have," she said. "Thank you, Mr. Darcy. Can you say the same?"

From her tone, it almost sounded like a challenge, or perhaps a test. She knew enough of my sentiments from my earlier information to predict what my honest answer should be. Was she wondering if I would do the socially expedient thing instead, saying I had enjoyed myself immensely? It would not do to begin the next stage of our relationship with a falsehood, however, so I gave an answer undisguised.

"I have enjoyed *some* parts of it, Miss Lambright." I said. "I have sincerely enjoyed my time with you as well as seeing your father and brother again. I enjoyed the supper, which was excellent. More than that, I will not claim."

She nodded thoughtfully. "I am pleased you have paid me the compliment of answering truthfully, Mr. Darcy."

"I shall always endeavor to do so, Miss Lambright. You have my word on that."

We carried on for a time with very little conversation until I estimated that the dance would soon conclude. I could not allow that to happen without at least giving Amelia some hint of my intentions, without asking from her a further indulgence of her time.

"Miss Lambright..."

"Yes, Mr. Darcy?"

"Might I have a word with you?"

"Certainly. Speak freely. I give you leave to say whatever you would like."

"Thank you, but I had a different circumstance in mind – something more... more private."

"More private?"

"Yes. I thought perhaps after this dance we might take a walk in the garden."

"Well, I hardly know, Mr. Darcy. What can you say to me in a garden that you cannot say in a ballroom?"

Was she willfully misunderstanding me, I wondered? Apparently, I would have to make myself abundantly clear. "If I could but speak to you in private for a few minutes, Miss Lambright, I have something very particular I wish to ask you."

She was quiet for some time, leaving me in suspense of an answer through to the very end of the dance.

The company began applauding their appreciation – to the orchestra and to our host, Lord Harcourt. Then suddenly everybody was in motion and talking all at once. And still I had no answer from my partner.

"Miss Lambright?" I prompted her. "May we take our walk now?"

"One moment, Mr. Darcy. My father needs me." So saying, she hurried away.

10

A Change of Plans

It had been an ill-judged plan from the beginning. I should have known that, as acting hostess of the ball, Amelia would not be free to do as she pleased. She would not be at liberty to cater to my request for more of her company. Her place was beside her father as the guests expressed their thanks and took their leave.

I lingered a while in the hope that there might yet be an opportunity, but then I realized the idea was meritless. It was extremely late already, and Miss Lambright would be tired. It would be unfair of me to detain her even longer on business that could easily wait a day or two. So I prepared to take leave myself.

I shook hands and exchanged a few words with Franklin Lambright. I thanked the viscount, who was looking a little frayed about the edges with the lateness of the hour. Amelia stood a few feet off, and I went to her next.

"You are going, Mr. Darcy?" she asked when I approached.

"Yes, Miss Lambright. Since it is so very late, I believe the question I meant to discuss with you must wait until another time. Might I call again, perhaps the day after tomorrow?"

"Of course. You are always very welcome here at Ravenshaw."

"And might I have a private audience with you then?"

With a look I did not know how to interpret, she said, "You may. A walk in the garden if you like, just as you suggested. I am sure my father can have no objection."

Taking her offered hand, I had the fleeting thought of kissing it. But I refrained from such a uselessly sentimental gesture. "Until then, Miss Lambright," I said, "good night."

So I went away without accomplishing my purpose after all. I slept as well as I could in the coach on the drive back to Pemberley and then went to my bed quite exhausted.

The post had already arrived by the time I arose again, and one of the letters was from my cousin Colonel Fitzwilliam. My cousin's Christian name is Richard, but to save confusion in a family replete with men of the very same appellation, he is, among his intimates, more commonly known as John (his middle name), Colonel, or simply Fitzwilliam. This is what he wrote:

Dear Friend,

I hope that you are well. I have been here in London these several weeks, partaking of social delights and, to please my father, pretending to look for a wife. Not that I would mind marrying if I discovered a young lady who not only fulfilled my father's requirements but mine as well. And yet I find that beautiful heiresses with exceptionally amiable dispositions are rather scarce this year.

I wanted you to know that I did drop round to check in with Georgiana at her new establishment a few days ago, as you had suggested. She seemed pleased to see me, and we had a very agreeable afternoon together. At my request, the dear girl spent some little time entertaining me at the piano-forte. I never tire of hearing her, and her playing seems to grow more and more accomplished.

Mrs. Younge was all affability and hospitality, and Georgiana appears happy in her charge, just as she has told you. There was much discussion of their imminent excursion to Ramsgate, to which, I gather, they are both very much looking forward. They were departing almost at once, so by the time you receive this, I suppose they will be enjoying the beauty and benefits of the seaside.

I will now mention a circumstance to you that is probably of no importance. You will be the best judge, however, since you know the man better than I do myself.

*I happened to espy Mr. Wickham in the neighborhood
that day, walking in the opposite direction and on the
other side of the street as I approached Mrs. Younge's. If
he had simply nodded or tipped his hat to acknowledge
me, I would have thought nothing about it, since there
could be any number of reasons he might be in that part
of town. But instead, he made some effort to conceal his
face with his hand and then ducked down the first alleyway
he came to. Nevertheless, I am sure it was him. As I say, it
is probably of no importance, and yet I thought you should
know.*

*Now I must get this to the post so that I can return to
my full schedule of bachelor duties. Knowing how ugly I
am, Cousin, you may find this difficult to believe, but there
are many young ladies who seem to delight in my
company. I must not disappoint them!*

Yours, etc.
R. J. Fitzwilliam

I had neither heard nor seen anything of Wickham since I
rejected his repeated requests for the Kympton living, so I had no
idea of his whereabouts or activities. It did not surprise me,
however, to learn that he was in London. London would exactly
suit an enterprising young man with more schemes for easy
pleasure than for useful occupation. That he was seen just down
the street from my sister's school was a circumstance worthy of
more note. I also trusted Fitzwilliam's instincts, which I had rarely
known to be in error. If he found Wickham's behavior suspicious,
I was inclined to credit his opinion.

The news made me uneasy, although I could not have said
exactly why. Low though my opinion of Wickham was, I would
never have considered him a threat to Georgiana's bodily safety.
Besides, she was now away from town on a holiday in Ramsgate
with Mrs. Younge, well supervised and chaperoned, according to
our agreement, so there was no reason to fear.

I set the letter aside and returned my thoughts to my all-important visit to Miss Lambright at Ravenshaw on the morrow. But it was no good. The business with Wickham kept niggling at me, worrying my brain until I could think of nothing else. Finally I decided that my only course of action was to go, rather than to Ravenshaw, to Ramsgate to reassure myself that all was well with Georgiana.

Miss Lambright would be expecting me, however, so I would need to send a message to explain my delay. I could not write to her directly, of course, so the pertinent information would have to reach her through her father – preferably without tipping my hand to him of what I had intended. I owed it to Amelia to put the question to her first without the chance of undue influence being brought to bear by her parent. So, deeming a little disguise necessary and justified, I wrote:

> *Dear Lord Harcourt,*
>
> *Once again, I thank you for your hospitality and for a very fine ball the other night. As I took leave, I believe I said something to your daughter about the possibility of my riding over again in a day or two, for I had hoped to spend more time with Franklin while he remains at Ravenshaw. Unfortunately, I must forfeit that pleasure, for urgent business calls me away, and I cannot say how long I will be detained. Please apologize for me to your daughter and son. I will write as soon as I have a better idea when I may be at liberty to come to you again.*
>
> *Sincerely,*
F. Darcy, Esq.

I sent this to Ravenshaw by messenger in the morning, at which time I myself set off by carriage for Ramsgate. I have often thought since how very different might have been the outcome for all concerned if I had done the reverse, sending a letter to Ramsgate and myself to Ravenshaw.

~~*~~

I was not overly concerned. In fact, as I thought about it rationally, I was nearly convinced that the entire journey would prove unwarranted. It would ease my mind, however, and a few days at the seaside with my sister could never be viewed as a waste of time. I had once been to Ramsgate before, and I began to anticipate renewing my acquaintance with the town and exploring its environs, this time in the agreeable company of my young, impressionable sister. I would delight in being the one to show her some of its hidden charms.

Georgiana would be surprised to see me, but pleased as well, I trusted. I knew where to find her as this was one of my stipulations for her going, that Mrs. Young should supply me with all the pertinent information. I was glad that I had had the foresight to inquire about this in advance, just as a matter of course, never expecting I would have cause to actually use the information for more than sending a letter. But now I did.

My sister was indeed surprised, but not nearly so much so as Mrs. Younge seemed to be upon discovering me at the door to her suite of rooms at the inn where they were staying. That lady expressed pleasure at finding me there, but it did not ring true. From the odd look on her face, I could see that she was in fact extremely discomposed, which in turn triggered my own alarm.

"Is anything wrong here, Mrs. Younge?" I asked at once. "Where is my sister?"

"Oh! Why, nothing is wrong at all, Mr. Darcy!" she exclaimed unconvincingly. "It is only that I am astonished to see you." She checked over her shoulder, and I noticed that she kept the door as little ajar as possible, blocking my view. "I... I am sure I never had any idea that you meant to pay us a visit. Of course you are very welcome. If you will wait there a moment, I will just get Miss Darcy."

She closed the door again, leaving me standing awkwardly in the passageway. I could hear excited murmurings and a bustle of activity within. Presently Mrs. Younge opened the door again, wide this time, to reveal my sister beside her.

Georgiana smiled at me, but it was not a smile of pure joy. There was something else present in her flushed cheeks, furrowed brow, and in the tremor of her voice. "How good of you to come all this way to see me, William," she said, glancing nervously at Mrs. Younge.

I looked from my sister to her guardian and back again, and it struck me at once that there was some secret collusion between them. "What is it, Georgiana?" I asked. "What is the matter here?"

Mrs. Younge began to object and disclaim, to apologize and to excuse. I paid no heed, however; my attention and my gaze were fixed unwaveringly on my sister, awaiting some kind of response from her. It did not take long for her resistance to crumble. She fell into my embrace with a choking sob. I knew then that I would have the truth from her if only we could get away from Mrs. Younge. So I guided Georgiana through the door, down the steps, and out into the street.

"Wait!" Mrs. Younge called after us. "Georgiana, come back!"

"Ignore her," I told my sister. "This is between you and me."

My mind worked feverishly, imaging all sorts of things as we walked on in silence. I cared not where we went, but we soon found ourselves in a quiet area near the shore. By then, I was calm enough to where I hoped I could address Georgiana with patience and not frighten her with an overly forbidding aspect.

I stopped, gently turned her to face me, and tipped her chin up until she, somewhat unwillingly, met my eyes. "Now, start at the beginning and tell me what this is all about," I said.

"Oh, William!" she began. "I am so confused. I am afraid I have behaved quite badly and that you will be very angry when I tell you. Can you ever forgive me?"

"Of course I can, my dear," I said more calmly than I felt. "Have no fear. We will sort this out together, whatever it is."

I held my breath as Georgiana began to pour forth her story: how Wickham had appeared, seemingly by chance, the first night of their being at Ramsgate; how Mrs. Younge had allowed, even encouraged, his attentions day after day; how the plan for a secret elopement had come about, Wickham declaring it the only way to ensure they could always be together.

"We were so much in love that it seemed to justify anything! And I thought perhaps you would not mind in the end, seeing as how Mr. Wickham had been such a friend to you in the past, and my own father thought well of him. Mrs. Younge made no objection either. Although I suppose I should have known there was something not quite right if we could not tell you about it until afterwards. Have I been very wicked to contemplate such a thing, William? I see now how it might have grieved you not to be consulted."

I hugged Georgiana tightly to myself, saying, "I should have been grieved indeed."

I did not trust myself to utter another word immediately, for inside me had risen up a great rage against Mrs. Younge and against the friend of my youth. Alongside it, a horror for what might have happened had I not arrived in time. My own dear, innocent sister – a child of fifteen – might have fallen prey to that unscrupulous man and been ruined forever. Yes, I was angry, very angry, but not with Georgiana. I would deal with Wickham in good time, but my first concern was for my sister.

"William?" she said tentatively.

"Yes."

"I do hope you will hold no grudge against dear Mr. Wickham. Now that you know we are in love, perhaps we can still be married, only in London or Derbyshire with all our friends about us, as we should have planned it from the beginning."

Then I realized; I was *not* in time. Although I might have prevented the elopement, I was too late to save my sister from all harm. She would at least suffer grievously when I told her the truth – that I would *never* allow the marriage and that Wickham's true object was undoubtedly her fortune, not herself. However that conversation could wait, I decided. At present, I only prayed for nothing worse than a broken heart.

"We will talk about that later," I said, "but now I must ask you one thing more, Georgiana, dear. And you must answer me honestly, whatever the truth may be. Agreed?"

"You are frightening me, William. What can it be?"

The question must indeed be asked and answered so that I would know what action was required. And yet it was a question that filled me with dread... and one that should never need to be mentioned to a girl of fifteen at all!

Bracing for the worst, I asked, "Has Mr. Wickham laid a hand on you?"

Georgiana looked too confused by this to reply, and so I tried again.

"Sometimes, when a couple is planning to marry soon, there is a temptation to... to anticipate their vows." Still no reply. "To become physically intimate. To behave as man and wife before..."

Georgiana looked stricken and began violently shaking her head. "No! Oh, no, William! There has been nothing improper of that sort going on; I swear it. He is not so unworthy as you imply. You must believe me!"

I exhaled. "I do, and we need never mention it again. Now, I must take you home."

"To my lodgings at the inn, do you mean?"

We began retracing our steps in that direction. "Yes," I said. "We are going there first, but then to Pemberley."

She began to cry. "I may not stay in Ramsgate? But when will I see my dear Wickham again?"

"Mrs. Younge has acted wrongly by not chaperoning you properly. You must see that, Georgiana, and that I can no longer entrust you to her care. As for the rest, we will discuss it later, as I said."

We arrived back at the inn, and I knocked once more on Mrs. Younge's door. "Has he gone?" I asked grimly when she opened.

"I'm sure I have no idea who you mean, Mr. Darcy," she lied. "There is nobody here but me. Come in and see for yourself if you like."

I sent Georgiana to her room to collect her things. While she was gone, I gave Mrs. Younge a piece of my mind and extracted from her the whereabouts of Mr. Wickham, whom she at last admitted to having known before. When Georgiana returned, carrying her portmanteau, I said, "You will hardly be surprised, Mrs. Younge, to learn that I am removing my sister from your charge. You are a disgrace, madam."

I escorted my sister away at once and settled her in my carriage, which, fortunately, I had left standing by. Then acquiring paper and pen at the inn, I wrote this short but pointed note:

> *You are a rogue and a scoundrel, sir, and if I could do so without harming others, I would immediately expose you to the world as such. But I swear that <u>nothing</u> in all of creation will constrain me if anything else of a similar nature should happen. If you value your safety, therefore, you would be wise to remove yourself from the vicinity at once and keep well out of my sight henceforth. For I shall not be responsible for my actions if I ever catch you within ten miles of a certain person again. I trust I make myself clear.*

I addressed the note to Wickham, and though I did not sign it, I expected that when it was delivered he could be in no doubt as to the identity of the sender.

11
Fitzwilliam Consulted

It was too late in the day to attempt making much progress towards our eventual destination, and yet lodging options in Ramsgate were limited. Besides, I had that afternoon developed a sudden disgust for the town. So I determined it best to make for a place I had stayed before in Canterbury, and thence to London the next day.

I knew I must speak to Georgiana along the way, while we had complete privacy, not leaving it to the last minute either, much as I dreaded saying to her what I must – destroying all her illusions, forever changing her view of the world and of men in particular. Would that I could have kept her safe and at the same time preserved her child-like innocence. But I could not. The trouble she had already encountered made that clear. Perhaps if I had chosen to disillusion her a little sooner, she would not so easily have been victimized by Wickham. I could not undo that error in judgement, but I could at least help her to learn from what had happened – and what had very nearly happened – so that she would be wiser in future.

But how much to tell her? That was the question I struggled with as we drove along those first few miles.

I must reveal enough of Wickham's faults, past behavior, and his true intentions to prove he was by no means a respectable young man deserving of her love and loyalty. That did not admit a doubt. Georgiana must understand why they could not be allowed to marry or she would never give him up, at least not in her heart. But must I also describe in horrifying detail what might have become of her if Wickham had succeeded? – the heartache, the degradation, the probable abuse that would have awaited her once he had gained his object: control of her fortune.

I did my best to walk the fine line between enough and too much information, but it was every bit as tortuous as I had feared.

Georgiana at first denied the truth of what I told her, staunchly defending Wickham against every charge. Because of this, I was forced to be more blunt, to use stronger language than I had hoped would be necessary, until I finally succeeded in convincing her. However, I could by no means count it a victory that I had reduced my sister to such a pitiful state.

Once Georgiana accepted the veracity of my explanations, she also accepted my shoulder to cry on. And of course there were tears aplenty. What followed was arguably worse, however. It was an unnatural calm so profound that I feared for Georgiana's health. She would not speak. She would not eat that night at our lodgings, nor the next morning before we set off for London. She moved about as if in a daze, doing the very minimum that was required of her and no more.

I apologized again and again for not properly forewarning her against such a danger, as well as for the part I had been required to play in spoiling her dreams, asking her to tell me that she understood and forgave. She would nod, even give me a half smile, but there was no light in her eyes to reassure me, no color in her cheeks, no spark of life and hope.

It was a relief when we at last arrived at Darcy House, where I hoped the familiar surroundings would lend both my sister and me some comfort. I did finally persuade her to take a little wine before retiring very early to her room and to bed. I was nearly beside myself with worry – for her wellbeing and for what to do to help her. All that occurred to me was to send for Fitzwilliam at once.

~~*~~

I called for Fitzwilliam's help in this crisis because he was not only a near relation and friend, but as Georgiana's other guardian, he had a right to be kept informed and a responsibility to help determine what was best to be done.

Fortunately, my message reached him directly and he came at once.

"What is this about, Darcy?" he asked jovially when I met him in the entry. "I would have you know that I left a very fine dinner to come, so it had better be serious."

"Yes, it is, I'm afraid. Do step in here, Fitzwilliam," I told him, leading him to the library, where we could talk in private. It would not do for the servants to hear any part of what I must impart to my cousin. Closing the door behind us, I continued. "It concerns Georgiana."

"Georgiana?" he said, instantly sober. "I thought she was amusing herself in Ramsgate."

"She was, but it was not all innocent enjoyment, I discovered. I have now fetched her home again and just in time. She is upstairs asleep."

"Then do not keep me in suspense. Is your sister ill?"

"You shall know everything presently, but we may as well sit down." We did so, and then I hastened to commence my explanations before Fitzwilliam became any more agitated. I told him all, every particular of what had transpired in Ramsgate, including what Georgiana had confessed of the plan for a secret elopement and how I acted thereafter. "So you see how near to tragedy we have come," I concluded. "Thank God for your letter, Fitzwilliam! Had you not written when you did, had you not mentioned Wickham's suspicious behavior, it would have been a very different outcome."

"And thank God you listened and acted! When I think how easily either of us could have overlooked or ignored the warning signs… And yes, the outcome then is something I cannot countenance. To think of that darling creature upstairs forever under the power of such a man, ruined…"

Suddenly restless, I stood and paced. "I am to blame for placing her in danger," I confessed. "My conscience clearly tells me so. I should have been more vigilant. I should have chosen an establishment for Georgiana more carefully and certainly not allowed her to go to Ramsgate on holiday without me. I should have educated her long ago about the ways of unscrupulous men, the deceptive ploys of fortune hunters. Everywhere I look I see my own errors, but all too late."

Fitzwilliam shook his head. "Not too late; just in time. And if there is blame on your side, Darcy, you share that with me. We are equally responsible for Georgiana's wellbeing. But let us remember who the real villain is here. Do you think he has truly relinquished his object now? Thirty thousand pounds would be difficult for a man like Wickham to walk away from after coming so close."

"Indeed. We must continue to guard against him and others of his ilk. The danger will remain until Georgiana is safely married to a man of good character. Toward that end, we must also ensure that knowledge of this unfortunate incident never comes out. I am convinced that no real harm has been done, but you know the damage even a hint of scandal can do to a young lady's reputation, and therefore her marriage prospects."

"True, although it is difficult for me to think of our dear girl being ready for marriage any time soon. Why, she is not yet sixteen!"

"I heartily agree with you, Fitzwilliam, but she herself was recently persuaded to believe otherwise," I said soberly. "If she is thinking of marriage, we had best be too. Although I would keep her perpetually at home and under my protection if I could, the more realistic solution is to see her respectably settled when she is eighteen or nineteen."

"A brilliant marriage, I trust you mean," my cousin said sardonically. "That is what will be expected of her by the family. That is what is expected of us all!"

"No doubt. However, especially after what has so recently occurred, I am inclined to demand far less. I am inclined to think more of mere respectability and kindness than prestige. I would even be glad to see her married to a man like my friend Charles Bingley. He is not high born, of course, but he is a gentleman whom I know to be honorable, trustworthy, and to already hold Georgiana in some affection. I will condition for nothing more when the time comes."

A little calmer by this time, I resumed my seat before continuing. "For now, though, I would simply like to see her restored to herself. This business has brought her spirits so low. I mean to take her home to Pemberley for the summer, but I have no thought beyond. What would you advise me to do to see her well and cheerful again, Fitzwilliam?"

"Oh, good heavens! I am hardly qualified; I know nothing of the workings of a young girl's mind!"

"No more do I. Nevertheless, there is nobody else, not unless you think it would be of use asking your mother or Aunt Catherine for assistance."

"Hardly! I have no doubt of your receiving strong – and probably diametrically opposed – opinions from those two venerable ladies if you asked. But as to the sagacity of that advice, I am far less confident. Moreover, if that is what your father had wanted, he would have made one of them Georgiana's guardian instead. No, I believe there is good reason he did not."

"Agreed. Then we must do the best we can on our own, at least until one of us has a wife to lend her aid."

"A wife? You must not look to me for that, friend! Despite what I have told my father, I have no thoughts of matrimony at present." Then he looked at me narrowly. "But perhaps you are thinking of yourself. Yes, I see it in your eye. You *have* been thinking of marrying! Is it to be Miss Bingley? Do tell. When am I to wish you both joy?"

Fitzwilliam had said it in jest, but I did not really mind him knowing my intentions. In fact, I might have told him myself if he had not guessed it. So I only denied the distastefully erroneous detail. "It is *not* Miss Bingley I think of."

His hand holding his chin, he puzzled aloud. "Hmm. Then who can it be? For you have not been to town to peruse the goods available on the marriage market this season. Oh, I have it!" he declared triumphantly. "It must be our cousin Anne, of course! Lady Catherine will be so pleased."

"Very droll indeed, Fitzwilliam. You have had your fun, but that will do. No, I am thinking of Viscount Harcourt's daughter, Miss Amelia Lambright. I suppose you could say that I have been courting her these several weeks past, and I was about to ride over to propose when I received your letter."

"Truly? I am all amazement. Is it a love match, then?"

"I would hardly characterize it in that way. I have a great regard for Miss Lambright and for her family, and it is a highly suitable match, one my father suggested to me years ago in fact. I believe Miss Lambright and I will deal very well together. Now, however, ought the whole thing best be delayed? I cannot judge whether such an event would be likely to cheer Georgiana or only distress her more."

"I see your difficulty, Darcy." He was silent for a minute or two, and I did not disturb his ruminations. Presently, he spoke again. "If you are not too impatient to give up your freedom, old man, I would advise you to wait. It does seem a bit cruel to go ahead with your own wedding plans just after breaking up your sister's."

"When you put it like that, Fitzwilliam, there is no question. My plans will certainly keep until Georgiana is feeling more herself again."

"And then perhaps some visitors to Pemberley this summer would help to distract her from her troubles. I am glad to offer my own humble services for one. I believe she usually finds me amusing."

12

Return to Pemberley

It was a melancholy journey north out of London – melancholy and painfully silent. Georgiana steadfastly fended off my every effort to engage her in any conversation beyond the bare necessities.

The recent events had worked an irrevocable alteration in our relationship. Although I did not know it at the time, my sister had crossed over some invisible boundary. Gone forever were the carefree days of childhood, the days when her dreams were simple and she would tell me everything she was thinking. We retained a certain closeness, but now she frequently kept her own counsel rather than confiding in me, and my glimpses into her heart became far rarer.

I suppose these changes were inevitable. All children must grow up and exert their independence, separating themselves from their parental figures to some degree. And yet I cannot help but feel these changes were unfairly hastened in Georgiana's case. It was an early lesson for me as well, one that gave me sympathy for what every parent must feel. Mothers and fathers work tirelessly toward the moment when their children will be grown and can make their own way in the world. And yet they pay a heavy price when that goal is finally achieved.

The deafening silence continued after we reached Pemberley, at least for a time. Then, ever so gradually, week by week, Georgiana began to show some symptoms of recovery – a painfully slow return of spirits. She began occasionally speaking to me of her own accord, I noticed. Her appetite improved a bit, and she spent less time isolated in her own apartments, occasionally taking some air instead. The tone of her music, which was her one great consolation throughout this and every other difficult period, improved as well, moving from the playing of universally somber pieces to things with more light and life to them.

When I judged that Georgiana might be ready, I proposed having some guests to Pemberley. "What would you say to our inviting a few friends to stay?" I asked her over breakfast one morning in the middle of July. "Fitzwilliam or the Bingleys perhaps?"

She frowned. "I suppose you have told Fitzwilliam all about… about my disgrace in Ramsgate."

"I have told him about Ramsgate, yes, as was only right, since he is also your guardian. However, there was no talk of any disgrace on your part, my dear. It was not you but others who have dishonored themselves, as Fitzwilliam agrees."

This seemed to mollify her a little.

"Still," she said presently, "I will be embarrassed to see him again, knowing he has heard of it. Must we invite him?"

"No, certainly not. We could have the Bingleys instead, or perhaps the Lambrights. You remember Viscount Harcourt and his daughter Amelia Lambright. Whilst you were away this spring, I renewed my acquaintance with them, visiting Ravenshaw some three or four times, where I was treated with great civility, I must say. It would be a courtesy to return their hospitality, if that would be agreeable to you. They know nothing of recent events, of course, nor shall they. So there would be no worries of that sort, not with either party in fact." When she did not respond, I added, "Consider it, anyway. There is no rush."

Georgiana nodded but said nothing more on the subject that day. I hoped – for her sake as well as my own – that she would agree to Amelia and her father. Bingley would have been a cheerful addition to our family party, but having him usually meant having one or both of his sisters as well. Given the choice between the Bingley sisters and Miss Lambright, I knew which would be the better influence for my sister, nowhere near fully recovered from her disappointment. Besides, my courtship plans had been interrupted long enough.

I had written to Lord Harcourt a second time with my excuses when I knew I would be delayed still longer in coming to them, saying my sister was unwell. I could not leave Georgiana in order to go to Ravenshaw, not until she was stronger. However, I did not wish to insult Amelia – or encourage my rivals either – by prolonged inattentiveness, not if it could be helped. If she and her father came to Pemberley, even just for the day, that would serve to forward things neatly, I believed. Amelia could see Pemberley again, now with the implied invitation to imagine it her future home. She could renew her friendship with Georgiana as well, which I hoped would smooth the way for when my sister learnt Amelia was to become my wife.

A week later, Georgiana told me that she would not find a visit from the viscount and his daughter disagreeable, especially if it were a short one. So the invitation was issued and answered, and we were to expect them a fortnight later. It was a bonus to learn that Franklin would be accompanying them to Pemberley.

The day before they were due to arrive, I said to my sister by way of a hint, "You have been too little amongst people of your own level, Georgiana, especially young ladies of quality. You will have one such before you tomorrow."

"I think some of the girls at school were very agreeable," she proposed hesitantly.

"Perhaps they were, but after observing Miss Amelia Lambright, I am sure you will perceive the difference. She is everything respectable and refined. She would make a fine friend for you, though she is a few years older."

I wished to say more. I wished to advise Georgiana to learn from and emulate Amelia. I wished to suggest that the connection between the two young women might soon have opportunity to develop into one of a more intimate and permanent character. I hoped that she would also perceive the superiority of a young gentleman like Franklin Lambright to a man like George Wickham!

I said none of this, of course. With Fitzwilliam's warning words in mind, I resolved to move slowly, to be patient with Georgiana, not chiding her over past mistakes or abruptly foisting my marriage plans on her. I only hoped Amelia would be likewise patient with me.

I am not normally plagued by nervous disorders. However, that day was an exception, for it was very important to me that all went well with our guests – that the viscount and his daughter should approve of Pemberley and that Georgiana should approve of Amelia. I did not require my sister's endorsement of my chosen bride, naturally, but I earnestly desired to have it. After all, I had pursued this course of action partly with her in mind, that my marriage might benefit Georgiana as much as myself. If she should dislike my choice, therefore, half the benefit would be lost. If she should be violently opposed, it would spell disaster.

Then I reminded myself that the idea of anybody's violently disliking Amelia was unimaginable. And it was true; Miss Lambright was not at all the sort of person to inspire violent emotions of any kind.

13
Noble Visitors

My misgivings were soon tolerably allayed once our guests arrived. During the initial greetings, all three made much of seeing Georgiana again after so long. Georgiana herself was characteristically reserved but not unfriendly as she welcomed them to Pemberley. Miss Lambright behaved with uncommon solicitude, I thought, sitting near my sister and drawing her into conversation. Lord Harcourt was left primarily to my share, with Franklin dividing his time and attention evenly between the two discussions.

"Well now, this is capitol indeed, Darcy!" said the viscount thirty minutes into our agreeable visit together in the drawing room. "I have often had the desire to see Pemberley again."

"I am ashamed it has taken me so long to invite you, Lord Harcourt. It should have been done years ago."

"Nonsense, my boy. Perfectly understandable under the circumstances, all you have had on your plate since your father's death. And it is 'Harcourt' to you, remember?"

I nodded.

"Now, shall I tell you what I should really like?"

"By all means, sir."

"I should very much like for you to take me on a riding explore of the park before dinner. Not all of it, mind you, for I suppose there are not enough hours in a day for that! Only let us peruse some of the best Pemberley has to offer. The weather is not too hot for such an outing, and the ladies are doing very well together, as you see. They will not miss us. Perhaps Miss Darcy would care to give my daughter a tour of the house whilst we are gone, since it has been so long. Would you like that Amelia?" This last he said loud enough to attract her attention.

"What were you saying, Papa?"

"That perhaps you might like it if Miss Darcy were to show you about the house a little."

Miss Lambright glanced at me and colored noticeably. She was probably thinking of the implications of such a suggestion, as indeed I was myself. But here, I was proud of my sister for speaking up immediately to rescue her guest from obvious discomfort, although Georgiana could have had no notion of its true cause.

"You must have no scruples on my account, Miss Lambright," she said. "I am not the least bit tired, I assure you, and I would be very happy to show you the house."

It was a natural interpretation of Amelia's hesitation, for Georgiana knew our guests had been informed of a recent unspecified illness.

"Very well, then," I said after some further reluctance. "It appears it is all settled." There was clearly nothing else to be done. "Will you be joining us, Franklin?"

"I certainly will, if you can provide me a mount."

I was surprised when the viscount then hurried to discourage his son in this, saying, "You must feel no obligation to ride with us, Franklin. It is only a little whim of mine that Mr. Darcy is kind enough to indulge. Would you not prefer to stay and keep the ladies company?"

"Although I should be delighted to spend more time in Miss Darcy's company," Franklin replied with grace and diplomacy, "I would no doubt be only underfoot in this case. No, I shall take myself out of the way and leave the house entirely to the ladies. That is their area of particular interest – their natural domain, one might say – whilst men must prefer the out of doors."

Seeing that Lord Harcourt raised no further objection to his son's accompanying us on the ride, I sent word on ahead to the stables to have my own horse and two others saddled at once. I regretted having to abandon the ladies for so long, primarily on

Georgiana's account. But otherwise it was by no means an onerous duty, for time spent in the saddle on a fine day is never tedious to me, and I could not help taking a measure of pride in showing the men some of the best that the grounds of Pemberley could boast.

I judged that the three of us would have just time enough to travel the path along the lake and the outflowing stream as far as the bridge, which was a pleasant route regardless of the season, and then climb through the hills to the high point of the estate – the bald prominence, from which nearly all the rest might be seen – before returning to the stables and then the house to join the ladies for dinner. And so that is what we did.

There was nothing particularly remarkable in our conversation along the way. Both Lord Harcourt and his son were as complimentary of what I showed them as could be expected of men who have seen other large and prosperous estates before, their own being of a similar size and grandeur. Beyond these standard civilities, however, the viscount seemed rather quieter than was his normal style, and I could not help wondering if something had displeased him.

Then I had an idea of what the trouble might be. Perhaps Lord Harcourt had been hoping for a private word with me, an opportunity with which his son had unwittingly interfered. Had he concocted this impromptu plan of a ride in order to ascertain my intentions towards his daughter, perhaps even expecting me to seize the chance provided to come to the point, asking his permission to marry her?

I would never know, of course. If so, however, I was grateful for Franklin's presence, though his father was not. It thereby spared me an awkward conversation with Lord Harcourt – one I would earlier have welcomed and yet now must postpone for Georgiana's sake.

"Care for a gallop?" I asked the others when we were within sight of the stables again. We gave the horses their heads and let them do the rest.

Lord Harcourt seemed to have recovered his good humor by the time we sat down to dinner, which was a great boon to keeping up an acceptable amount of talk. Father and son spoke of our tour of the park, primarily for Amelia's benefit. Her comments about the house were more reserved, presumably for the same reason as before, her consciousness of the implications. Franklin, who sat across from Georgiana, went to the trouble of cultivating a conversation with her, through which they discovered a mutual interest in music.

"Will you play for us before we go, Miss Darcy?" he subsequently asked.

"If you like," Georgiana replied, dropping her eyes demurely.

"I would like that above all things. I cannot play myself, but I appreciate the skill of those who can tremendously. I suppose you have been taught by the best masters in London."

"I believe Mr. Winterbrook is considered a very fine music master, yes, but I would not wish to raise your expectations too high, Mr. Lambright. I am perhaps not as talented as some of his other pupils."

"I cannot suppose that to be true. Besides, you are young yet. You will become more and more proficient with time as you continue to receive his instruction. Will you be returning to town to carry on with your studies, Miss Darcy? If so, I hope that I might be so fortunate as to occasionally see you there, now that we have renewed our acquaintance."

A cluster of unhappy emotions briefly bloomed over Georgiana's countenance. She turned to me in her confusion.

We had been taking each week as it came that summer. And although I had been making some discreet inquiries, I had not yet broached the difficult topic with my sister of where and how she was to continue her education after the disaster of Mrs. Younge's. "Our plans for the autumn are not yet firmly established," I said. "For now, the quiet of the country is all we require."

"Naturally, naturally," voiced the viscount. "Nothing so good for the health of body and mind as the peace of a country life. That is what I always say."

After dinner, and after we had listened to Georgiana play for half an hour, Lord Harcourt and his offspring began taking leave. Franklin offered Georgiana his arm as we all made our way outside to send them off. I did the same for Amelia, and falling a little behind the others gave me my first chance of the afternoon to exchange a few words with her in relative privacy.

"I hope you have spent a pleasant day with us, Miss Lambright," I said.

"Yes, Mr. Darcy, very pleasant indeed."

We walked on. "I so appreciate your generous attentions to my shy sister. She is at a… a difficult age, especially for a girl without a mother. It would please me very much if the two of you could be on friendly terms."

Amelia cast me a sidelong look before answering, but I could not judge what it might mean. Had I said too much? Had I implied more than I should have or intended to, making her uncomfortable? In any case, she only said, "We have made a good beginning today, I daresay. Miss Darcy is a sweet girl, and her performance at the piano-forte was wonderful. With her natural reticence, I am amazed that she did not seem to mind playing for us."

"I understand what you mean; it does seem a contradiction. But she has told me that, generally speaking, she is more comfortable playing for than talking to people, because music is the language in which she is most fluent."

"What a lovely idea! In that case, I envy her musical fluency. I am not nearly as eloquent in that tongue."

Having heard Miss Lambright play, I could not honestly dispute her claim. Something else was required. "I am certain you possess other gifts that are just as valuable, Miss Lambright."

We had by this time reached the waiting carriage. Pausing there a moment, she smiled mildly. "Thank you, Mr. Darcy, and good bye," she said, then allowed me to hand her in to her brother.

The viscount shook my hand, saying, "Do visit us again soon, Darcy. You are always most welcome at Ravenshaw." Then to his daughter in the carriage, "Isn't that so, Amelia?"

"Of course, Papa," Amelia replied.

"There, you see? Bring your sister too, if you like."

"That is very kind of you sir," I said. "However, please pardon me if my present commitments prevent me from coming as soon as I would like."

He harrumphed and cleared his throat. "Naturally. Naturally. I suppose you know your own business best."

I bowed. He joined his family in the carriage, and they drove away.

14
A Sister's Opinion

lthough I was satisfied with how the visit had come off, I was just as interested in Georgiana's opinion. Lord Harcourt's carriage was not even lost from view when I received the first indication of her feelings.

My sister and I were still standing on the porch together, and I began by complimenting her on how well she had managed her hostess duties, even though, as I well knew, it was not something with which she felt comfortable. "...but then, the Lambrights are such well-bred and agreeable people, which makes everything easy. Do not you agree?"

Georgiana did not answer. She only turned on her heel and ran back into the house. I could not be sure at first, but I suspected she was crying. And so I followed.

"Georgiana!" I said in hot pursuit. "What on earth is the matter? Georgiana?"

She paid me no heed. In fact, her pace only quickened as she mounted the stairs, no doubt intent on achieving the security of her own apartments – her safe haven, where she knew I would not intrude myself without her leave to do so. I was just as determined to keep her from escaping, however, at least until she had told me what the trouble was. I caught her door before she could close it in my face. "Now, my dear sister," I said from the doorway, "tell me what has you so dismayed. Did Mr. Lambright do or say something at the last to upset you?"

"No!" she cried angrily, dropping down in her favorite chair. "He was a perfect gentleman, of course. Was that not the point you wished to make?"

I was baffled by such an accusation. "Forgive me, Georgiana, but I have not the pleasure of understanding you. What can you be speaking of?"

She looked at me as if I had been an imbecile. "Of Franklin Lambright, of course! You said it yourself: he is well-bred and agreeable."

"Yes," I said slowly, still struggling to reach beyond this first statement, with which I heartily agreed, to whatever my sister apparently saw as the obvious conclusion that followed. "But why should Mr. Lambright's being a perfect gentleman upset you?"

"I should not need to tell you, for it was all your own doing! Oh, how can you be so unkind as to tease me about it?"

I was at a complete loss for what to do when she began to cry again. By this time, I knew better than to expect rational behavior from my adolescent sister, especially where questions of romance were concerned, but I still had no idea how to best cope with such an excess of sensibility. I drew near to her, kneeling beside her chair and speaking in my most soothing voice.

"Upon my honor, I do *not* tease you, Georgiana. Please help me to comprehend your meaning."

"Do you think me a fool? Mr. Lambright was meant to make Mr. Wickham look inferior by comparison, of course. No doubt you invited him here for that purpose and told him how to behave – to be gallant and pay me handsome attentions."

There it was at last: an answer, although still not a reasonable one. I took a deep breath, telling myself that I must remain calm in the face of this latest challenge. There would be no hope if we *both* lost our heads. "Now listen carefully, Georgiana. I did no such thing. As you will doubtless recall, I was not even aware that Franklin remained at Ravenshaw when I issued the invitation. If, however, your eyes have indeed been opened by Mr. Lambright to what a gentleman ought to be, then I must thank him."

"I suppose now you wish me to marry *him* instead of dear Wickham!"

At this, my struggle for calm was lost. "*Dear Wickham?* This is fine talk! I thought you understood – and agreed with – the reasons why George Wickham is not an eligible candidate, that he is not worthy of your further consideration. And as to my wanting you to marry Franklin Lambright instead, that is utter nonsense. You are much too young to marry anybody at present. If I was hoping for one of the Lambrights to make a favorable impression on you, it was Amelia, not Franklin. If I was thinking of a nearer connection to that honorable family, it was to be through myself, not…"

I stopped abruptly but too late. The words were out of my mouth, and Georgiana had heard them. She stared at me wide-eyed. Now I wondered, belatedly, what price I should pay for losing control of my temper. Or would it be my sister who would pay for my loose tongue?

I saw comprehension beginning to dawn in her face. She blinked away her tears and said, "You wish to marry Miss Lambright." It was a statement, I noticed, not a question.

I rose to my feet and strode a few paces away, allowing myself a little time and space to construct an answer. "Well… perhaps," I hedged. "That is to say, it is an idea I have been considering, yes."

Again, I could see her mind working.

"Does she know it?" she asked evenly.

"I believe so. I have not yet mentioned marriage to her, not in so many words, but I think she can hardly be without a strong suspicion."

This conversation was meant to have taken place some weeks hence, when I judged that Georgiana might be strong enough to tolerate it. However, because she had actually grown more composed instead of less so since we had inadvertently begun the topic, I ventured to proceed one step further.

"What would you think of the idea, my dear? Should you mind having Amelia for a sister-in-law?" When Georgiana did not immediately answer, in my discomfort, I blundered on. "It would be a very desirable connection on both sides, as everybody must admit. The Lambrights are an old and respected family, and our own father thought highly of them. In fact, it was he who first suggested the idea of Miss Lambright to me years ago. She is a congenial lady, do not you agree? Entirely suitable, too. She would become a sister of sorts to you, a more mature woman to help and guide you."

I had run out of words, and still Georgiana did not answer. Although eminently to be preferred to noisy hysterics, her thoughtful calm was unnerving.

At last she spoke. "You tell me of her many advantages but not one word about affection. William, are you in love with Miss Lambright or are you not?"

I should have anticipated this question from my sister, whose whole being had lately been consumed with nothing but emotion, consumed with her unfortunate passion for Wickham and then with the grief of losing the idyllic future she had imagined with him. I should have anticipated the question and been prepared. However, I was not. Suddenly called upon to justify my plans in terms my young sister could understand, I was nearly confounded.

"Of course I have a degree of affection for Miss Lambright," I began cautiously "affection and respect, as I believe she does for me. That is all that I require. Choosing a marriage partner is possibly the most important decision each of us will ever make. Accordingly, it is wisest to use one's head and not be led astray by emotion."

"Like I was, do you mean?"

"Well... yes, I suppose so. Although I did not mean to mention it, Georgiana, you yourself have learnt by painful experience that the heart cannot be trusted to choose the wisest course. But we need not go over that ground again."

"Still, to marry without love, William? I cannot countenance the idea! Surely it must be possible to choose with both head and heart agreeing together!"

"Perhaps, but that is not the question at hand. I only ask you once more, what should you think of having Miss Lambright for a sister-in-law? You were friends once. Could you be so again, do you suppose, and possibly more? Should you be able to accept her as an elder sister? It is important to me that my choice in this matter does not destroy your happiness."

"My happiness is already destroyed, William," she said flatly, her earlier emotion spent. "You may as well marry to make *yourself* happy – Miss Lambright or somebody else. What does it matter to me? Only let it wait a little, I beg you. Let us remain just as we are for now. I do not think I could bear such another disruption so soon."

Not the answer I had been hoping for, this. There were no words of praise or approval for Amelia. She was not to be preferred over any other, only viewed as an unpleasant "disruption." Georgiana's continuing thoughts of Wickham were most disturbing. Clearly, her recovery had not progressed as far as I had hoped. Clear it was as well that my proposal to Miss Lambright must be put off yet a little while longer.

I left Georgiana with my solemn assurance that I would take no serious action immediately. More than that, I could not promise. Although I wished to be kind to my unhappy sister, I also needed to be fair to Miss Lambright and her father. I still held out some small hope of its being possible to do both.

15
Town and Country

Miss Lambright was momentarily set aside... again. As the summer came to a close, all my efforts were directed at setting up an acceptable new situation for Georgiana in London. She would not be going to another school, however, for I would not make the mistake of entrusting her safety entirely to a stranger again! No, I decided – and she reluctantly agreed – that her masters and teachers must come to her at Darcy House, where Fitzwilliam and I and a host of servants loyal to me could keep a close watch.

Toward that end, I engaged a woman of extensive education and exemplary character – this time I had researched more carefully, taking nothing for granted – to serve as Georgiana's constant companion and tutor for all basic subjects, including comportment. Her name was Mrs. Annesley, and she would ensure that her charge never went anywhere unprotected. She would, I hoped, also provide the feminine perspective about which Fitzwilliam and I were so ignorant.

This arrangement would mean my spending more time in town than I liked, and much traveling to and fro, but it could not be helped. For I agreed with Georgiana that Pemberley all the year round would be too isolating for her. London had the advantage of the best masters, the best culture, and the best of her friends. A little inconvenience to myself was not to be considered.

By the end of August, everything was in place for our departure. I had consulted at length with my steward, Mr. Adams, concerning every detail I could anticipate for the management of the estate during my long absences. The trustworthy, experienced, and highly capable Mrs. Reynolds, of course, needed no instruction from me in the running of the household. Mrs. Annesley had preceded us and was already in residence at Darcy House. She was prepared to begin her educational duties as soon as we arrived in town, her knowledge supplemented by masters engaged to teach dance, music, and so forth. Finally, I had by post apprised Fitzwilliam of all these arrangements in full. As he spent the majority of his time in London, I knew I could depend on him to do his part.

I hovered very close indeed those first few weeks after our arrival in town to be assured that Georgiana was comfortably settled and to see for myself that she got on well with Mrs. Annesley. I also wished to be certain there were no unsavory characters, such as Wickham, attempting to insinuate themselves into my sister's world.

Besides Fitzwilliam, however, the only young man who came was my good friend Bingley. And although he was kind and solicitous of my sister, as always, it was primarily myself to whom he wished to speak.

After seeking my advice earlier, as he was wont to do, a letter from him had arrived announcing momentous news; he had very precipitously taken a house in Hertfordshire, to which I was urged to come and give my approval as soon as might be. His visit to us in Berkeley Street now, a fortnight later, was, I gathered, to make certain I would accept the invitation.

"I took the house immediately, for is as fine a place as ever you can imagine!" he told Georgiana and myself in high spirits shortly after his appearing at our door. "Well, I suppose that is not precisely true, for to be sure, it is nothing to Pemberley. But it will do very well for *me*, I think."

"Do let us be seated," I entreated him, perceiving at once that this would not be a brief conversation. "You can make free to tell us all about it, but we may as well be comfortable first."

"Certainly. Certainly," he said. "At least I will try, and yet I scarcely know if I can sit still in all my excitement."

The three of us took our ease in the drawing room.

"What a stroke of luck that I found it when I did!" Bingley continued at once. "For I had nearly made up my mind to take that place I told you about before, which would have been a disaster, I am now convinced. What was I thinking of in considering Devon? Devon! Can you imagine?"

"Devonshire is quite beautiful, Mr. Bingley," said Georgiana, "or so my brother has told me."

"It is true," I confirmed. "I have twice been as far as Exeter, and I remember the scenery as quite pleasing. It is a different style of beauty from the northern counties perhaps, but no one could have accused you of bad taste in considering the possibility of residing there."

"Perhaps not," he said, seeming impatient to regain control of the conversation. "I am not a champion of the sea air, though. Oh, it is all very well in the summer; on a hot day, the breezes must be quite congenial. But not in the winter! I'm sure I should have been quite cold and desolate then. No, Hertfordshire is the place for me – all the comforts of a country life and yet close to one's friends and to town when one needs to be."

Finding no fault with this logic, I said, "Then I applaud you in arriving at a very sensible decision."

He looked pleased. "Darcy, you must come back with me at once to see the place. Indeed, you must! And Georgiana too, if you like."

"What is your new house called, Mr. Bingley?" asked my sister.

"Netherfield. It is a charming name, is it not, Georgiana?"

"Yes, indeed! I like it very much."

"I knew you would. I so much like the sound of it myself that I could say it again and again." He laughed. "In truth, I must confess that I do! It is by way of practicing, you see. I say, 'my estate, Netherfield' or 'I soon return to Netherfield, my estate in Hertfordshire.' How noble it sounds!"

His enthusiasm was contagious… to Georgiana, at least.

"Oh, yes! May we go, William?" she asked, turning to me expectantly.

"Certainly not," I replied calmly. "I will not have your studies disrupted only for the purpose of seeing a house. You have just now got settled, and if memory serves, you have your music lesson with Mr. Winterbrook this week. I know you would not wish to miss it."

"That is true."

"There will no doubt be other opportunities to see Mr. Bingley's fine house."

"Indeed there will be, Georgiana!" he agreed. "I have the lease of Netherfield for a twelve-month at the minimum."

"Very well, then," she said with a small sigh, gracefully relinquishing the idea, which had been, after all, but the wish of a moment.

Then my friend returned his efforts to persuading me. "You must come by yourself, then, Darcy, for you have not the same impediment."

"Perhaps it might be arranged," I said, looking at Georgiana and pondering the prospect of leaving her on her own, without the protection of my immediate presence.

"My sisters will be there as well, along with Mr. Hurst," Bingley added, as if this should have been the only necessary inducement previously lacking. "I secured their promise before I came here."

I nodded my comprehension. "Ah," I said when I could think of no other tactful response.

"They are quite keen that you should join us – especially Caroline, I confess. I daresay you will like Hertfordshire, Darcy. Oh, I know that the local society cannot compare with London, but *I* find country manners charming. In fact, I have already been called upon by two or three of the most prominent gentlemen of the area, who could not have been more friendly and obliging. I have heard much of the reputed beauty of the young ladies round about as well."

"I believe you have now hit upon the reason for your hearty welcome, Bingley. No doubt these gentlemen are looking to get their daughters – beautiful or not – credibly married and off their hands."

"Scoff if you like, Darcy, but you shall not spoil my good mood. Although I am earnestly anticipating meeting more of my new neighbors, especially those of the fairer sex, we need not impose them on you if you do not like it. I daresay we shall be a very merry party at Netherfield, even should we keep entirely to ourselves."

Here my sister joined in, understanding my hesitation and supporting Bingley's cause by saying, "You should go indeed, William. I do not need you here any longer. Mrs. Annesley and I are going on very well together now. Go and see Netherfield, and then tell me all about it on your return."

Admittedly, I was more than a little curious to see the place for myself. And after over a month languishing in London with very little to do, I was highly amenable to the idea of some diversion, even if it were only a change of house and the questionable company of the Bingley sisters. Besides, Hertfordshire was within an easy distance, should I be needed at home again. So I decided that, if I could confirm with Fitzwilliam that he would be available to keep an eye on things at Darcy House while I was away, I would go to Netherfield and see what all the fuss was about.

I regretted that decision almost immediately.

16
Meryton Assembly

Netherfield Park itself was no disappointment. Indeed, just as Bingley had described it, the house was very fine, with spacious rooms, tasteful furnishings, an excellent library, and well-kept grounds. It was entirely suitable for a young gentleman on the rise, like Mr. Bingley. The simple possession of such an estate would lend him more consequence – a more substantial presence among his peers and betters. In fact, my friend seemed to be walking a bit taller already, I noticed, as he showed me about the place.

No, the chief disadvantage to Netherfield proved to be not the structure on the outside but the human element within. Well, truth be told, one human in particular: Miss Caroline Bingley.

I was of course not unfamiliar with her supercilious ways by this time. *Both* sisters had perhaps felt the elevation in their family fortunes too strongly, but in Miss Bingley's case came something additional, something irksome to myself in particular. She had apparently taken up the notion of rising still further by marriage. There was nothing remarkable in that, except she seemed to have settled on *me* as the means to her end. So I had always, when I saw her, a certain amount of noxious flattery, flirtation, and frivolity to put up with.

On this occasion, however, I found I could tolerate it less well than usual.

I will not give Miss Bingley all the blame, for I believe any alteration in the case was primarily on my side. I had now the example of Miss Lambright's natural dignity and straightforward manner in my mind, by which comparison Miss Bingley's dubious character and designing ways could not help but suffer. Secondarily, ever since the near tragedy at Ramsgate, I had struggled in vain to throw off a persistent cloud of gloom. I will not compare my injuries to Georgiana's, but Wickham had robbed me of something as well; he had stolen my equanimity.

In part, I had come to Netherfield hoping for a cure. Bingley's ebullient nature and cheerful company had often proved an effective antidote in the past. It was part of what I had learnt to value in him since the inception of our unlikely friendship, formed through a mutual acquaintance. In a curious way, our opposing natures seemed to balance each other to our mutual benefit. My seriousness and judgement steadied him, I believe, and his natural lightheartedness somehow lifted me, counteracting my tendency to sink into brooding over every evil in the world about me.

I was not confident of alleviation this time, however. In excess of two months had now passed since Ramsgate, and yet I still found an optimistic outlook difficult to support. I still found it a more than customarily arduous task to bear with the indiscriminant wants and expectations of others. Moreover, I was in no humor to tolerate fools gladly. I soon found I was in no humor at all to tolerate Miss Bingley.

Good manners required me to do so, however, to endure with as much grace as possible Miss Bingley's coquetry and much more. I might have acquitted myself well enough, too, but for Bingley's insistence, shortly after I arrived, that we must all attend a ball, an assembly in the nearby town of Meryton, despite his earlier insinuations that there would be no need of imposing the local society upon me.

As I have stated before, I am no admirer of a ball in general, and this ball, I was certain, could be no exceptional case. In fact, as a public rather than a private affair, it was bound to be more odious to me than most. I suppose I could have refused to attend outright. And in hindsight, I often wonder what might have happened if I had. But I went.

The room was hot, noisy, and overcrowded with an unrefined group of people in whom I detected little beauty, breeding, or reason for interest. Worse still, I knew no one at all beyond my own party, which is always a severe handicap to me.

Had I been of a more positive mindset at the time, perhaps I might have successfully overlooked some of these inherent disadvantages... or at least behaved as if I had. Had I been born with Bingley's easy temperament, I mightn't have noticed anything to overlook in the first place, for none of these drawbacks seemed to trouble my friend in the least. But alas, I do not share his carefree nature, and I could not pretend to enjoy myself that night. I could not pretend to like being stared at, gossiped about, and generally undressed by uncouth strangers from the first moment until the last.

Because I was reserved – dancing little and barely speaking to anybody beyond my own party – I was well aware of being universally condemned by the end of the evening. I was declared over proud and above my company, not entirely without cause, I will allow.

Again, Bingley seemed oblivious to all of this – the intrusive public scrutiny as well as my personal discomfort. Instead of finding fault with the circumstances, he found fault with me. Although I had earlier danced with each of his sisters, I had passed the time since either walking about the perimeter of the room or remaining fixed where I could unobtrusively observe the proceedings. That was not good enough for Bingley, however.

"Come, Darcy," he said, interrupting his own dancing to press me about it. "I must have you dance. I hate to see you standing about by yourself in this stupid manner. You had much better dance."

"I certainly shall not," I declared in answer to this unwarranted attack. "You know how I detest it, unless I am particularly acquainted with my partner. At such an assembly as this, it would be insupportable. As you see, your sisters are engaged, and there is no other woman in the room whom it would not be a punishment to me to stand up with."

"I would not be so fastidious as you are for a kingdom!" cried Bingley. "Upon my honor, I never met with so many pleasant girls in my life as I have this evening; and there are several of them who are uncommonly pretty."

Here, I had to concede that at least in his most recent partner, the eldest Miss Bennet, he was not mistaken.

Now, however, I come to the most infamous portion of the evening, notorious both for my ill-considered behavior and for its unanticipated and lasting effects. In Bingley's determination to engage my interest in what the assembly had to offer, he drew my attention to another young lady.

"There is one of Miss Bennet's sisters sitting down just behind you, who is very pretty, and I dare say, very agreeable."

"Which do you mean?" I asked, turning round to see for myself. The dark-haired young woman to whom Bingley had referred was indeed reasonably pretty, I decided, at least to a certain taste. She had a cherubic face set with chestnut eyes that sparkled like jewels. I had in fact noticed her before, her light figure and gracefulness of movement as she danced earning my mild approbation at the time. Still, I observed little of fashion or manner to admire in her.

Meanwhile, Bingley had continued. "Is it not a shame – a clear injustice, even – to see so fair a lady sitting down in want of a partner? Now, be reasonable, Darcy. Do let me ask Miss Bennet to introduce you, so that you may invite her to dance."

I was unlikely to allow myself to be goaded into doing something I had already decided against for good reason. And when I momentarily caught the lady's eye, it hardened my resolve, for she seemed to be laughing at me, or perhaps it was a look of challenge. Neither sat well with me. In that instant, I realized that she must have been over listening our conversation as well. She had heard Bingley's compliments to herself and his offer to me of an introduction. Just as her friends and neighbors about us had already judged me that night, this Miss Bennet was now waiting to hear and to criticize whatever I might say.

So, allowing my distain to show, I withdrew my eye and gave her something to hear that she would not like. "She is tolerable," I began in a tone of hauteur, "but not handsome enough to tempt me; and I am in no humor at present to give consequence to young ladies who are slighted by other men."

It was entirely true. It was also unforgivably rude, of course, and no matter what the circumstances, a gentleman should *never* be that. My conscience smote me at once and repeatedly thereafter, both for my questionable assumptions about the young lady and for my childish response. However, I was hardly so repentant as to not resent Bingley's provoking me to act in such a way, to act against my own principles.

As for the lady I had supposedly injured, however, I could not detect that she suffered one jot for what I had said. In fact, she could not seem to suppress her merriment at being so well entertained. When she presently left her seat and walked by, she gave me a look – such a look! – and a saucy smile to be sure I knew she had heard me and did not care. Next, she went to her friends, who all then seemed to be laughing with her, looking at me and enjoying a good joke at my expense. I could have been wrong about this assumption as well, but I did not think so.

Consequently, my discomfort grew still more pronounced. I endured the balance of our time at the assembly in a heightened state of mortification, nurturing an overpowering wish that I should never be forced into company with the laughing lady or her friends again.

It would be impossible to overstate my profound relief at leaving the ball behind at last for the sheltering privacy of Netherfield. But then I found that the ball must be talked of and its gentle agonies relived at length.

"An altogether capital evening!" declared Bingley with satisfaction upon our settling into the drawing room for half an hour before bed. "I swear that I can never remember meeting with a collection of pleasanter people or prettier girls before in my life – in London or anywhere else. They were all ease and friendliness, no undue formality or stiffness. Just what I like. With such kind attentions as they bestowed on me, I soon felt myself acquainted with the whole room!"

"You cannot be serious in such complete approbation, Charles," said Mrs. Hurst, who then in vain looked at her husband to support her opinion. Mr. Hurst, studiously employed in pouring himself a strong drink, could not be bothered. Miss Bingley came to her sister's aid instead.

"Indeed, he cannot, Louisa. Such a provincial company as we endured tonight does not deserve even to be mentioned in the same breath as the best society of London, and our brother well knows it."

"I know no such thing! In truth, I find the country manners of my new neighbors thoroughly charming, and I grow more and more pleased with myself for deciding to make my home amongst them."

Miss Bingley's eyes rolled heavenward then returned to earth to alight upon me. With mischievous glee, she asked, "What say you, Mr. Darcy? I fancy you will have a shrewd opinion; you always do."

"Yes, what is your view, Darcy?" Mr. Bingley surprisingly inquired likewise.

I looked at my friend. "Are you sure you wish to know it?"

"Certainly," he said, sounding, in fact, very far from sure. "I know you did not enjoy the ball as I did, but you must have something to say in favor of Meryton."

I thought a moment before speaking. "The best thing I can say about the good people of Meryton… is that I am very glad they will be *your* neighbors and not mine."

Though I had not meant it as such, the sisters thought my words a good joke and laughed heartily.

I continued. "However, my opinion in the case is of little importance. Only take care the friends you make, Bingley; that is my advice. If you are too trusting, people will take advantage of you."

"I daresay your advice is well and good as a general rule, but you shall not make me think ill of Miss Bennet. None of you shall be able to do that, I am determined, for she is as beautiful as an angel – in her character as well as her looks."

94

"The beauty of Miss Bennet's person, I will not dispute," said I. "I think it remarkable, though, that you can be so confident of her character on such a short acquaintance. She may turn out to be all you say, but I always feel an instinctive mistrust of anybody who smiles over much."

"Too true," said Miss Bingley. "I could not agree more with what you say, Mr. Darcy, that one must be on one's guard when making new acquaintance, especially amongst those of less elevated rank. But in the case of Miss Jane Bennet, I believe we may be easy. I myself found much to like and admire in her. Louisa?"

"What? Oh, yes, I am of the same mind. Jane Bennet is a sweet girl, and I should have no objection to knowing her better."

"Nor should I," echoed Miss Bingley.

"Good! Good!" said their brother, smiling and rocking heels to toes and back again.

This was encouragement for my friend but unwelcome news for me. Although I had no particular objection to Miss Bennet herself, at least not as a casual acquaintance, I feared everybody's desire to know her better would inevitably involve our party in closer contact with her family – including the laughing sister – and all the rest of the locals. I could foresee no possible advantage or pleasure in the idea.

I kept this and the rest of my teeming thoughts to myself, however. I had nothing else useful to offer the others on the topic of the evening's events, for I could reflect on neither the ball itself nor my own actions that night with any satisfaction. But most of all, I remained haunted by the mocking look I had seen in Miss Elizabeth Bennet's eye, for that was her name, I learnt. Although why it should have troubled me so, I could not say.

17
Closer Acquaintance

As I had predicted, when once some definite acquaintance with the local society had been established, there was nothing to prevent its progressing on to the next level and then the one after that. A regular intercourse between Netherfield and the other principle houses of the area soon began.

It started with the ladies of Longbourn waiting on Miss Bingley and Mrs. Hurst, who then returned the visit in form. I had no involvement at this early stage, naturally, but then came the evening parties, which I could not reasonably avoid.

Bingley's enthusiasm for accepting every invitation (as well as issuing some of his own) did not surprise me, for he craved society of every sort. And, as I had often observed before, he was never one to deprive himself a chance to fan the flames of his current infatuation, which was now clearly Miss Jane Bennet. I had seen it all before.

I was amused, however, at his sisters' equal eagerness to attend every gathering. They had no such particular inducement, and they were more apt than not to afterward criticize what they had found there. This sport itself, I soon realized, was their chief amusement in the exercise. Everybody except their pet – Miss Bennet – became a target for their raillery: the absurdity of the self-important Sir William Lucas carrying on about St. James's, the unfashionable way in which Mrs. Long insisted on wearing her hair, the vulgar manners of Mrs. Bennet and Mrs. Phillips. These were all laughable in their estimation.

Perhaps I was just as guilty, though, for my silent reflections were often similar to those they chose to voice aloud. I am ashamed to admit that much of my private censure in those early days at Netherfield was reserved for Elizabeth Bennet. She really was not handsome after all, I told myself, certainly nothing to her elder sister or many other ladies of my acquaintance. On closer inspection, I became convinced that her nose, although nicely shaped, deviated slightly to the left. And her perpetual laughter might have a charming lilt to it, but it came too often and was sometimes a bit too loud for polite society. As with Miss Bingley, I also compared Elizabeth Bennet to the lady who had become my standard: Amelia Lambright. Any differences between the two (of which there were a copious number), I put down without hesitation as another mark against Miss Bennet.

Although I renewed my earnest intention of paying her no heed whatsoever each and every time I had the misfortune to be in company with her, I always failed miserably. I could not understand it. I only could suppose that, having thoroughly disconcerted me with her satirical eye at the very outset, she had somehow gained a certain power over me. I might find new faults with her breeding, behavior, and features on each successive occasion; I might achieve my aim to avoid speaking to her for a whole evening together; but I could not seem to actually ignore her, as I steadfastly vowed to do.

She irritated me. She confounded me. The simple truth was that despite my best efforts, Elizabeth Bennet interested me. She was like no one else I had ever known.

It was for the sake of mere intellectual curiosity, therefore, when I finally abandoned my original policy and gave myself permission to observe her discreetly. This unusual young woman was an oddity, a novelty, like a new species of plant or a peculiar insect. Such a specimen could be studied with scientific detachment as a form of mental exercise – a benign entertainment, if you like. My interest in the young lady represented nothing beyond, or so I told myself.

As is to be expected when carrying on any scientific observation, some of my initial ideas modified as I studied my subject further. For example, I began to think that the bright expression of her fine eyes revealed a liveliness of mind and an uncommon

97

degree of intelligence. I began to consider it possible that her easy laughter bespoke – rather than a propensity toward ridicule – simply a playfulness of spirit. All this without having exchanged more than a few sentences with her.

Observing Miss Bennet *was* an enjoyable pastime, I found. Unfortunately, I was not as circumspect as I should have been, and ultimately my covert scrutiny did not go unnoticed.

It was at Sir William Lucas's house, where a large party was assembled one evening. I had been standing close enough to hear an inconsequential exchange between Elizabeth and Colonel Forster. When it was over and the colonel walked away, she happened to catch sight of me there. Then after a few whispered words with her friend Miss Lucas, who was beside her, she turned to me.

"Did not you think, Mr. Darcy, that I expressed myself uncommonly well just now, when I was teasing Colonel Forster to give us a ball at Meryton?"

Although momentarily taken aback by so direct and unexpected a question, especially from that quarter, I soon rallied. "Yes, uncommonly well and with great energy," I said. "But dancing is a subject which always seems to give a lady enthusiasm."

She laughed at this. "I am afraid you mean to be severe on us, Mr. Darcy."

"Not at all, Miss Bennet. It is a simple observation. According to my own experience, there are few topics upon which ladies can speak with more length and zeal than a ball."

"You astonish me, sir. And gentlemen? Do they never like a ball just as well? Do not *you*, Mr. Darcy?"

She added this last before I could respond to the first. And from her challenging look, I was sure she meant to allude to that earlier occasion – my unfortunate behavior at the Meryton assembly. I returned her look while I considered my reply. I did not wish her to go away knowing she had beaten me. I wished to say something cunning – or even cutting – to put her in her place. And yet nothing at all clever came to mind.

"I am not partial to a ball myself," I said at last. "However I will not presume to speak for *all* gentlemen."

"Why ever not?" she asked archly. "You seemed to have no scruple in speaking for all ladies a moment ago."

Clearly, the advantage of wit was all on *her* side that evening, and there was nothing for it but to surrender. "You are quite right, Miss Bennet. I should not have done so. My apologies to you as well, Miss Lucas."

"Apology accepted, Mr. Darcy," said Miss Lucas, lightly.

I bowed.

"And now," Miss Lucas continued, "I trust that my friend is finished tormenting you, for it will soon be her turn to be teased. I am going to open the instrument, Eliza, and you know what follows."

Miss Bennet's attention thus mercifully diverted from me, she said, "You are a very strange creature by way of a friend, Charlotte! – always wanting me to play and sing before anybody and everybody! If my vanity had taken a musical turn, you would have been invaluable, but as it is, I would really rather not sit down before those who must be in the habit of hearing the very best performers."

Here she glanced at me again.

Miss Bennet did not really look put out about being asked to play, however. And upon Miss Lucas's persevering, to which I added my own small word of encouragement, Miss Bennet relented in good humor.

Her playing was not brilliant. At least from the aspect of technical proficiency, her skill was certainly nothing to my own sister's. And yet I had to admit that her singing voice, along with her easy, unaffected style, made her songs highly enjoyable nonetheless. In fact, those several minutes while Elizabeth Bennet was at the piano-forte comprised the most pleasing part of the evening for me – not only for the sake of the music itself, but for giving me the perfect excuse to watch the fair performer openly without fear that anybody should think it remarkable. She was also enough distant to secure me against any further verbal assault.

Indeed, it was Miss Bingley instead who accosted me later, saying, "I can guess the subject of your reverie, Mr. Darcy."

"I should imagine not," I replied.

Undaunted, she carried on. "You are considering how insupportable it would be to pass many evenings in this manner – in such dull society. And indeed I am quite of your opinion. I was never more annoyed! The insipidity and yet the noise; the nothingness and yet the self-importance of all these people!" she sneered. "What would I give to hear your strictures on them!"

"I am not up to the task tonight, Miss Bingley, I assure you – not in my best wit, I have discovered. Besides, your conjecture is totally mistaken. My mind was far more agreeably engaged."

"Oh? Do tell!"

I hesitated but then decided there was no reason to avoid saying the truth. Perhaps it would even serve to discourage my faithful admirer a little. "I have been meditating on the very great pleasure which a pair of fine eyes in the face of a pretty woman can bestow."

Miss Bingley, smiled coyly, fluttering her lashes at me. "May I know who has the credit for inspiring these agreeable reflections?" she asked.

"Certainly. It is Miss Elizabeth Bennet."

"Miss Elizabeth Bennet!" repeated Miss Bingley with sarcasm. "I am all astonishment. How long has she been such a favorite? And pray, when am I to wish you joy? You will have a very charming mother-in-law, I must say."

In this predictable manner, she carried on for some minutes. I listened with perfect indifference. Miss Bingley and her jokes possessed no power to wound me. Besides, I knew that her insinuations held no merit, as I supposed did she. Although I might admit to admiring Miss Bennet's fine eyes, although I might be somewhat intrigued by her, I also knew that I was perfectly safe from her unique set of charms, contained, as they were, in an entirely inappropriate vessel. I had already chosen the impeccably suitable Miss Lambright to become my wife, and Miss Bennet could run her no possible competition.

18

Houseguests

"I shall be *so* bored," announced Miss Bingley a few days later. "Louisa, is there nothing that can be arranged to lend a little novelty to our employments? With the gentlemen away so long, I daresay you and I shall be at each other's throats before the day is gone."

We had informed the ladies of our intention – Bingley, Mr. Hurst, and myself – to dine with the officers in Meryton that day. That is what had set up Miss Bingley's lament.

"Perhaps," offered her brother, "the Miss Bennets would be willing to come and bear you company in our absence. Invite them to dine, if you like."

There passed a look and a nod between the sisters.

"Yes, perhaps," Miss Bingley tentatively began.

"But certainly not *all* of them," continued Mrs. Hurst.

"Heavens, no!" agreed her sister. "That would not be fair to expect of Cook on so short a notice. And we must not deprive Mrs. Bennet of all her daughters at once."

"I think perhaps only Miss *Jane* Bennet," suggested Louisa.

"I quite agree. As the eldest, it is right that she be shown special attention."

"Very true. That is only proper and fitting."

"We can always invite the others…"

"…some other time. Yes."

"Exactly."

Bingley, who had watched this like-minded conversation volley back and forth between his sisters, only shrugged. "Just as you think best," he said, and we went away.

When we returned quite late that night, we were informed by the ladies that Miss Bennet had indeed come to dine, but having arrived on horseback and soaked clear through with rain, she had subsequently taken ill and been put to bed upstairs.

"There was no question of sending her home in such a state," explained Mrs. Hurst.

"No question at all," echoed her sister, shaking her head sadly.

"Of course not," Bingley agreed, with a wistful glance overhead.

"We have put her in the blue room," Miss Bingley explained. "And a message has been sent to Longbourn."

"Very well," he said. "Miss Bennet must be shown every possible attention while she is here. Caroline, I trust you will send for Mr. Jones if there is any reason at all to be uneasy."

"Naturally. I hope I should know my duty to any guest in this house, Charles."

By the morning, the rain had ceased, leaving dirt and puddles everywhere, as I discovered on my early walk. Afterward, I had joined the others in the breakfast-parlor when our meal was interrupted by the surprise of Miss Elizabeth Bennet's being shewn in to us. From the mud at her hem and the warm glow of her complexion, it was clear that she had not been delivered in the calm and comfort of a carriage.

"Please forgive the intrusion," she said.

"Miss Bennet!" cried Miss Bingley in astonishment. "Have you walked all this way... alone and at such an early hour, too?"

"I have. It was nothing, though; I enjoy walking. When I heard of my sister's situation, I could not be easy without seeing her for myself. How does she do?"

"We were with her ten minutes ago," explained Mrs. Hurst. "There is no danger, but she is too unwell to leave her room. A maid sits with her now."

"We are much obliged to you all, I am sure," said Elizabeth.

"You are very welcome," Bingley declared, "and you shall be taken to your sister at once. Caroline?"

"Yes, of course," she said with a sigh of resignation. Leaving her breakfast, she stood to perform her duty.

Over the rest of our meal and throughout the day, there was much discussion of our visitors upstairs. The more recent arrival's appearance and actions were thoroughly canvassed: her wind-blown hair and soiled hem, and the questionable necessity and propriety of her lengthy, solitary walk from Longbourn. Much fault was found with these by the Bingley sisters. Then later, they moved on to a critique of her manners and a review of the Bennets' low connections, the lamentable conclusion being that there was very little chance of any of their five daughters marrying well.

Predictably, Bingley saw no deficiency in either of our guests, even defending against the disparaging remarks about their relations. "If they had uncles enough to fill all Cheapside," he cried indignantly, "it would not make them one jot less agreeable to me."

"But it must very materially lessen their chances of marrying men of any consideration," I sensibly pointed out. "That you cannot deny."

My other sentiments, which I kept mostly to myself, fell somewhere in between my friend's too generous approbation and his sisters' snide jokes and criticisms. I could not think well of Elizabeth Bennet's questionable exertions that morning, especially at the expense of propriety. And yet I had to admire her energy and her devotion to her sister. While in some respects the exercise might have been inadvisable, I could not deny that it had also heightened her complexion to a becoming brilliance.

Again, it was these contrasts and contradictions that made her such an interesting study. And it seemed I would have an extended opportunity for my observations, since she had been invited to stay at Netherfield to nurse her sister as long as it should be necessary.

~~*~~

More Bennets arrived the next morning – the mother and the two youngest girls – along with the apothecary to ascertain the invalid's condition. The conclusion was that, although there was nothing alarming in her illness, it would be best if she were not moved until she was fully recovered.

Apparently satisfied with this arrangement and returned downstairs, Mrs. Bennet became quite cheerful, commencing to copiously thank Mr. Bingley for his hospitality, to compliment him on his very fine house, and to hope he would never wish to leave it again. Bingley, who could say nothing wrong, was obviously her darling; I, equally obviously, was not. My one attempt to join in the conversation – an innocent remark about the confined and unvarying nature of a country society – was met with her determined misunderstanding and rebuff. Nothing could have induced me to speak to the woman again after that, and I was very glad when she and her younger offspring were gone again.

The unpleasant interlude did add one more observation about Elizabeth to my book, however. Accustomed as I had become by this time to being challenged and teased by her, I was somewhat amazed when she turned to defend me against her mother's abuse. "Indeed, Mama," she said, "you are mistaken. You quite mistook Mr. Darcy's meaning." Although her defense made no apparent impression on her mother, *I* noticed it.

While we men spent most of the day out of doors, I believe the ladies passed much of their time upstairs with the invalid, who continued to slowly mend. But after she was asleep, the rest of us were reunited first for dinner and then in the drawing room in the evening.

Rather than all combining our efforts together for cards, as we had the night before, this time we took up various pursuits. Bingley and Mr. Hurst played at piquet with Mrs. Hurst looking on. Miss Bennet applied herself to needlework of some sort. I settled at the writing desk. The post had earlier brought me a note from Fitzwilliam assuring me that all was well with Georgiana in

London, which had prompted me to sit down that evening to write her a long letter of news and encouragement.

Even this simple task could not be accomplished in peace, however, for Miss Bingley, hovering close at hand, made it her business to monitor my progress, to compliment me on my style of writing, to offer her assistance in the mending of my pen, and to praise the virtues of my intended recipient. I had to get on as best I could, therefore.

My dear Georgiana,

I trust this finds you well and content and that your studies with Mrs. Annesley are progressing apace. You know the degree of importance I place on the improvement of the mind, and I am looking forward to receiving a good report of your advancement when I return.

Netherfield is all that Mr. Bingley told us – house, grounds, stables, etc. All are suitably grand and commodious. No doubt he will enjoy giving you the full tour whenever you are able to come. Or Miss Bingley, who is here and is to keep his house, as you know, would be just as glad to take up that office herself, I daresay. She sends her compliments to you, and she says she longs to see you again. There. I have done my duty by delivering this message from her.

Did your lesson with Mr. Winterbrook go well? I suppose he, after finding you had already mastered the others, has now given you a new and even more challenging piece of music to learn. I will anticipate hearing it soon. Very little in this world gives me more pleasure than listening to you play. I know you have heard me say it before, but it is still true.

We have musicians here also, of course – Mr. Bingley's sisters and a Miss Bennet, who happens to be staying as well – but none to compare to your degree of accomplishment...

"Oh!" exclaimed Miss Bingley, loudly enough that I could not disregard her. "Mr. Darcy, do tell your sister I am delighted to hear of her improvement on the harp. And pray, let her know that I am quite in raptures with her beautiful little design for a table, and that I think it infinitely superior to Miss Grantley's."

"Will you give me leave to defer your raptures till I write again?" I asked. "At present I have not room to do them justice. Or perhaps you might like to write to my sister yourself."

"Oh, it is of no consequence," she said dismissively. "I shall tell her some time or other when I see her."

I have just been interrupted again by Miss Bingley, who is anxious that I should tell you how delighted she is to hear of your improvement on the harp, etc., etc. Also something about your design for a table. As I have told her, she must write to you herself if she wishes her many ideas communicated in full.

We have been to a dance at the local assembly rooms with a great many strangers. I mention it for the sake of honesty and completeness, but otherwise, I have nothing of an interesting or diverting character to tell you about it. As you know, I do not perform to best advantage in such a setting, and this was no exception.

I have mentioned to you that a Miss Bennet is staying. In truth, there are two of them – sisters. The eldest, Miss Jane Bennet, was here to dine with Miss Bingley and Mrs. Hurst when she became ill. Then her younger sister Elizabeth arrived to nurse her back to health. I have seen nothing of the former, confined as she is to her sick bed. The latter, however, joins us when she can, and she is a very different sort of young lady from any I have ever met with before – an interesting mixture of intelligence, arch-ness, and wit. Most intriguing. I have undertaken a kind of study of her, but despite all my careful observations, I still cannot make her out. I wonder what your opinion would be of the lady, although I think it unlikely the two of you shall ever meet. Her inferior connections will tend to ensure that...

...You must pardon yet another interruption, Sister Dear, for I was drawn away from this letter some minutes to debate with Mr. Bingley and Miss Elizabeth Bennet a futile hypothetical case about the virtue or vice of acting precipitously. Does the tendency, which Mr. Bingley claims for himself as a virtue, bespeak admirable decisiveness and rapidity of thought, or mere carelessness? I suppose, knowing me as you do, you can have no doubt as to which side of the question I argued. Miss Bennet took up Mr. Bingley's part, however, and nothing was agreed upon in the end. So you see, you are not missing much of value by being absent from us.

I am urged now to finish my letter so that we might have some music, and I suppose I must not be disobliging to my hosts. I will write again soon.

Love and salutations,
Your brother William

~~*~~

With Miss Bennet recovering well, her sister was no longer needed so often to attend her, leaving her free to walk about out of doors or whatever she liked during the daytime. But she was consigned mostly to our company during the long evenings.

Obviously, my initial hope of avoiding her could not be sustained under these circumstances. To say we grew comfortable in each other's presence would be going much too far, but there was an increasing familiarity with each other's ways. The sharpest edges of our awkwardness had been dulled somewhat, rubbed away by repeated contact. And I learnt to match her boldness, even occasionally taking the initiative of beginning a new topic with her myself.

Late the second night of her residence at Netherfield, with Miss Bingley at the piano-forte playing a lively Scotch air, I decided that I would see what would happen if I were to fling a challenge in Elizabeth's path, as she made so free to do with me. After watching her a little, I drew near and asked, "Do not you feel a great inclination, Miss Bennet, to seize such an opportunity of dancing a reel?"

She met my eye, but to my surprise, she only smiled and remained silent.

"Perhaps you did not hear me, Miss Bennet. Shall I repeat the question?"

"Oh, I heard you before, but I could not immediately determine what to say in reply."

"It is a simple enough question, I should think, requiring as little as a 'yes' or a 'no' to discharge your responsibility."

"A *deceptively* simple question, Mr. Darcy, for I perceive that there is more behind your inquiry than idle curiosity. You wish me to answer in the affirmative, I imagine, that you might have the pleasure of despising my taste."

"Do I? Your imagination must be very shrewd indeed to have divined a motive that I myself was unconscious of. Well done, Miss Bennet. I see I can never expect to get the better of you."

"I hope that may be true, Mr. Darcy," she said with an archness that was a good deal counteracted by her smile. "I always delight in overthrowing those kinds of schemes and cheating a person of their premeditated contempt. I have therefore made up my mind to tell you that, no, I do not want to dance a reel at all. Now despise me if you dare."

By saying this, I suspected she wished to affront me. As I looked into her flashing dark eyes, however, I found myself more bewitched than injured by her. My reply softened as well. "Truly, I do not despise you, Miss Bennet. You have indeed succeeded in cheating me, though, out of my premeditated pleasure of seeing you dance."

The next night, I again fell into a very direct conversation with her – more than I intended – which began lightly enough with her and Miss Bingley taking a turn about the room. It was Miss Bingley's idea, who then invited me to join them. I declined, observing that my entering into their promenade would only interfere with the real purpose of the exercise.

"It is one of two things," I explained. "You may choose this method of passing the evening because you are in each other's confidence and have secret affairs to discuss, in which case I should be entirely in the way."

"That is not our motive, I assure you, Mr. Darcy," said Miss Bennet. "But you said two things. What is the second possibility?"

"Why, that you are both conscious that your figures appear to the greatest advantage in walking. If so, I can admire you much better as I sit here by the fire."

"Oh! How shocking!" cried Miss Bingley.

And she was correct. I could not at all account for what had caused me to say such a forward thing, especially in the hearing of one I had known comparatively briefly.

Miss Bingley then called for me to be punished for such a speech, and her companion suggested teasing, that for me to be laughed at must be a great punishment indeed.

The details of what followed now escape me – something about the difference between pride and vanity. I *do* recall, though, that as it went on, Miss Bingley faded from the conversation, leaving Miss Bennet and myself locked in a verbal joust, the friction between us escalating to the end.

I remember I said, "There is, I believe, in every disposition a tendency to some particular evil, a natural defect, which not even the best education can overcome."

"*Your* defect is a propensity to hate everybody," declared Miss Bennet at the last.

"While yours is willfully to misunderstand them," I replied with a measured smile.

It was just as well that Miss Bingley broke the heavy tension by hastily calling for some music, for I cannot imagine otherwise where we would have gone from there.

Sleep did not come quickly to me that night. I was suddenly uneasy with the degree to which Elizabeth had captivated my interest, and also with the suspicion that I might have paid her too much attention. Nothing could be allowed to come of it; I was still enough master of myself to know that. And yet I considered it was at least conceivable she did not.

For both our sakes, I believed it would be best if henceforth we saw and spoke to each other as little as possible. I silently rejoiced, therefore, when I heard the next morning that it was the Miss Bennets' intention to depart early the following day. Elizabeth had been at Netherfield long enough.

I resolved at once to be particularly careful that no sign of admiration should escape me during that final day – nothing that could elevate her with any hope of featuring in my future felicity. If such an idea had been accidentally suggested to her mind, it must be swiftly and categorically crushed. Accordingly, I scarcely spoke ten words to her. So committed to this course was I that when we were left half an hour by ourselves, I did not look at her once. I adhered most conscientiously to my book, periodically turning pages that I had not read.

This pretense may have been entirely unnecessary for her sake, but it was important for me in breaking away from the undeniable attraction I felt for her. Relief, not regret, was the sensation uppermost in my mind, therefore, when Elizabeth Bennet joined her sister in the carriage and finally drove away.

19

Disturbing Encounter

To have the Miss Bennets gone from Netherfield was such a relief that I abided Miss Bingley's presence and her unwanted attentions almost cheerfully, as the lesser of two significant evils. She varied between her usual flattery and her new occupation of teasing me about Elizabeth Bennet. The realization that she might be jealous was another hint that I must be more careful. If Miss Bingley had perceived my regard for Miss Bennet, then surely it was possible Elizabeth herself had noticed as well.

We had two days of relative peace, keeping to ourselves, before Bingley proposed calling at Longbourn for the purpose of respectfully inquiring after Miss Jane Bennet's health. I did not object, for such a visit would comprise less than fifteen minutes, and I could surely withstand any woman's charms that long – even Elizabeth's, should she happen to be there. It would in fact be an excellent opportunity to exercise my renewed commitment of distinguishing her with no sign of admiration whatsoever.

Accordingly, Bingley and I set off for Longbourn on horseback early in the afternoon. We never did arrive at our destination, however, for as we passed through Meryton we found what we went in search of – and more.

"Look there!" said Bingley, riding beside me. He nodded in the direction of a company of people in conversation at the side of the way. Distinguishing some of the Miss Bennets amongst them – Miss Jane Bennet, Elizabeth, and their two youngest sisters, it turned out to be – we went directly towards them.

There were three gentlemen talking animatedly with them as well, none of whom I immediately recognized. As we approached, I could see that one was a stout young man clothed in the garb of the clergy, and the second was an officer in regimentals. The third man was tall and had his back to us. Bingley continued forward to begin his civilities to Miss Bennet, but I pulled my mount up short. There was something familiar in the third man's profile and posture that gave me warning prickles up my spine. Then he turned and my fears were confirmed; it was Wickham.

Wickham drew back a little in alarm when he saw me, and he went quite white in the face.

For a moment I froze as well, not knowing what to do. This was the first occasion of my seeing the man since I had learnt of his treachery towards my sister, and my surprise quickly turned to anger as the bitter remembrance of those events flashed before my mind's eye once again. If I had met the villain in some secluded place with a sword in my hand, the outcome might have been entirely different. Fortunately for us both, however, the constraints of the situation prevented my doing anything rash.

Wickham, recovering from his initial shock, grimly nodded and touched the brim of his hat. Against my will, I was then obliged to return the salutation, just.

Another minute and it was over. Bingley took leave, rejoined me, and we rode on.

"I am relieved to see Miss Bennet looking so well!" exclaimed Bingley. "Remarkably well, in my opinion. Her sisters too. Would not you agree? And I met all her friends. But where were you, Darcy, and where were your manners? You ought to have joined us and been introduced. I hope no one will take it amiss that you did not. As long as I have known you, sometimes I still do not understand you – your odd little moods and whims."

"What was *he* doing here?" I grumbled, ignoring all the rest.

"Who do you mean? The clergyman is a Mr. Collins, a cousin of the Bennets, who is staying with them. The officer is Mr. Denny of the regiment stationed here."

"No, the other one: Mr. Wickham."

"So you know his name?" Suddenly, realization dawned on his face. "Oh! Do you mean to tell he is *that* Mr. Wickham? – your old friend from Derbyshire?"

"Yes, but he is no friend of mine. Not anymore."

"I had no idea, Darcy, or I should have been a good deal less friendly to him, although of course you have never explained exactly what he is supposed to have done."

"As I have told you before, the particulars are something I cannot speak of. It is enough for you to know that he has behaved in an infamous manner that can never be forgiven."

"Yes, yes, just as you say; I do not doubt your word. But then I am sorry to tell you that it will be difficult to avoid crossing paths with him again, for he is to take a commission in Colonel Forster's regiment and remain in Meryton all winter."

I sighed heavily. "Heaven help us."

Bingley and I returned to Netherfield, and I am afraid I was not fit company for the rest of the day. My thoughts were consumed with Wickham and the strange, seeming coincidence of running across him in Meryton. I could not like it. No, I could not like it above half.

After much consideration, however, I concluded it could be nothing more than that – a coincidence – for Wickham clearly had been as shocked and distressed at seeing me as I was him. He could have had no reason to suppose I would be in that neighborhood. Perhaps he even feared the retribution I had threatened, in case Georgiana should have also been nearby.

She was not, however. She was many miles away in London. But the sight of Wickham had suddenly given me a powerful need to confirm for myself that she was well. I freely admit it was perfectly irrational. After all, if Wickham was in Hertfordshire and she in London, I could never have been *more* certain that she was safe from him at present. Nevertheless, I was soon resolved that I would return to her the next day.

"Leaving tomorrow?" questioned Bingley that evening, when I told my friends what I had decided. "My dear fellow, you cannot be serious. As yet you have spent no time at all with us."

"It is above three weeks, nearly four," I corrected.

"But I had depended on your company for a full two months, at the very least."

"Had you? I know not why, for I never pledged myself for so protracted a visit."

"I thought it was understood."

"Yes, you cannot go away now, Mr. Darcy" repined Miss Bingley. "It would be a very sad loss to us all."

"Nevertheless, I *am* going. I have been away from my sister too long as it is."

I stood firm against these voices of ready persuasion, and with the promise that I would return for the ball Mr. Bingley had decided to give, I was at last honorably released.

Travelling to town might have been primarily for my sister's sake, as I had said. But the plan comprised a number of other advantages as well: being free, at least temporarily, from Miss Bingley's smothering attentions; leaving behind the distasteful possibility of seeing Wickham again; and removing me from the dangerous temptation of Miss Elizabeth Bennet.

~~*~~

Allowing for travel time, I would still have the better part of five days with my sister before setting off again, which was a period more than ample to suit my purposes. I intended to see how Georgiana fared, to discover how she was getting on with Mrs. Annesley and with her studies, and to confer with Fitzwilliam about what, if anything, had transpired in my absence. I addressed the last first, by going by his house in Grosvenor Street as soon as I arrived in town late that Wednesday afternoon, on the chance that I might find him at home. Luck was with me.

"Darcy!" Fitzwilliam exclaimed upon seeing me. "So you have come home at last. Do come in and be seated. I am very glad."

"Good to see you too, Fitzwilliam," I said, shaking his outstretched hand. "Thank you for receiving me."

"Of course! Although in truth, I can spare you no more than fifteen or twenty minutes, old friend. I am engaged to dine with the Amhersts tonight, I am afraid."

As I was sitting down, I paused to raise an eyebrow at this, remembering a prior conversation.

"I know, I know," said Fitzwilliam from the chair opposite me. "But one must be civil. Besides, their cook is one of the finest in any London house." He laid a hand on his belly, closed his eyes, and inhaled reverentially. "If old Amherst wanted me to marry *her* instead of his unappetizing daughter, I believe I should be a lost man!" He laughed. "Which reminds me, what of your marriage plans, Darcy? Any progress on that head?"

"None at all. I have written the viscount twice since I came away, just to let him – and Amelia – know that I have not skulked off into the night never to return, but..." I sighed. "Well, there is little more that I can do at present."

"As they say, *absence makes the heart grow fonder*. Staying away a while is a very sound plan to assure that the lady will be eager to say yes when you finally *do* come to the point. My compliments on your strategy."

"I wish it were only that, but you know the truth of the matter. Now, how does Georgiana do? I came straight here and have not seen her yet."

"She is well, at least I believe so," he said with a look of bewilderment.

"What do you mean by that, Fitzwilliam?"

"I don't mind admitting that I am a little mystified. I have received good reports from Mrs. Annesley and the housekeeper, and I have seen the girl herself on half a dozen occasions. I can find nothing amiss, but your sister seems to always have some excuse to avoid spending more than a few minutes in my company, which is not like her. She says she is tired, she must return to her lessons, practice her music, or some such thing. I could not even convince her to accompany me to the latest concert. Is she really so out of spirits that fine music cannot tempt her? Or is it just *me* that she objects to, do you suppose?"

115

"Unless I miss my guess, she is only embarrassed. She knows that you have been made aware of what occurred in Ramsgate, and for that reason, I daresay she can barely look you in the eye."

"Hmm. No doubt you are correct. That would certainly explain it. But she need not be ashamed; she was not the principle wrong-doer in the unfortunate affair."

"As I have repeatedly told her. I have, in fact, just seen the true villain himself."

"What?" Fitzwilliam said, sitting up in surprise.

"It is true. Yesterday, in Meryton. I cannot find out that it is anything more than an odd coincidence, though, him turning up in that location at the same time I happened to be stopping nearby. Bingley spoke to him, and he has accepted a commission in the regiment of militia stationed there. That is the simple explan-ation."

"Still, it seems somehow suspicious."

"Yes, I know. Once a man is known to have a devious nature, everything he subsequently does seems suspect. In any case, it made me uneasy to be away from Georgiana any longer. Unfor-tunately, I have to drive back on Tuesday, for Bingley is giving a grand ball and cannot spare me. He is in love again, you see," I explained wryly.

Fitzwilliam laughed. "Is he, now? Does this make the second or third time this year?"

"The third."

"So he wishes to impress his new ladylove by throwing her a fine party. That is natural enough, I suppose, but it is no reason to make his friends miserable. You, for one, will be dreading this ball, I think."

"Precisely. You know how ill I can abide such affairs. I shall know almost nobody... nobody except a person or two I would rather avoid."

Amusement sparked in Fitzwilliam's eye. "Can we possibly be speaking of the gentleman's sister? Is Miss Bingley still hopeful of a return of her affections?"

"You have divined the problem exactly."

"Oh, but you have said there are two you wish to avoid. Is the other also a lady in love with you? Such trouble as this, some men would scarcely complain about, you know."

"No, your guess is off the mark in this case. The second is indeed a lady, but she does not live to please and flatter me. Quite the opposite, I assure you."

"What? Do you mean to say her goal is to torture and insult you? That seems unlikely."

"Nevertheless, it is true."

He laughed. "You are not known as a charmer, it is true. But she must be a queer sort of woman to not be impressed by your wealth and consequence, if nothing else."

"She is unusual, I grant you, and my dearest wish is that I should never be required to spend time in her disagreeable presence again."

"I am astonished, Darcy! I would like to meet the venerable lady who has frightened you to such an extent!"

"I am not afraid of her – not in the way you mean, at least – and I offer you this proof. I am going to the ball, though she will certainly be there."

"And shall you ask her to dance?"

"Why should I do that? I do not even like her."

"Oh, I don't know. Perhaps to demonstrate that what you say is true – that you are not afraid of her – that is, if you think you are up to the challenge."

"You should come with me and ask her to dance yourself. No doubt you and the lady in question would get on famously, since you both take great delight in vexing me."

"Ha! An excellent notion! I would be glad to take her off your hands if you think she would suit me. She must be quite pretty, you know, lively, and an heiress as well, for I have no money of my own, remember."

"Then, no, she would not do."

"Not pretty enough?"

"Not rich enough by half. I do not believe Miss Bennet has any fortune or connections worth speaking of. Otherwise, you might like her very well indeed, for she meets your other requirements."

"A great pity. Still, I stand by what I said before. I should like to meet this woman and be my own judge."

"That is unlikely to happen. You move in very different circles. I will not see her again myself after this ball is over and done."

That thought, meant to consign the lady to her proper place in my mind, failed to placate my irritated feelings as it should have. In fact, the idea of never seeing Elizabeth Bennet again began to weigh heavily on my mind from that moment forward.

Georgiana was surprised but pleased to see me when I arrived in Berkley Street, and it was not long before I had satisfied myself that she was as well as could be expected – her state of mind and also the progress of her studies. I did not mention to her, of course, that I had seen Wickham, for there was no reason to break open old wounds, still not fully healed.

"Shall you be home long?" she asked me.

We had settled side by side on a sofa in the drawing room.

"Only for a few days," I explained. "I must return to Netherfield on Tuesday for a ball Mr. Bingley is giving. I will just stay the one night, however. Two at the most."

"A ball! How delightful!"

"Should you have liked to attend, do you think?"

"Oh, no! But I should very much have liked to find a hiding place from which I could watch. Fine ladies and gentlemen dancing and making merry: it would be a beautiful sight to behold. And the music will be of the first quality too, I suppose."

"No doubt. Mr. Bingley has spared no expense, I understand. But do not worry, my dear," I said, laying my arm about her shoulders and giving her an affectionate squeeze. "You will have many balls to enjoy when you are a bit older. We will give one at Pemberley for your eighteenth birthday, perhaps. How does that sound to you?"

"It sounds very well indeed until I think of so many people looking at me. I am afraid I should not know how to behave."

"Ah, but you will have learnt by then. With two more years, I daresay your confidence will have grown significantly as well."

In the minute of silence that followed, I imagined that day. Would Amelia Lambright be beside me as my wife by then? Very likely so. And what eligible gentlemen would be there to court my sister, properly this time? Bingley, perhaps, having long recovered from his current *tendre* for Miss Bennet. Perhaps Amelia's brother Franklin as well, and some of our other friends from town. It would be a proud moment for me to see Georgiana admired and valued as she should be.

"Shall I play for you now, Brother?" Georgina asked, interrupting my private reverie.

"Yes, please. That is exactly what I need."

20
The Netherfield Ball

I was not sorry for having spent a few days in town visiting my sister, though it did oblige me to make an extra trip to and fro. Departing quite early Tuesday morning, I arrived in Hertfordshire in good time, despite the muddy condition of the roads from a week's worth of rain.

Netherfield was a flurry of activity, alive with preparations, and nobody took more than a passing notice of me. It would have been as well if that might have continued directly through the ball. I knew it could not, however. With Bingley the host, I would be required to exert myself more particularly than under other circumstances. I would be required to dance several times in order to satisfy his idea of reasonable civility. This I was resigned to do.

When the guests began to arrive, I was alert for two things. First, I examined the wearer of every red coat to be certain Wickham was not amongst them. Fortunately, he was not. Secondly, I watched to discover what ladies might suit me most as partners. Mrs. Hurst and Miss Bingley naturally qualified, by virtue of their general good breeding and my familiarity with them. There were some others of Bingley's acquaintance from town as well. I thought I might find appropriate partners amongst them, so that I would not be required to select from the daughters of the local gentry.

But what of the Miss Bennets? I supposed that, as Bingley's special guest, I should dance with Miss Jane Bennet. She was modest, pretty, and well mannered, so that would be no great punishment to me. And I had taken Fitzwilliam's challenge about Elizabeth Bennet under consideration. I would ask her, I had decided, but I thought it likely (and even preferable) that she would find some excuse to decline my invitation.

This prediction was only strengthened when I approached her some little time after her arrival, determined to do my duty without further delay.

"Good evening, Miss Bennet," I said, bowing. "I hope you are well, and all your family."

She scowled at me as if I had said something distasteful. "You!" she said in an accusatory tone. "*Mr. Darcy.*"

"Yes?" I waited for her to make herself clear.

"Some of our pleasantest young men, I am told, have been kept away from this ball by the most artificial of reasons, but nothing has prevented *you*, I see."

It was a perplexing observation, one for which I could not begin to perceive the purpose... nor the most appropriate response to it. "That is true, as to myself," I said after some hesitation. "I cannot at all account for the presence or absence of others, however."

"Can you not? I find that difficult to believe. Please excuse me, sir."

With an expression of disgust – it could be called nothing less – she turned away and immediately left me.

Again, Miss Bennet had managed to confound me. My innocently polite inquiries had been summarily repulsed for no apparent reason, and her abrupt departure had left me no opportunity to ask for the pleasure of her company in the dance. How I had offended on this occasion, I could not begin to understand. I would try again later, I determined, but only once more. If I was similarly rebuffed, that would make an end to it.

I watched Elizabeth dance the first two with a man whom I recognized as her cousin, Mr. Collins, which seemed to do nothing to improve her ill humor. Not that I could blame her if she did not like it; Mr. Collins was frequently moving wrong, I observed, giving all the shame and mortification which a disagreeable partner can. Had she been kinder to me earlier, I might have felt some compassion for her plight. As it was, however, I found myself

121

enjoying her obvious discomfort and wagging my head at her in amusement when once our eyes met.

I danced the next two with Miss Bingley, passing in the set Elizabeth and her new partner – an officer unknown to me but more to her liking than her last, it seemed, judging from the smiles she bestowed on him. At the conclusion, I was determined to try her again and have done, one way or the other. I found her talking to her friend Miss Lucas. When she looked up from her conversation, I did not hesitate.

"If you are not otherwise engaged, Miss Bennet," I said boldly, "will you do me the honor of dancing the next with me?"

I surprised her, I think. She glanced first at her friend and then dropped her eyes, playing for time, it seemed to me. Finally she looked up again. "Thank you, Mr. Darcy. I would be delighted," she said, although she looked anything but.

It was my turn to be surprised... by her acceptance.

So we would dance together after all, and perhaps there had never been two consenting parties less pleased about the prospect.

I could never *truly* be sorry for the chance to admire Elizabeth Bennet more closely – her bright eyes, her dark satiny hair, curled and adorned with ribbons and pearls, her cheeks glowing with the warmth of exercise, her figure set off to best advantage by the white gown she wore. However, she had already made it clear she distained my company. Also, I wondered belatedly, how I was to reconcile this attention with my earlier resolution against distinguishing her with any sign of my regard. Perhaps, I told myself, my indifference would be felt by her just as keenly if I were to show no interest in conversation. I would do my duty as her partner but nothing beyond.

There was little time to consider these questions further, however. The music presently resumed, I claimed Miss Bennet's hand, we took our places in the set, and were soon in motion.

I remained steadfastly mute in the beginning, determined that my fair partner must be the one to break the silence if she so chose. When she finally did so with a prosaic observation about the dance, I replied with the minimum number of words possible: one. "Indeed," I said and resumed my silence.

A few minutes later, she tried again. "It is your turn to say something now, Mr. Darcy. I talked about the dance, and you ought to make some kind of remark on the size of the room or the number of couples."

"As you wish. 'This seems exactly the right sized room to accommodate the number of couples present.' Happy?"

"Very well. That reply will do for the present. Perhaps by and bye I may observe that private balls are much pleasanter than public ones. But for now we may be silent."

If *she* wanted to remain silent, it was my turn to disallow it. "Do you talk by rule then, while you are dancing?"

"Sometimes. One must speak a little, you know. It would look very odd to be entirely silent for half an hour together."

I wondered if this was a fling at me for the thirty minutes I had spent alone with her at Netherfield the week before, steadfastly ignoring her.

Then with an arch smile, she added, "For anybody with a taciturn disposition, in fact, it must be considered the perfect place for conversation. Due to the demands of the dance itself, one may easily arrange things as to have the trouble of saying as little as possible."

We continued on in this bantering fashion, which I was beginning to find not altogether disagreeable. But then Miss Bennet raised the stakes.

"When you met us the other day in Meryton," she said, "we had just been forming a new acquaintance."

I knew at once she referred to Wickham. No doubt she had noticed the exchange of glares between us in the street and decided to quiz me about it, to see how I would react to being reminded of him. I did not respond well. I am certain my countenance conveyed some of what I was feeling, but I did not speak until I had recovered some mastery of myself.

"Mr. Wickham is blessed with such happy manners as may ensure his making friends. Whether he may be equally capable of *retaining* them is less certain. I should think not."

"I find him very amiable, but his is a sad story, full of misfortunes. One in particular. I understand he has lost *your* friendship in a manner which he is likely to suffer from all his life."

What had she heard about the matter? Nothing to my credit, apparently, especially if she had had the story from Wickham himself, which seemed likely. It was neither the time nor an eligible place for setting her straight, however. Besides, she did not seem inclined to take an interest in whatever my side of the story might be.

Then as we were stopped a minute at the bottom of the set, Sir William Lucas came to advance things from bad to worse by making cheerful allusions to the probability of a wedding between Bingley and Miss Jane Bennet. My eyes were at once drawn to the happy couple, who were dancing together again and laughing. The sight raised urgent questions in my mind. Were Sir William Lucas's assumptions his and his alone, or had the entire neighborhood (and perhaps the lady herself) been overtaken by the same expectations? Let it please God to be the former. But if the latter instead, it was my clear duty to warn my friend that, while he had been enjoying Miss Bennet's smiles, he had unwittingly entangled himself in a way that it would soon be difficult to honorably escape.

I know not how I managed to do any credit to myself or my partner after such a disconcerting interruption, to carry on dancing without always setting my foot wrong or to converse with any coherency at all.

My partner, undaunted, had more probing questions for me. "I remember hearing you once say, Mr. Darcy, that you hardly ever forgave, that your resentment once created was unappeasable. You are very cautious, I hope, in allowing it to be created in the first place."

"I am," I said firmly.

"Never allowing yourself to be blinded by prejudice? It is particularly incumbent on those who never change their opinions to judge properly from the start. Do not you agree?"

I had had enough of the inquisition. It was time to turn the tables. "May I ask to what these questions tend?"

She smiled and adopted a lighter, more teasing tone again. "Merely to the illustration of your character," said she, "I am trying to make it out."

"And what is your success?"

She shook her head. "I do not get on at all. I hear such different accounts of you as puzzle me exceedingly."

This I could readily believe, especially if Wickham had her ear. "That seems reason enough to draw no conclusions about me at present. The performance might reflect no credit on either of us. And, as you have just so kindly cautioned me, there is danger in judging a person wrongly."

"Oh! But there is the difference between us. Unlike you, I am perfectly willing to change my mind when I am shown to be wrong. Besides, if I do not take your likeness now, I may never have the pleasure of another opportunity."

"If that be the unhappy case, Miss Bennet, neither will you have the opportunity to correct your mistakes. But I would by no means suspend any pleasure of yours."

I said this last more coldly than I meant to. Still, it seemed to have the desired effect, forestalling any further impertinent questions from my beautiful but exasperating partner. We were both silent until the dance finished, and we parted with only the civility of a bow and a curtsey between us.

The rest of my dance partners that night could not hold a candle to Elizabeth for gripping my attention with both hands, for keeping me balanced on edge for what might happen next. Although some of the other young ladies were just as pretty and light on their feet, they all behaved more conventionally, and our time together passed without incident. They were, without exception, soft-spoken and polite. They smiled and complimented. They most assuredly did *not* challenge every word I spoke or had spoken in the past. They voiced no unfavorable opinions about my character or conduct. Had it not been for the fact that I had already endured enough agitation of that kind for one evening, I might even have been tempted to accuse these good ladies of dullness.

Although the half hour spent with Miss Bennet had mightily disturbed my equanimity, because of other powerful feelings she continued to arouse in me, I was soon thinking more charitably of her again. Yes, she had challenged me, but a little testing might be said to be beneficial for keeping one's mind sharp. She appeared to have judged me unfairly where Wickham was concerned, but the blame for that would more rightly be laid to his account than hers. I could not decide whether there had been more pain or pleasure comprised in the encounter; one thing it could never be called, though, was dull.

It was fortunate for me, then, that other convincing evidence against the Bennet family presented itself before I could be completely run away with by unruly, nonsensical feelings – evidence why I should not even think of such an unsuitable woman as a partner in anything more consequential than a dance. Nor should Bingley be considering her sister.

I was distressed to see my friend continuing his marked attentions to the eldest Miss Bennet as the dancing concluded for the supper break, at which time I unexpectedly found myself accosted by her cousin. Mr. Collins was now known to me by sight, but we had never been introduced. Indeed, there was no reason we ever should be. And yet, without an invitation to do so, he approached, solemnly bowed, and began speaking to me.

"Mr. Darcy," he said, "allow me to introduce myself and pay my respects to you." Not waiting for me to allow or disallow his taking this astonishing liberty, he hurried on. "Indeed I must beg leave to apologize for not doing so sooner, for it has only just now come to my attention that you are the nephew of Lady Catherine de Bourgh. Have I been rightly informed?"

"You have, but pray, what business is my aunt of yours, sir?" I asked in irritation.

"Well may you ask, Mr. Darcy, well may you ask. My name is William Collins. Perhaps your aunt has spoken of me? No? It is of little matter. You need only know that by the beneficence and kind condescension of your noble relation, I am so fortunate as to hold the living of Hunsford, where, I assure you, I steadfastly endeavor to serve her ladyship in a highly commendable manner and with deep humility, ever conscious of my great good fortune in enjoying her generous patronage. I flatter myself that even she would say that I discharge all my duties to her and to the parish in a manner worthy of the trust she has placed in me."

"In so saying, sir, you presume that my aunt could never bestow a favor where it is not deserved. I doubt that is the case." I am afraid my sarcasm was lost on the man. I made him a slight bow and moved away at once, lest he should begin another long, unwelcome speech.

Since I had not danced the last before it, I had no partner as my natural companion for the supper. This was as I had planned it, and I was happy to simply take whatever empty place I found, hoping to enjoy the repast without being obliged to speak very much to anybody at all. For I was already weary of being forced to talk to strangers while dancing.

Unfortunately, I could not so easily avoid *hearing* some of the conversation about me, one of a particularly irksome nature. A shrill female voice near me cut through the other noise, and looking up, I found it was Mrs. Bennet. She seemed to be holding forth about the very subject that had already raised much concern in my mind that night: her sanguine expectation of a forthcoming union between her eldest daughter and my friend, and the manifold benefits to her family to be derived from it.

I did not care to listen, but Mrs. Bennet was making it difficult not to, despite what appeared to be Elizabeth's efforts to restrain her mother. The rest of the Bennets – the younger sisters and even Mr. Bennet – comported themselves little better, and I ended the evening having learned lessons of importance. I was now fully determined to disentangle my friend from so degrading a connection as he seemed to be in danger of undertaking, and I was absolutely cured of contemplating such a connection myself.

21
Withdrawing to London

Bingley had business that took him away to town the following day. I had intended to be gone then as well, but something caused me to delay my own departure. It was the thought that it would be far better for all concerned that my friend should not return to Netherfield so soon as he intended, or indeed, ever again.

After being alerted to the danger by Sir William Lucas's accidental information at the ball, and then hearing Mrs. Bennet's boasting on the same subject, I had watched my friend closely throughout the rest of the evening. Bingley had fancied himself in love several times before, but now I could for the first time perceive that this was at least somewhat different. His partiality for Miss Bennet went beyond what I had ever witnessed in him before. And, also for the first time, I believed it entirely possible that he meant to actually marry her if he could.

Miss Bennet I also watched, and although she seemed pleased enough with Bingley's attentions, I noticed she did not invite them by any obvious participation of sentiment. I detected in her looks and actions no symptom of peculiar regard for him. Her behavior was demure and her countenance so serene that at length I concluded her heart was not likely to be easily touched. More importantly, it seemed probable that her heart had not yet been engaged or endangered by my friend.

I was convinced, however, that Miss Bennet was exactly the sort of compliant and dutiful daughter who would never disappoint her family by rejecting an offer from a man of consequence, even if she did not care for him. If Bingley asked, she would accept him, and then it would all be too late. They might make each other miserable for the rest of their lives.

Something had to be done to rescue my friend from his own folly, and soon. He must be brought to reason. He must be kept away from Miss Bennet until his passion cooled and the expectations of others subsided.

I was willing to undertake the campaign on my own if need be, but it struck me that I might possibly find allies for the cause at Netherfield. I would have to tread carefully at first, however, until I knew their true sentiments, for Miss Bingley and Mrs. Hurst had been staunch defenders of Miss Bennet in the past. I could only hope that recent events had served to open their eyes, along with my own.

So I let Bingley depart on Wednesday without me. I remained behind to test the waters. "Your brother seemed to enjoy himself exceedingly last night," I casually remarked to the sisters over dinner. Mr. Hurst was present as well, of course, but I did not expect to interest him in my cause, not with a good meal set before him. "Did he dance with anybody other than Jane Bennet? I did not observe that he did."

"Oh, yes," said Miss Bingley, "one or two others, I believe, but no one to rival Miss Bennet for beauty."

"One cannot wonder at your brother's admiring her, I suppose," I added and waited. Here was the opening for one of them to confirm what I hoped they were also thinking.

Mrs. Hurst, after a short hesitation, said, "Miss Bennet is a sweet girl, to be sure. It is very sad that she should have such an unfortunate family, such low connections."

"As we had ample proof of last night," continued Miss Bingley, rolling her eyes. "Louisa and I were both saying how we could barely keep our countenances one time and another – the wild little sisters, the ridiculous cousin, the vulgar mother, to say nothing of Miss Eliza Bennet's impertinence."

"True. Your brother will have a deal to put up with when he marries her," I said. "But if he is truly in love this time..." I left that idea hanging.

"Surely it is not as serious as that!" cried Louisa.

"I watched them closely last night," I said, "and I believe the danger is very real. A proposal cannot be far off, unless I miss my guess. It seems the entire neighborhood is expecting it too."

"Then something must be done at once to prevent it!" Miss Bingley exclaimed. "A pleasant flirtation, such as we have seen before, would do Charles no harm. But he must not be allowed to completely throw himself away forever on a Miss Bennet. If he cannot see that for himself, he must be taught to know his own good. Mr. Darcy, you must assist us. No time must be lost."

Of one mind, we determined to follow Bingley to London, to join our efforts in dissuading him, and to keep him away from Netherfield and Miss Bennet for his own good.

The sisters were grateful when I proposed myself as the primary agent of the intervention, for as much as they generally made free to express their opinions to their brother, they could not completely forget the respect they owed him as head of the family. I was on a more equal footing with Bingley and had the extra advantage that he was already in the habit of relying on my judgement more than his own. I hoped he would accept my counsel on this most important occasion as well, and his sisters would be there to add the strength of their own convictions on the subject if needed.

Although Bingley was surprised that we had all followed on his heels, he had not the least suspicion of our reason for doing so, at least not until I cornered him in the sparsely furnished library of his bachelor town house and fastened my gaze on him. "I'm sorry Bingley, but it is no good. It will not do."

He smiled good naturedly at my declaration and began to look about himself. "What can you mean, Darcy? Is the room in disorder? Do you despise my limited collection of books? Oh, I know it is nothing to yours, but I have always meant to expand on it. Now perhaps I shall not, though. Perhaps I shall just add these few volumes to the fine collection at Netherfield instead. I have not much time for reading anyway, especially when I am in town."

"No, my friend; it is not this library. It is in fact something to do with Netherfield, something of a serious nature. Do sit down and give me your full attention while I explain." When he had done so, I continued. "I believe it would be wise for you to stay away from Netherfield for a time, not to return within the week as you had planned."

He looked up at me, puzzled. "How long do you mean? Two or three weeks instead?"

"A good deal longer than that, Bingley. Perhaps some months hence you might return without harm, but no sooner. It is unsafe."

"Darcy, you are speaking in riddles. Unsafe? What nonsense is this?"

"My apologies; I will be more direct." I searched for the right way to approach the heart of the delicate topic. "Are you aware that your very particular attentions to Miss Bennet have given rise to the general expectation of a forthcoming betrothal between yourself and the young lady? Indeed, I believe the idea to be very widespread in the neighborhood of Meryton. In short, you are quite near to becoming irrevocably entangled, Bingley, and you must withdraw before it becomes too late to honorably do so."

"Withdraw? What can you mean by making such a suggestion? I care nothing about the sort of gossips as you refer to. Besides, they may be right! I know I have not told you before, but I have a good mind to marry Miss Bennet, as they say. And who could blame me? She is an angel and you know it!"

I anticipated that disputing this assertion, exaggerated though it might be, was unlikely to advance my cause. So I turned the light from the charms of Miss Bennet to her far less charming family – their want of connection and their want of propriety, and how fatal such a disadvantage could be to a young man trying to establish himself in society. Bingley blinked at me but looked unmoved by such generalities. So I proceeded to present the unpleasant specifics. The issue was too critical to spare his feelings; he must be made to look at the painful truth.

I therefore relayed to him all the evidence of clear impropriety I had observed at the ball and before from Miss Bennet's relations.

To most of these things, I soon discovered that Bingley had been oblivious, his attentions being almost fully engrossed at these times by his ladylove. When I described them truthfully and earnestly, he did look shaken. But then he soon rallied.

"Even if it was as bad as you say, Darcy, what is that to me? I need not care about society's opinion of such connections. Besides, I would be marrying Miss Bennet, not her relations, and she is the model of modesty and propriety. Can you deny it?"

Again, I saw the futility of debating Miss Bennet's virtues. "You are naïve to say so, Bingley. You know I care little enough for the *ton* myself, but you disregard society's good opinion at your peril. If you have no lofty aspirations of your own, think of your sister and your future offspring. You have a duty to do what you can for them. And, in a very real sense, when you marry, you marry the girl's family as well. They would be a burden to you all your life."

"Suffering the inconvenience of a few awkward relations would be a small sacrifice," he said defiantly. "Nothing at all to compare to our happiness in each other's company. I love Miss Bennet, Darcy, and you may as well know it! I am now quite determined to marry her, despite what you say."

This was a miserable result. While doing my best to divide my friend from an inappropriate female, I had merely succeeded in pushing him into her arms! I paced up and down the room in silence, thinking. Bingley's resistance was more robust than I had anticipated, and there was only one more argument I could make. I hesitated to mention it for the pain it was sure to give my friend, but there was no help for it.

"You speak of sacrifice, Bingley, but are you willing to sacrifice Miss Bennet's happiness to achieve your own?"

This time he looked staggered indeed, falling backward in his chair as if I had dealt him a blow to the chin. While I had the advantage, I pressed ahead.

"If you make her an offer, no doubt she will accept you. She would feel too much obligation to her family to do otherwise, for she will have been reminded every day of her life that she must make a good match to save her mother and sisters from the poverty. She will accept you merely out of duty and pay for it the rest of her life. Is that what you want?"

"Then... Then you are persuaded that she is indifferent, that she does not care for me?"

I paused, aggrieved by my friend's crestfallen look, before reminding myself that this was all for his ultimate good. Giving a little pain now to save him a lifetime of regret was surely the kindest course.

"I'm sorry, Bingley, but I think you have mistaken her true feelings. You have deceived yourself into believing that she returns your regard in equal measure, that her smiles are especially for you when they are only a sign of the same cheerful manner and amiability with which she treats everybody, including myself. I have watched Miss Bennet carefully – and with more objectivity than you can possibly claim – and I am convinced. I have never seen any symptom of peculiar regard. No doubt she likes you as an acquaintance, but I believe her heart is untouched. Therefore, you can safely withdraw without harming her, and that is what you must do. It will be for the best. Your sisters will support me in this, I assure you."

Bingley's head dropped into his hands and his elbows onto his knees. He remained in this attitude for a matter of minutes while I waited patiently. At last, he raised his eyes and said morosely, "I did think Miss Bennet cared for me, but I can understand now how I might have deceived myself without knowing it. Sometimes one sees just what one wants to see."

"Exactly."

"What a presumptuous fool I have been," he cried, shooting to his feet of a sudden, "thinking of nobody but myself and my own happiness!"

"Now, now, Bingley," I said, placing a steadying hand on his shoulder. "There is no need for all that. The important thing is what you do from here. I know you will want to do what is right, even if it is painful to yourself."

"Certainly. I would not wish to place Miss Bennet under an unpleasant obligation. I would not hurt her for the world. So you think I had best not see her again?"

"Precisely. It would be the kindest course, for everybody concerned."

After some further discussion and assurances, I shook Bingley's hand and left him in the library.

Miss Bingley, who had been waiting in the drawing room with her sister in case their help was needed, intercepted me on my way to the front door, extending a hand and an urgently questioning look to me.

I took and patted her hand briefly before letting it go again. "Never fear," I told her. "I believe all will be well. Be kind to your brother, for he is hard hit. But he is now convinced of doing the right thing, of giving up Miss Bennet."

I firmly believed at the time that I had done the right thing as well, that I had nobly saved my friend from a most unfortunate alliance, that I had in fact saved him from being ruined by the dizzying effects of love, which had so clouded his judgement. I was also relieved for myself, for having thereby been likewise removed from the seductive dangers to be found in Hertfordshire.

22
Winter Outlook

My mission successfully accomplished, I went home to my sister in Berkley Street.

The weeks that followed were relatively uneventful. Georgiana continued her studies with Mrs. Annesley and the visiting masters. I conducted what business I could in town and kept in close correspondence with my steward concerning matters at Pemberley. We neither accepted nor extended many social invitations.

Franklin Lambright, who was back in town, called on us, which Georgiana bore with relative composure. I saw Bingley frequently to encourage him as well as to make sure his resolve against seeing Miss Bennet held fast. Fitzwilliam came to say he had been summoned home for Christmas but would return to London with the coming of the new year.

That, I decided, would be my cue to travel north myself. By then, I would have been away from Pemberley in excess of four months, and although I trusted those managing my affairs in my absence, it would be high time I showed my face to reassure everybody that the master was still actively interested and in control.

"How long will you be away this time," Georgiana asked when I told her of my travel plans. She was doing better and better all the time, and she did not seem distressed by the idea of my leaving.

"Not long. Two or three weeks, perhaps. A month at most. But I shall not go until Fitzwilliam is back in town," I assured her. "He will look in on you while I am gone, as he did when I was away in Hertfordshire. If you need anything at all, call on him."

She dropped her eyes and only nodded.

Noticing this, and as we were quite alone, I continued. "You really should try to get over your embarrassment where Fitzwilliam is concerned. He is a true friend and deserves to be treated as such."

"I know, and I am sorry," she said, eyes still downcast.

I reached over and took her hand. "Georgiana, Fitzwilliam is devoted to you. If you asked him to sail to China and back, he would set off tomorrow! He does not think at all the worse of you for having made a mistake or two. He is no saint either, you know. No one is. Understand?"

"Yes, William."

"Good. And will you try very hard to meet him in the old, friendly way next time?"

"I will try." She was quiet for a few moments before she added a question. "And shall you see Miss Lambright while you are in Derbyshire?"

"Yes. It would be discourteous not to visit our friends at Ravenshaw after so long away."

"And shall you ask her to marry you?"

"That is my intent."

"When will the wedding take place?"

"Assuming she accepts me, do you mean?"

"Yes, but she will, of course."

"Then I should imagine Miss Lambright and her father will have something to say about when the ceremony occurs. I will not press for anything before the summer, though. I should like to see you finish out your studies here first in the spring, and then spend the summer at Pemberley again. Hopefully we can prevail upon Mrs. Annesley to accompany you there as well. Does that sound agreeable to you?"

"Summers at Pemberley will be very different once you have a wife, William."

"Indeed, but we have weathered changes together before. And this one will be all for the good, I believe. We have been much too quiet in recent years with just the two of us. It is time we begin gathering a little more family about us, and soon Miss Lambright – Amelia – will be a sweet sister to you. That is my hope."

Georgiana produced a brave smile. "I am sure you are right, William. If Miss Lambright will make you happy, then I shall be glad to have her as my sister."

I kissed her cheek and said, "Thank you, my dear. That means a great deal to me."

Accordingly, I sent off another letter to Lord Harcourt, promising a long-overdue visit to Ravenshaw in January or early February. He responded by suggesting a particular date and further recommending that I come prepared to be his guest for more than an afternoon; I was to spend at least a night or two, he said. I thought it an excellent suggestion, particularly at the time of year when the days were short and travel most awkward. Then there would be no rush because of a darkening sky and an impending departure. I was determined that this time nothing should keep me from carrying out my intention of proposing marriage to Miss Lambright at last.

I had lately seen how easily Bingley had succumb to the temptation of a pretty face, quickly fancying himself in love. And even I, who had liked to consider myself a disciple of sensible behavior and master over my own emotions, had discovered I was not completely immune to the attractions of a lively wit and bewitching eyes. It had shocked and distressed me. It had taught me to be more on my guard.

I had been so fortunate as to escape the danger unharmed this time. I was profoundly thankful for that. And now the best protection against any further stumbles of that sort would be to return to my carefully laid plans. Once Miss Lambright and I were engaged and everybody knew it, that kind of temptation would be at an end.

The other safeguard – equally effective – would be to never place myself in Elizabeth Bennet's way again. It seemed easily done, since we moved in very different segments of society. The Bingleys and the Hursts were our only acquaintances in common, and as long as Mr. Bingley kept away from the one sister, I should not be likely to come into contact with the other.

Christmas came and went as the primary bright spot in an otherwise dreary month. The weather had been particularly bleak – cold and gray as a stone with the only variety to the frigid rain provided by an occasional snow. But snow in town was not the beautiful blanket of white it was in the country. Before the crystalline flakes even touched the earth, they were made dirty by the soot of the air. Then they were almost immediately churned into the mud of the streets and lost.

By the time Fitzwilliam returned, I was ready and eager to be gone, though I knew from his report on the roads that the journey would not be an easy one. Nevertheless, I was prepared to put up with the challenges entailed without complaint. I had long since reconciled myself to the inconvenience of the distance involved with getting back and forth to London, convinced that it was more than compensated for by the privilege of living in Derbyshire.

The long hours on the road held one disadvantage that I had failed to take into account, however, that is in leaving me far too much time to do nothing else but think.

I began well enough, devoting my mental energies to planning all the various tasks I meant to accomplish whilst I was at Pemberley, intending to work through them as expeditiously as possible so that I could return to Georgiana.

Among other things, I would discharge my quarterly consultation with Mrs. Reynolds concerning household affairs, reviewing her books for the past three month and listening to her prediction of future needs and expenditures. It was a mere formality, for Mrs. Reynolds had expertly managed Pemberley House for more years than I could remember, and she was as dependable as the day was long. The primary advantage of the exercise was in having the pleasure of spending a little extra time in her company.

Likewise, a long conference with Mr. Adams was overdue. He was a highly capable and trustworthy steward, managing the day-to-day business of the estate as well or better than I would have myself. And no doubt I could have left him entirely in charge for a year or more at a time without any significant harm being done. I would not so abandon my responsibilities, however, so I required him to keep me fully up to date. A month never went by without at least one tenant complaint, a report or two of poaching, an urgent repair being needed here or there, or something even more consequential. I wished to know it all, and I reserved for myself the task of making every weighty decision.

Beyond these concerns, visiting Ravenshaw and completing my business there was the most pressing matter. Accordingly, I gave considerable thought while I travelled to how I should proceed. But then I would find my mind drifting from Amelia Lambright to Elizabeth Bennet, and not always with productive results.

I might start by reminding myself of every way in which Amelia was superior – her birth, her connections, her even temper, her calm and proper behavior – but then I would end somewhere else. I quickly put Elizabeth's outspoken, impertinent opinions on the ledger against her... until I recalled something she had said that made me laugh, until I remembered how my blood had hummed, how alive I had felt when we had fallen into one of our spirited debates. I pictured Amelia's pleasing appearance in my mind's eye – her thin, statuesque frame and regal bearing, her fair hair and ivory complexion – and then Elizabeth's dark, sparkling eyes would intrude to overpower them as easily as the brilliance of the sun overpowers the pale glow of the moon.

Time and again I found it necessary to call myself to account, to take myself to task for my weakness where Elizabeth was concerned. Though I had been removed from her by several weeks of time and distance, her inconvenient influence lived on. I had failed to completely vanquish it.

I did not view these importunate thoughts as cause to hesitate in my resolve to marry Miss Lambright, however. On the contrary, they were a powerful reason to proceed according to plan, for they only reiterated the danger comprehended in allowing oneself to be swayed by something as ignoble as animal attraction, as unreasonable as emotion, as ungovernable as the heart. These were exactly the things I had set myself against from the beginning, and wise I was to have done so. Without that strong compass to guide me, I could now perceive how easy it would have been to stray away from the correct course.

I could only hope that Miss Lambright would relieve my suffering by accepting me at once, thereby securing my future and my peace of mind from further torment.

23
Coming to the Point at Last

I had two days at Pemberley to rest from the journey, which had indeed been arduous. A bridge had washed out, necessitating a detour of nearly fifteen miles. And when I at last arrived at the inn I always patronized, every regular room was taken. The innkeeper, who apologized again and again, offered to put somebody out for me, but I would not hear of it. Instead, I made do with a very small but clean chamber designed to accommodate a servant, and was glad to have it. Add to all this a horse who threw a shoe, and it made for one of the more memorable but less pleasant return trips.

Then on the appointed day, I was back in the carriage again, bound for Ravenshaw and my momentous appointment with Miss Lambright.

I was pleased – and relieved – to be about this important business at last, and yet I did not mean to charge in like some impatient oaf and overwhelm Miss Lambright at once. Since I would be staying until at least the following day, there would be time for courtesy and restraint. There would be time for the exercise of civility and gracious behavior.

After I had paid my respects to both Lord Harcourt and his daughter, I anticipated no difficulty in finding an opportunity to speak to Miss Lambright alone. Indeed, I was reasonably certain Harcourt would be expecting me to make such a request.

When I arrived at Ravenshaw, I was received as warmly as I ever had been, which seemed to bode well. Harcourt pumped my hand vigorously, saying how exceedingly glad he was to see me again. Amelia looked very well, I thought, a warm glow of health in her cheeks and perhaps a bit more animation than before. Was this for me, I wondered? Was she as pleased to see me as her father was and cheerfully anticipating what I had come there to do?

We three spent an hour in comfortable conversation in the drawing room and then continued in the same style as we went in to dinner. Towards the end of the meal, I was about to ask Harcourt to grant me the honor of a private audience with his daughter at any time convenient, when he seemed to offer me just that.

"I hate to desert you, Darcy," he began, "especially when it has been so long since we have seen you, but I am afraid it cannot be helped. Tomorrow I must go into the village on business that simply will not wait."

"I hope it is nothing serious, my lord," I responded.

"Harcourt, please. And no, urgent but not too serious is how I would describe the situation. You will please excuse me. And perhaps you will not mind it if Amelia keeps you company for an hour or two in my absence." He said this last with a glint in his eye and a knowing grin.

I returned his smile. "I cannot think of anything I would enjoy more, sir."

Thus, I had a fair idea of Lord Harcourt's approbation. Next I looked at Amelia to see if I could judge how she bore these allusions to what would certainly take place the following day, but I found her expression inscrutable. She was neither giddy with happiness, which I would not have expected in any case, nor did she seem at all disconcerted. Although her well-schooled countenance gave nothing away, I knew I could depend on a straightforward answer from her on the morrow, or so I thought.

~~*~~

With a wink in my direction, Lord Harcourt left us in the front hall immediately after breakfast, and then at last I was alone with Miss Lambright. For a long minute or two, we said nothing at all;

the only sound to be heard was the rain that began pelting against the windows.

"The roads will be wet," Amelia said finally. "I hope Papa will not run into any trouble."

"Fortunately, he does not have far to go."

"True," she agreed. Then as if she had decided on some definite course of action, she said, "Well, Mr. Darcy, I thought we might take a tour of the picture gallery upstairs. It is a quiet, pleasant place to walk, and it must have been a very long time since you have seen it."

I bowed my assent, and then we both remained silent until we had reached our destination. Amelia paused to point out the first two or three pictures, giving the names of the depicted ancestors, before dropping the pretense that either of us was interested. Then we walked on and I knew it was time for me to begin.

"Forgive me for staying away so long, Miss Lambright. It was not at all what I had intended or wished to do."

"It is above five months since I have seen you, Mr. Darcy – five months since I visited Pemberley and six since we danced together at Ravenshaw. You asked for a walk with me in the garden that night."

"How well I remember. Then circumstances prevented me from returning to claim that walk."

"Today is no time for a walk in the garden."

"No, indeed, but though the setting must be different, I would like to discuss the same matter with you now as I had meant to do then."

"Very well, but you should feel no obligation to do so, Mr. Darcy. Many things may have changed in the intervening months. I am perfectly sensible of that."

"Nevertheless, with your permission, I shall continue."

She nodded. "Just as you please."

We strolled along at a very leisurely pace, which suited me fine. I knew it would be easier to say what I needed to say without being looked at.

"Miss Lambright," I began. "Or may I call you Amelia?"

"Of course."

"Amelia, I wish to first express my great respect and admiration for your family and for you in particular. I think you cannot be without suspicion that I came to Ravenshaw last spring with the idea of finding in you a suitable partner for myself and a mistress for Pemberley. I was not disappointed in any way. We seem to deal very well together, and an alliance between us must be considered advantageous on both sides." Here I finally stopped to face her. "In short, Miss Lambright, I am asking you to marry me, perhaps in the summer. Will you do me that honor?"

She walked away a few paces before turning to answer, although it was more of a question instead, and not at all what I had expected.

"No talk of love, Mr. Darcy?"

"Well... no," I said. "I once promised that I would always be honest with you, and so I will tell you only what is true. I hold you in considerable esteem and friendly affection, which I believe is most important when choosing a marriage partner, but I cannot say that I am in love with you. Neither do I consider this a disadvantage, you understand, because romantic love often leads a person astray. I have chosen you with an informed mind and with family loyalty and honor in view. I thought perhaps you might think similarly about such things."

She considered for a moment. "In general I do, Mr. Darcy. I am not in love with you either, and I also believe that mutual esteem and friendship are vital. At one time, I would have been easily persuaded that these things were enough for a successful match – that, plus my father's approbation, which I already had in your case. In fact, if you had offered for me last summer, as I expected you to do, I was prepared to accept your proposal at once. We might already have been married by now!"

Bewildered, I asked, "But now the situation is altered?"

"It is somewhat, and yet I cannot tell you exactly how or whether it will make any difference in the end. I apologize for being so ambiguous, Mr. Darcy, but I must ask if you can be patient with me. I am not prepared to give you a definite answer at this time."

My first impulse was to say no, that it would not do at all, that I required and deserved the straightforward answer I had expected. But fortunately I took a moment to reflect first, and I decided that attitude would not serve me well.

I had wanted and expected to have the matter settled without further delay, but was that fair? Since I had kept Amelia in suspense of my question for fully six months, it did not seem unreasonable that I should now be kept in suspense of her answer for a time. "Certainly, I can," I said at last, and we began walking again. "There is no rush. If you need time to consider your reply, you shall have it."

"Thank you for your forbearance, Mr. Darcy. I am very sensible of the honor of your proposal, I do assure you, and I mean no disrespect in not accepting it outright. However it is better to be certain before proceeding. Do not you agree?"

It was a significant blow to my pride, I admit, but not to my heart. "Of course," I said after some further contemplation. "And what shall we tell your father? If he indeed wishes us to marry, which seems to be the case, he may not be so patient. He may consider that we have been skirting about the issue long enough."

"I will manage Papa. I will simply explain that you and I have come to an understanding, which must remain private for now. I believe he will consider it a step in the right direction and be satisfied for the time being."

"And... And how am *I* to think of this 'understanding'? If it is not a definite engagement, what is it precisely? I want no confusion or recriminations later."

"I *am* sorry, Mr. Darcy, truly I am, for asking to leave things in such an indeterminate state. Here is what I am suggesting, though. You are to understand that although I like you very much, I may cry off at any time. You are free to do the same, of course."

"I shall not."

"Nevertheless, if neither of us does cry off within... Shall we say six months? Then we will go ahead and marry at once. Does

146

that seem reasonable? We could still be wed in the summer, just as you suggested a moment ago. If not, then no one except my father will be the wiser, and I trust he will forgive us both eventually."

I did not like the secrecy and the delay. I did not like the uncertainty. But there was some logic in the plan; I would have expected nothing less from Miss Lambright. And if all went well, I would achieve exactly what I had wanted in the end. It was giving Amelia what she needed to be comfortable and the only sacrifice was my wounded pride.

I should not think of it as a personal rejection, I decided. Since what I had offered Miss Lambright was a mutually beneficial alliance, not my heart, I could not be offended if she wished to negotiate terms more to her taste, as was customary in any business contract, even a contract of marriage. It was best to keep all emotions, including pride, out of the equation. That was just as I had designed from the beginning.

"I accept your terms, Miss Lambright," I said abruptly, holding out my hand to shake hers.

She smiled and took it.

24
Comfort and Conscience

The rest of my stay at Ravenshaw was less awkward than I might have imagined. The viscount was obviously pleased with me for finally coming to the point, and he accepted his daughter's wishes for the rest. I liked them both too much to dwell on my disappointment, especially since I had every hope of things coming right in the end.

Naturally, I said nothing to anybody about these developments when I returned to Pemberley the following day. I went about my business as if nothing at all had occurred, which was, unfortunately, more or less the case. I might be getting married in the summer, or I might not. I might soon have the pleasure of providing Georgiana a sister and Pemberley a new mistress... or I might not.

I could do no more at present to influence the outcome, so I endeavored to dwell as little as possible on the unsettled state of affairs. Instead, I turned my attention from Miss Lambright to my first and truest love: Pemberley.

It was delightful to be home again after so long away. Even in the dead of winter, even without anybody to share it, there was nowhere I would rather have been. Pemberley was where I felt I most truly belonged, where I felt the purest sense of my own identity as a man. I was Fitzwilliam Darcy of Pemberley. Yes, I could function in other places, and most people would probably notice no difference in me. But *I* knew. I felt it. I was never as confident or complete when I was away from my home. As if I sensed a critical component of myself had been left behind in Derbyshire, I was never fully at ease anywhere else.

There were challenges aplenty at Pemberley too, of course, but at least I met these challenges with my home ground on my side. Pemberley itself was my friend, and my friend would always be on my side, wishing me to succeed.

So, although I knew I should return to my sister in London without too much delay, I could not persuade myself to rush through my duties or neglect the opportunity of taking as much refreshment as possible from my country surroundings before facing the gloomy prospect of town again. While at least half of every day was given over to genuine estate business, I always found time – and an excuse – to take a ride through some part of the park or other, whenever the weather made the exercise at all eligible. A personal visit from the master to each of the tenant farms would not be taken amiss, I trusted. Then there was the quarry works and the timber works to inspect. A heavy snow curtailed my rides for a few days, but the dogs were eager to get out and romp in it with me.

As the last week of January approached, however, I knew it was time to begin making preparations to depart Pemberley. I visited Ravenshaw once more, just for an afternoon, and found things unchanged there. Miss Lambright did not cry off, but neither was she ready to make our provisional engagement definite. So I went away again still not knowing my fate. I left Pemberley and returned to London without knowing if I was to be married in the summer or not.

How I wished that I had never breathed a word about my plans for Miss Lambright to anybody! But Georgiana and Fitzwilliam would both quite naturally be wondering about the outcome. I only intended to have that humiliating conversation once, so I sent for my cousin as soon as I returned, to get it over with.

Sitting Fitzwilliam and Georgiana down together in the drawing room of Darcy House, with the door closed, I told them, "You will both wish to know about my visit to Ravenshaw while I was in the north. The facts are these: I did indeed propose to Miss Lambright but she was not prepared to accept me."

Georgiana said nothing. Fitzwilliam did not hold back.

"She refused you? I cannot believe it!"

"No, she did not refuse me, not precisely."

"If she did not accept and she did not refuse, what else is there?"

"Something in between, I suppose. Miss Lambright wishes to keep the matter to ourselves at present – so you must both understand you are not to say a word – and we shall revisit the question in six months. If nothing occurs in the interim to put her off the idea, we will be married in the summer, as I had suggested to her in the first place."

"Well, I never heard the like of it! Can she be a sensible girl to not accept you at once? You must be vexed by such an ambivalent response, Darcy, and who could blame you? Perhaps *you* had better be the one to cry off."

"I am sure she meant no disrespect," suggested Georgiana.

"Quite right, my dear," I said. "I know I could, and perhaps should, feel insulted. And I admit it was a blow to my pride at first. Still, I like and respect Miss Lambright and her family too much to be peevish about it. I shouldn't be surprised if this kind of thing happens all the time, especially between families of equal consequence; we simply do not hear of it."

"You are more generous than I should be in your situation, Darcy. That is all I can say."

"By being patient, I may well get what I want at last. But for now, there is an end to it," I said decisively, hoping to bring the matter to a close.

Georgiana had one more question, however. "And your heart will not be broken if you do not get your way?"

"Certainly not. This was meant to be a beneficial alliance, not a love match. You know that."

"Yes, I know that is what you said, William, but I thought perhaps you might have fallen in love with Amelia just the same. I am glad to know you are safe from that kind of pain."

I could tell that my sister was thinking of her own heartbreak, and so it was definitely time for a change of subject. "Yes, thank you," I said. "Now tell me about your visit to our friends in Grosvenor Street. How did the dinner come off?"

I knew from a letter that had reached me at Pemberley that Georgiana had been invited to the Hursts' and that she intended to go. She would have seen Miss Bingley also, since that lady resided with her sister, and no doubt the brother would have been there as well.

Georgiana's descriptions were not comprehensive, but she talked more of the dinner than I might have expected in months past. Added to the fact that this conversation occurred in Fitzwilliam's presence without any particular reticence, and I took it as an encouraging sign of her steady improvement.

I had been back in town only a few days when another invitation for my sister and myself arrived from Grosvenor Street. It was for supper and cards this time. Since I was desirous of seeing Bingley, who was sure to be amongst the guests, and hearing from his sisters how he did, with Georgiana's agreement I accepted for both of us at once.

I was glad to find upon our arrival that the party consisted only of Mr. and Mrs. Hurst, Miss Bingley, Mr. Bingley, Georgiana, and myself. I was not long in discovering my friend as yet unreturned to his former carefree ways. Although he made an effort to appear so, I was not deceived. Still, it had only been two months since he was obliged to give up Miss Bennet, and I told myself that his total recovery was not to be expected so soon.

Over supper, some pointed looks from Miss Bingley alerted me to the idea that she very particularly wished to speak to me. I was no less eager for a private conference, anticipating that I would then hear her report on her brother and whatever had transpired in my absence. Working together, we so well maneuvered as to be the two odd persons out when the others settled to play whist, giving us a good half an hour to talk quietly at the other end of the drawing room.

"Your brother's commitment has held?" I asked at once, knowing no further explanation would be necessary to make myself understood.

"It has," Miss Bingley answered with a sly smile. "I am quite certain he has not seen her, though it has been more troublesome to achieve than we had imagined."

"What do you mean? He has not been back to Netherfield, has he?"

"No, not that, but Miss Bennet is here!"

Her words had seemed too loud, and I glanced up to be sure Bingley had not heard before asking at a near whisper, "In London?"

"Yes, these four weeks!"

"How came that to be the case?"

"She is staying with her aunt and uncle in Gracechurch Street. I have seen her myself. It could not be helped, believe me." She rolled her eyes derisively. "You can imagine, however, that I have been at great pains that Charles should know nothing about it, for I fear the temptation to see her again, with her so nearby, would be too great for him. He is not strong like you and I, Mr. Darcy."

"How is it that you happened to see Miss Bennet yourself?"

"I ignored her letter announcing her arrival in town, as if it had gone astray, but then she *would* call on me and she would ask after my brother too, of course."

"That is only natural, I suppose, due to that certain level of past acquaintance."

"I flatter myself, though, that I have done a famous job of discouraging her on all fronts. I wish you had been here to see it, Mr. Darcy. First, I waited as long as was decently possible before returning the call to that unfashionable part of town. Then I said enough – without actually telling a complete falsehood, you understand – to allow Miss Bennet to believe that my brother must know and not care that she is in town, that he has the idea of never returning to Netherfield again, and that perhaps he is really partial to Miss Darcy!" She laughed behind her hand. "Moreover, I behaved with such cold indifference that I daresay she will give up my acquaintance altogether now, which will remove her only connection back to Charles. Have I not done well, Mr. Darcy?"

After listening to Miss Bingley's recitation, I was too much troubled to give her the praise she so obviously desired.

"But Mr. Darcy, why do you frown?"

"Deceiving Miss Bennet is nothing to gloat over, Miss Bingley. It speaks of duplicity, which is not something I can admire."

"What? I hope you do not mean to criticize, Mr. Darcy, for I did only what we *all* agreed was necessary! You said yourself that we must do whatever it might take to keep Charles from seeing her again."

"I know I did."

"Well then, have you changed your mind? Because I daresay one word from me would send Charles off to Gracechurch Street at a run! Is that what you want?"

I sat without speaking for a minute, thinking about what it was exactly that was bothering me.

I still believed that separating my friend from Miss Bennet had been the necessary and right thing to do – a kindness to him at no appreciable cost to the lady. But when confronted by the means Miss Bingley had deemed necessary to sustain that separation, my conscience began to complain that I had been a party to something underhanded. She had used the art of concealment, and now that she had told me that Miss Bennet was in town, I would be obliged to keep that information concealed from my friend as well, or sacrifice all we had achieved so far. And yet disguise of every sort was abhorrent to me.

"No, Miss Bingley, that is not what I want, but I am sorry to have involved you in this business. And I am sorrier still that you should have so much enjoyed your part. I had thought your friendship with Miss Bennet would have made deceiving her quite painful to you. Or maybe that was the true deception – your pretense of liking her in the first place."

Without waiting for reply, I rose to return to the others, whose game I felt sure would soon be breaking up.

25

A Summons

A few weeks passed without any complications with Mr. Bingley. Partly thanks to me, for better or for worse, he continued in complete ignorance of Miss Bennet's presence in town. And, true to Miss Bingley's prediction, the lady in question made no attempt to resurrect their waning friendship.

No word arrived from Ravenshaw, which I also counted as good news. For if Amelia had definitely decided against me, I was sure to have heard.

The significant piece of correspondence that *did* reach me was from my aunt, inviting me and Georgiana to Rosings Park. Although it was worded cordially, I recognized it for what it was. When Lady Catherine de Bourgh issued an 'invitation' to one of her underlings, which included nearly everybody of her acquaintance below a duke, it was meant to be taken as a command. I was no exception.

It was a visit of duty, which I felt myself bound to pay. But I could at least spare my sister if she so chose. Lady Catherine might exercise some direct line of imagined authority over me, but I held the direct authority over Georgiana. Since she, not surprisingly, declined to go to Rosings with me, I proposed myself an alternative companion.

"Must I?" Fitzwilliam protested, when I asked him.

"Of course not, but you know your turn will come soon enough otherwise. If you go with me now, you will have already done your duty and may expect to be exempt from any further invitations for at least three or four months." When he did not yet seem convinced, I added, "And this way, neither of us shall have to face the harrowing specter of Rosings alone."

As I had hoped, Fitzwilliam laughed, and he soon agreed to go.

Through his military contacts, Fitzwilliam had been discreetly monitoring Wickham's activities, and so we knew that he would be fully occupied in Meryton with his regiment, which was the only reason I felt it safe for both Fitzwilliam and I to absent ourselves for a fortnight or a little more. Also, Georgiana continued to do well under the disciplined tutelage of Mrs. Annesley, whom I had learnt to trust and value as a true godsend.

Accordingly, Fitzwilliam and I journeyed south to Kent the week before Easter, expecting a visit very much like all the others we had, separately or together, endured in the past. This assumption, however, could not have been more erroneous, for we had no more than just arrived when my aunt accosted me with a most surprising question, one sounding more like an accusation.

"Darcy, what is this I hear of your acquaintance with Miss Elizabeth Bennet? She tells me you are well known to her. Can it be so?"

I could not at first imagine how my aunt should even be aware that such a person existed, let alone that she might have actually spoken to her. Then I remembered Mr. Collins; that had to be the connection. "Elizabeth?" I said. "Is she here?"

According to my aunt's hasty explanations, Elizabeth's friend Charlotte Lucas had somehow been prevailed upon to marry Mr. Collins, who I already knew held the living of Hunsford. Now Elizabeth was visiting at the parsonage and had actually been a guest at Rosings more than once.

"But you have not answered my question," she continued. "What is your level of acquaintance with this young lady?"

I mumbled some vague account of my familiarity with the Bennet family from my time at Netherfield, making it sound as trivial as possible. But then I instantly contradicted this assertion by foolishly suggesting that I should acknowledge the acquaintance with an immediate call at the parsonage, inviting Fitzwilliam to accompany me. I was not thinking clearly.

"Stay where you are, both of you," Lady Catherine command-
ed. Tomorrow or the next day will be soon enough to begin paying
calls of duty. For now, you must rest from your travels and give
your attention to those who have a higher claim to it."

My cousin Anne came in, I rose to greet her, and then I sank
back down to consider the situation, leaving the conversation
mostly to Fitzwilliam and my aunt.

"This is a disaster!" I told Fitzwilliam later, when the ladies
had left us for the night and gone to bed. We had retreated to the
billiards room, each of us with a glass in one hand and Fitzwilliam
with a cigar in his other.

"Do you mean about Anne? It would be difficult indeed to have
misinterpreted Lady Catherine's agenda for bringing you here, the
way she dragged me from the room to leave the two of you alone.
I suppose she thinks it high time you officially proposed."

"No doubt. She persists in clinging to the old idea that I will
marry Anne, though I have done nothing to encourage it."

"It matters not a bit what you think of it; Lady Catherine
intends to have her way, as always! Good thing she doesn't know
about Miss Lambright, eh Darcy?" He laughed, the traitor, giving
my shoulder a jab. He was clearly enjoying my discomfort.

"I should have expected more sympathy. Our aunt could just
as easily have set her sights on *you*, you know."

Fitzwilliam shrugged, looking not even a little bit repentant.
"Ah, but you are far richer, my friend, and that suits her ambitions
all the better."

I could have left it at that – let Fitzwilliam mistake the source
of my consternation and move on. But I needed to tell somebody
the true state of affairs, and regardless of his apparent lack of compassion, I knew I could absolutely rely on his friendship. "Anne is
the least of my worries, actually. In fact, she did me a good turn
whilst you were out of the room, apologizing for her mother's
machinations and letting me know that she expected nothing from
me."

"Really? Are you certain she was speaking of your supposed engagement? I rather thought she desired – or at least depended on – the match as much as her mother does."

I reviewed the conversation in my mind before answering. "I can only believe Anne is just as much a victim of her mother's ambition as I am. She said she regretted the 'untenable position' her mother had placed me in. She assured me that she had nothing to do with it. And then she said, 'Furthermore, you should know that I neither want nor expect anything from you.' Those were her very words, Fitzwilliam. Is that not clear enough?"

"It is indeed. You will still have the old dragon to deal with at some point, but at least you may have peace of mind where Anne is concerned. If she had had her heart set on the match it would have been too bad."

"Quite. I would have hated to see her hurt."

"So now you may marry Miss Lambright this summer if you please. But then what is this talk of disaster?"

I could only stare at him in defeat, waiting for him to put the pieces together. It did not take long.

"Oh! If not Anne, it must be this Miss Bennet who has you so shaken. Of course, she is the one you told me of before, the one you dearly wished never to see again! I remember. But wait, for somebody you supposedly loathe, you seemed awfully keen to pay her a call, once you knew she was only a stone's throw away at the parsonage."

"The thing is, Fitzwilliam, I do not loathe her," I admitted, "but she is dangerous."

"Really? Has she threatened you with bodily harm? Come now, Darcy, she cannot be as formidable as that!"

"She is a temptation I can ill afford, for she makes me forget what is important."

"A-ha! She makes you forget all about Miss Lambright. I would wager that is the real problem."

"Perhaps so, but not only that. Elizabeth is unsuitable in every way, and yet when I am in her presence…"

"Yes?"

"When I am in her presence, I begin to imagine that nothing else matters, which is nonsense. You know me, Fitzwilliam. My life is all about duty, honor, and expectations, about propriety and order. I have no elder brother to carry the load of responsibility as you do. It is all on my shoulders. I cannot afford to allow anything to distract me."

"Or any*one*."

"Precisely."

"Well, I say what I said before. I am most curious to behold the woman who can make you tremble so. Perhaps, if I find her as intriguing as you seem to do, I will nobly sacrifice myself, monopolizing all her time to spare you."

"By doing so, you would prove yourself a friend indeed," I said with a sigh.

I was grateful to my aunt for one thing, for postponing the inevitable at least a day. I would undoubtedly have to see Elizabeth, but I now had some forewarning. I had time to prepare and compose myself, to discipline my unruly feelings into better order than if I had been taken completely unawares.

The more I thought about it, however, the more ashamed I became of my cowardice. It had to end at once, I resolved. I would not go through life afraid of every charming woman I might meet. No indeed. I had mastered my emotions before in far more desperate situations than this. I had even resisted Elizabeth's own particular brand of attraction, successfully walking away in the end after the Netherfield ball. I would simply need to do it again. The sooner I faced and conquered this latest test, the better.

Thanks to Mr. Collins, I had that opportunity very soon indeed.

26

We Meet Again

An impatient Mr. Collins called at Rosings early that next morning – too early, in fact, for we were all still at breakfast. He was left to wait while we finished, and then we were obliged to join him in the drawing room: my aunt, Anne, Fitzwilliam, and myself.

"Mr. Collins, what can you mean by coming at this unseemly hour?" demanded Lady Catherine. "Most people have better things to do at this time of day than bothering their neighbors."

"A thousand pardons, your ladyship!" he exclaimed, bowing low. "If my early visit is inconvenient to you, I am mortified indeed. But as for myself, I consider that I never have anything better to do than to be of service to others. I could not help but notice yesterday the arrival of your noble guests." Here he nodded to Fitzwilliam and myself. "And I felt it my highest duty to pay my respects as soon as possible."

By all indications, he was prepared to hold forth at some length on the subject had not Lady Catherine cut him short. He then silenced himself at once to allow her to take command of the conversation, only intruding from time to time thereafter to apologize for some fault in himself, real or imagined, or to copiously praise her.

This second exposure to Mr. Collins did not much change my opinion of him, but it did somewhat explain my aunt's choice in giving such a man the Hunsford living. It was perfectly clear at once that Mr. Collins was willing, even eager, to bow and scrape to his "noble patroness," to prostrate himself at her feet, never challenging her opinions or instructions. No doubt he and his wife also made themselves conveniently available whenever she felt like holding court or needed extra hands for cards. I could never have abided his toady ways myself, but I could see how they would exactly suit my aunt.

At least Mr. Collins did not prolong his visit. Fifteen or twenty minutes along he said, "Unless I can be of any use to you by staying, your ladyship, I will take my leave now before I overstay my welcome."

Lady Catherine dismissed him and, with much ceremony and flattering civility, he prepared to go. I saw my opportunity and took it.

I abruptly stood to join him, saying, "Since you are so eager to be of use, Mr. Collins, perhaps you will be so good as to show me the way to the parsonage. I wish to follow your example, paying my calls promptly as well."

Mr. Collins bowed, looking very pleased with himself. "You are most welcome, Mr. Darcy. I should be gratified indeed to have my humble abode honored by your distinguished presence. I daresay the ladies will be equally delighted."

I doubted the last, at least as to Elizabeth. But I thanked Mr. Collins, excused myself and, with Fitzwilliam in tow, we made the short walk across the park to the parsonage.

I intended to be perfectly civil, but nothing more. I intended to meet Elizabeth with the flawless composure expected of a gentleman. I intended to give her no opportunity to find fault or to mock. I intended to give her no reason to suppose she possessed any power over me or to anticipate additional attentions from me. I intended to keep reminding myself that I wanted to marry Miss Lambright.

How well I succeeded, I cannot be sure.

'The ladies' Mr. Collins expected this call to delight consisted of Mrs. Collins (the former Charlotte Lucas), her younger sister Maria Lucas, and of course Elizabeth. I believe I bowed in the proper places and spoke the correct greetings, and then I hoped I might be left in peace for a time whilst Fitzwilliam put his gift of conversation to good use. He did so without delay.

Settling in a chair close to Elizabeth, he cheerfully set to work. I could not hear all of what was said between them, for I had Mr. Collins beside me to contend with, but I could clearly *see* how well entertained Miss Bennet was by Fitzwilliam. And he gave every appearance of equally enjoying himself.

It was exactly what I had wished for and what Fitzwilliam had offered to do for me the night before: to spare me trouble by monopolizing Elizabeth himself. And yet I was not happy. In fact, the longer they carried on together in this friendly manner the more irritated I became. I freely admit it was irrational, but true nonetheless.

I suddenly begrudged Fitzwilliam his easy manners with people, women in particular. I was provoked by Elizabeth's response – the smiles and obvious regard so quickly bestowed on my cousin but never on me. Mostly, I suppose, I was vexed with myself for caring.

When I could bear it no more, I crossed the room to demand *some* share of the conversation.

"May I enquire after your family, Miss Bennet? I hope that they are well."

She looked up at me with an expression of mild surprise. "They are all well indeed, Mr. Darcy. I thank you," she said. Then with a mischievous look, she continued. "My eldest sister has been in town these three months. Have you never happened to see her there?"

This was my reward for making an effort to be cordial. Elizabeth had, deliberately or accidentally, given me an uncomfortable question that reminded me of the unfortunate business between her sister and my friend. Did Elizabeth know of – or at least suspect – my interference there and blame me for it? There was just such a challenging look in her eye as to make me wonder, and I'm afraid my answer was more rambling than articulate as a result.

"I cannot recall," I began. "That is, I cannot recall that I did see Miss Bennet. Well, in fact, no… No, I was not so fortunate as to have the pleasure of meeting with your sister in London. But then, that is hardly surprising, is it? There are so very many people in town this time of year, and one tends to only come across those who move in one's own circle."

"Quite so, Mr. Darcy," she answered with a self-satisfied smile. "That is exactly what I thought you would say."

She held my gaze, waiting to see if I would speak again.

There were many things I might have liked to say or ask as I stared into the dark pools of her eyes. *Why do you dislike me so, Miss Bennet? What have I done to offend you? Is this teasing style of yours purposely designed to torment me, or do you have another motive? You have had your fun. Now please be good enough to leave me alone. Remove whatever spell you have cast, and I promise to soon be out of your way. Then I shall wish you very well and very happy all the days of your life!*

Of course, I said none of these things. And when I held my tongue, she turned her attention back to Fitzwilliam.

Presently I was released from this acute torment by its being time to go. But there was still Fitzwilliam and his satirical wit to deal with. Although he remained blessedly silent as we walked back to Rosings, his comments commenced almost immediately upon our arrival.

Only Anne awaited us there – another blessing. She asked, "Had you a pleasant visit to the parsonage? How did you find the Collinses?"

"The Collinses are well," I said peevishly, "and our visit was tolerable, I suppose."

"Tolerable, indeed!" cried Fitzwilliam. "Darcy, you astonish me. I have not been so well entertained in an age. Your Miss Bennet is delightful!"

"She certainly is not *my* Miss Bennet, Fitzwilliam, as you know perfectly well. I will not have you refer to her as such; it is a gross impertinence."

"I only meant that you knew her first, old friend. But now that I have met her myself, I would never concede to giving up the pleasure of Miss Bennet's conversation. And what eyes! They fairly sparkled today. Surely you noticed, Darcy, or you would have done if you had made some effort to speak to her yourself."

"I did," I said with some indignation, "and you saw the manner in which my efforts were received."

"I saw nothing so very extraordinary. But Anne," said Fitzwilliam, turning to her, "you must tell us your own opinion of the lady. You know her somewhat better than I do."

"Oh... well... I cannot really say. As yet, we are not well enough acquainted."

"Come now," he coaxed. "You must have formed some impression. Tell us what you think."

When I added my own gentle urging, for I was really interested in Anne's opinion, she relented.

"She is a very pretty creature, and I admire her liveliness of manner. Would that I had a portion of her self-possession."

Taking this at face value, Fitzwilliam proclaimed with satisfaction, "There! I knew we should have an insightful assessment from you, Anne. You may be quiet, my dear, but I daresay you are the more observant for it."

What *I* observed, however, was a certain sadness in my Cousin Anne's eyes, as if this honest admission had cost her dearly.

Anne was quite shy, like my sister, and had suffered from ill health for much of her life. I could imagine, therefore, that it would be nearly impossible that she had been able to refrain from making some unfavorable comparison between herself and the lively visitor, of whom she had just spoken so candidly. So perhaps I was not the only one to fall victim, injured in some way by Miss Bennet's charms. Although it must have been unconsciously done in Anne's case, I was of the opinion that there was some clear intent in mine.

27

Easter

After Fitzwilliam's success at the parsonage, no doubt he was a very welcome visitor there when he called more than once during the week that followed. I did not care to see it, though, so I stayed away. I also knew nothing good could arise from my spending more time in Miss Bennet's company. However, I had no control over who might come to church or whom my aunt might choose to invite to Rosings. Thus, on Easter Day itself, I could avoid Elizabeth no longer.

She was in church, sitting beside Mrs. Collins, while Mr. Collins led us through the Easter rites. With my eyes trained forward, I could not see her, but I was acutely aware of her presence all the same. And then upon exiting the church at the end of the service, my aunt stopped for a word with Mr. Collins.

"You did an acceptable job of the sermon, Mr. Collins," she said. "And I noticed that you made the corrections I suggested."

"I did, your ladyship, as always. I am gratified that you found the result was not deficient in the main."

"Yes, well, there is always room for improvement. Now, perhaps you and Mrs. Collins and your guests would care to come to Rosings this evening. We will be keeping to a family party throughout the day, you understand, but come round about eight. By then, we may be in need of a little fresh diversion."

Collins bowed. "You do us great honor, your ladyship. I thank you on behalf of myself and the others. We shall come promptly and do our best. You may depend on it."

Lady Catherine nodded and walked on. So did I.

I dreaded what was to come of this unfortunate invitation, imagining it would be like those long, awkward evenings at Netherfield all over again, only worse now that I had fallen more under Elizabeth's spell. She would freely bestow her arch smiles and pert opinions, and once again I would not know how to respond. Once again, I would be caught betwix and between, my mind telling me to stay away but being powerfully drawn to her nonetheless.

And so it was.

I began safely enough, thanks to Lady Catherine, who claimed me in conversation for herself and for Anne. There, I had little to do but to listen to my aunt talk. And yet, against my will, my eye repeatedly strayed to where Elizabeth and Colonel Fitzwilliam were carrying on together in a very lively manner, just as they had during our one common visit to the parsonage.

Then after coffee, Fitzwilliam led her to the instrument to collect on her earlier promise to play. I stayed where I was at first. But when my aunt began talking over the music, that was my excuse to move closer, stationing myself where I could see and hear the fair performer much better. That is all I meant to do, and yet it was enough to draw Miss Bennet's notice.

She paused her playing and turned to me. "You mean to frighten me, Mr. Darcy, by coming in all this state to hear me?" she said with one of her teasing smiles.

I noted it was half question, half accusation.

"...But I will not be alarmed, though your sister does play so well. There is a stubbornness about me that never can bear to be frightened at the will of others. My courage always rises with every attempt to intimidate me."

I immediately felt myself at a disadvantage, and yet I could not allow her to get the better of me so easily. So I plunged ahead in the same bold style. "I shall not say that you are mistaken, because you could not really believe me to entertain any design of alarming you; and I have had the pleasure of your acquaintance long enough to know that you find great enjoyment in occasionally professing opinions which in fact are not your own."

I was pleased – with myself and with her – when Elizabeth laughed unaffectedly at this characterization of herself. Then turning to Colonel Fitzwilliam, she said, "Your cousin will give you a very pretty notion of me, and teach you not to believe a word I say. I am particularly unlucky in meeting with a person so well able to expose my real character here, where I had hoped to pass myself off with some degree of credit." Then addressing me, "Indeed, Mr. Darcy, it is very ungenerous in you to mention all that you know to my disadvantage from our time together in Hertfordshire – and give me leave to say, very impolitic too – for it is provoking me to retaliate, and such things may come out as will shock your relations to hear."

Beginning to enjoy the game, I smiled and said, "I am not afraid of you, Miss Bennet."

Fitzwilliam cried, "Pray, Miss Bennet, let me hear what you have to accuse him of!"

"You shall," said Elizabeth, "but prepare yourself for something very dreadful. The first time of my ever seeing Mr. Darcy in Hertfordshire, you must know, was at a ball, and what do you think he did? He danced only four dances! I am sorry to pain you, Colonel, but so it was. He danced only four dances, though gentlemen were scarce; and, to my certain knowledge, more than one young lady was sitting down in want of a partner. Mr. Darcy, you cannot deny the fact."

My first fleeting thought at this speech was surprise that Elizabeth should have been following my movements to the degree that she knew precisely how many times I had danced at the Meryton assembly. That was interesting.

Mostly though, I was embarrassed to remember that night, when I had been in such a foul temper as to not think Elizabeth tempting enough to dance with. I deserved this mild rebuke and could only be grateful for her charity that it was no worse, for there was clearly more she could have said to my discredit.

"I had not at that time the honor of knowing any lady in the assembly beyond my own party," I said by way of explanation.

"True, and nobody can ever be introduced in a ball room, I suppose." She held my gaze for a long moment before breaking off and turning back to my cousin. "Well, Colonel Fitzwilliam, what do I play next? My fingers await your orders."

Although Elizabeth had changed the subject, I could not let it go. It was suddenly important to me that she should understand some of why I behaved as I did. "Perhaps," I continued, "I should have judged better had I sought an introduction that night. Perhaps I shall do so next time a similar occasion arises, rather than give unintentional offense. But on the whole, I find I am ill qualified to recommend myself to strangers."

Elizabeth looked bemused. "Shall we ask your cousin the reason for this?" said she, addressing Fitzwilliam. "Shall we ask him why a man of sense and education, who has lived in the world, is ill qualified to recommend himself to strangers?"

"I can answer your question," he said, laughing, "without applying to him. It is because Darcy will not give himself the trouble."

Although there was a degree of truth in Fitzwilliam's comment, I ignored it. "I certainly have not the talent which some possess of conversing easily with those I have never seen before. Unlike my cousin, here, I cannot catch their tone of conversation or appear interested in their concerns, as I often see done."

Elizabeth had an answer for this too, though. "My fingers," she said, "do not move over this instrument in the masterly manner which I see so many women's do. They have not the same force or rapidity. They do not produce the same expression. But then I have always supposed it to be my own fault. It is not because I am incapable but that I will not take the trouble of practicing enough to become a 'true proficient.' Let society and your aunt despise me for it if they choose."

It was time to raise the white flag of surrender in favor of finding common ground. I no longer cared anything for winning the debate, only for achieving a peace with the lady who sat before me, a provocative look in her eye. "You are perfectly right," I said. "You have employed your time much better. No one admitted to the privilege of hearing you can think anything wanting." Then I added, "It appears we have that much in common, Miss Bennet; we neither of us care to perform to strangers."

I meant the last part as an echo to something I remembered her saying while we danced together at Netherfield.

I have always seen a great similarity in the turn of our minds...

I had no doubt at the time that she meant it as another thorn to torment me. But now I could perceive there *was* a grain of truth in it, one that might constitute the basis for a bridge of commonality between us. However different were our talents and propensities, we did share a certain disregard for the popular mania of catering to society for advantage, of behaving always in a way as to make a favorable impression on people of power and fashion.

I saw it in Elizabeth's courage in the face of my intimidating aunt, her disinclination to flatter me, and now in her admission that she would not enslave herself to endless practicing just to be praised as accomplished.

Had she noticed my peace offering? Had she caught my meaning? Was she remembering her own words, as I was? Would she now be willing to lay her weapons down as well? I hoped to know by her response, but then Lady Catherine intruded, calling out first and then approaching.

As if in confirmation of what I had just been thinking, she declared, "Miss Bennet would not play at all amiss if she practiced more and could have the advantage of a London master. She has a very good notion of fingering, though her taste is not equal to Anne's. Anne would have been a delightful performer, had her health allowed her to learn."

My aunt talked a good deal longer. Elizabeth favored us with more music. But there was no opportunity to return to the former topic, no chance to confirm a change in how things stood between us.

Though frustrated in this, I meant to be more successful detaining Fitzwilliam in conversation, which I did when we were at last alone, our guests having gone away and the Rosings ladies having retired for the night. I desired to get at his true intentions towards Elizabeth, lest there be any unfortunate misunderstandings.

"I think it would be wise," I began, "if you did not pay Miss Bennet so much in the way of particular attentions as you have become used to doing since we arrived."

He looked at me in some surprise. "This is a new idea, Darcy. Did you not say before that it would be a great kindness to yourself if I did just that? Monopolize her completely, I believe we spoke of. What has changed?"

"I *do* take it as a kindness to me, certainly," I said with more earnestness than I felt. "And I thank you. Nevertheless, I begin to fear it may be no kindness to Miss Bennet, lest she begin to care for you and have her expectations raised. That is, unless you have decided she will suit you after all and your courtship is sincere."

"Courtship? Is that what you call it? Heavens, I had no idea it might appear to be any such thing! The lady is delightful, to be sure, but if she has no fortune, she will not do for me at all. What *would* we live upon, I should like to know? Do you truly think there is a danger of her mistaking my intentions?"

"It has been known to happen when a man calls so often and makes himself so agreeable. She may be unaware as to how your financial situation makes the match ineligible. She may know only that you are the son of an earl, which must seem very appealing to her."

"Oh, now you have wounded me, friend! If she were half in love with me, I should much prefer to think it my wit and charm that had worked the magic, not my father's title. But I take your point. I would not wish to do Miss Bennet an injury, so perhaps I had best be less generous in my visits to the parsonage, bestow my attentions less particularly on her, and even drop a graceful hint if opportunity arises."

"I do believe that would be for the best. I mean to do more of my share from now on, too, not leaving all the courtesy and civility to you. Perhaps I may visit the parsonage tomorrow in your place. I would not wish the Collinses to feel we were suddenly neglecting them."

"The Collinses, is it?" Fitzwilliam looked at me with suspicion. "Hmm. This is a different side to you from what I have ever seen before, Cousin, how you mean to take such care that those about you, even those you do not esteem, should never feel ignored."

I could think of no reply.

"I will not presume to tell you your business, Darcy. I will only suggest that perhaps it is you and not I who must proceed with caution."

28
A Subtle Shift

Although I had been given no opportunity to test my theory, it seemed to me that a subtle shift in my relationship to Miss Bennet had been achieved that night. Or perhaps I had misunderstood her feelings nearly from the beginning.

In any case, it now occurred to me that at some point she might have lost any true dislike of me, as I had of her, and that she now did not find my company so very disagreeable. Was it possible that the acerbic bantering style she typically adopted with me was simply her way, or only a remnant of former days, something she carried on because she enjoyed it – the challenging contest of wits and wills between us? Had it in fact become a style of flirtation – her smiles, her teasing, her pointed looks?

It was a revolutionary idea, I freely admitted to myself, but one that deserved further study. Perhaps Elizabeth even carried on with my cousin to make me jealous, which it had very effectively done. Look how I had been drawn within her reach by it that very evening, and how she had then brought me into the conversation. *She* had done it, not I. It began with the two of them – Elizabeth and Fitzwilliam – became the three of us together, only to end as an intercourse primarily between Elizabeth and myself, with Fitzwilliam all but forgotten.

I had to consider, as Fitzwilliam alluded to, that she might actually be wanting, even expecting, my addresses. I could not flatter myself that she was in love with me. No… No, but perhaps she had decided that such a match would be well worth her while, if she could achieve it.

She could not have known beforehand how captivating I would find her laughing eyes and her pert opinions, but she could hardly have failed to notice it since, so ill as I had concealed my fascination. Had she been intentionally drawing me in by her unconventional charms? Or perhaps it was unconsciously done. Either way, I was nearly a lost man, and she must know it. If I carried on my attentions to her much longer, she would soon expect me to make her an offer of marriage, an offer she surely would not refuse.

Hold on! Take Elizabeth Bennet as my wife? My mind had very blithely conveyed me far down the garden path indeed!

I pulled up short, giving myself a much-needed mental slap across the face, and taking myself to task for even contemplating such a thing. What about my promise to my father to choose wisely? What about my family's expectations? What about my plans with Miss Lambright? For God's sake, I had proposed to that lady only weeks before and was even then awaiting her reply! I clearly had no business thinking of another woman. And regardless of what Miss Bennet might hope or expect, I was not obligated to her in any way. I must take care to keep it so.

Oh, what an unfortunate coincidence of circumstances this was, that we should both find ourselves at Rosings! I had been perfectly safe when I left Netherfield. I had been prepared and reasonably content to go on with my life, never seeing Elizabeth again. What trick of fate had brought us together once more and why?

~~*~~

Nevertheless, despite my misgivings, I *did* go to the parsonage the next day – on my own, without Fitzwilliam – meaning to be strong against temptation and to show that I could be cordial and agreeable, much like my cousin. To my surprise, however, I found Elizabeth alone, the others having gone on some errand to the village.

I apologized for the intrusion on her privacy and was moving as if to go away again, when Elizabeth calmly invited me to sit. I took this as sign that I was not mistaken before in thinking there had been some improvement in her degree of regard for me. So I stayed and did my best at conducting congenial conversation with her.

It might have been easier – or at least more familiar – if she had thrown a few witty barbs and flaming arrows my way, the likes of which I had become accustomed to fending off and responding to. But there were none that morning, or at least they were well disguised. Elizabeth first commented on the abrupt manner of our quitting Netherfield in November and asked after Bingley's future plans for the house. Naturally, this occasioned some mild discomfiture in me, which I endeavored not to betray, but Miss Bennet's manner was one of only mild curiosity and perfect composure, leading me to suppose the discomfort with the subject was all on my side.

After a little silence, I discovered the next topic as I looked about the small parlor in which we sat, saying, "This seems a very comfortable house."

I could not have chosen better, for Elizabeth was as willing as I to speak about the parsonage and what naturally succeeded – my aunt's kind offices there, Mr. Collins's good fortune in his choice of wife, and whether or not Mrs. Collins found Hunsford an easy distance from her relations.

Elizabeth finished by admitting that it was possible for a woman to be settled too near her family. Although she framed the dialogue as if to mean it was of Mrs. Collins she spoke, it seemed more than likely to me that she thought of herself as well, and how little it must agree with her to settle very near to her mother.

I was pleased to think so. In any case, to show that I understood what I believed she had inferred, I leant forward and said, "You cannot have a right to such a very strong local attachment as Mrs. Collins, I think. You cannot always want to be at Longbourn."

From Elizabeth's look of confusion, I realized at once that I had overstepped my bounds. I did not think my assumptions had necessarily been wrong, but I had been wrong to embarrass her by speaking so openly. I drew back and quickly changed to a more neutral subject. The other ladies then arrived to join us, and I very soon went away again.

I did not see Elizabeth alone at the parsonage house or at Rosings again, but I happened to meet her on a ramble along a wooded ridge within the Park. I was taking the air in an attempt to sort out my thoughts when I chanced to come across her, moving along the same path in the opposite direction.

We each expressed surprise at seeing the other there, and then she said, "I often walk here, Mr. Darcy. It has become one of my favorite haunts." Then she added very pointedly, "In fact, I take this path from the parsonage and back again nearly every day."

"I understand, Miss Bennet," I said, and I could not help smiling to myself at her revealing this intelligence to me. "You have chosen well. The path is highly suitable for walking, and there are some pleasant views. May I accompany you the rest of your way?"

She nodded her assent, and so I turned back to walk with her. Little conversation seemed necessary; it was enough that we could enjoy the pleasantly warm day and the beauties of the Park together. I bowed and left her at the parsonage gate.

After her hint to me, though, which seemed nothing short of a clear invitation, I felt justified in looking for Elizabeth again in the same place. Two days later, we met with similar results. Then another few days and I found her once more. On this third *rencontre*, more conversation was required as we walked, for I had some specific questions on my mind.

It seemed to me that Miss Bennet must be feeling quite at home in Kent by this time. Whenever I met her on our walks, her color was high and she looked very well indeed, prompting me to ask, "How are you finding Kent, Miss Bennet? Does it agree with you?"

She glanced at me curiously. "It suits me very well, Mr. Darcy," she said, "at least this time of year. But then, spring is my favorite season. I daresay I should be content to roam anywhere in

England in the spring, so long as the weather is fine and there are rocks and mountains, or woods and groves such as these."

"You are very fond of a long walk, I collect."

"Yes, indeed. There are few things I enjoy more, and a dull day is always infinitely improved by an hour spent taking the air. Would not you agree, Mr. Darcy?"

"Oh, yes. The streets of London are not always so inviting, however. Country air is what I like."

"As do I."

We walked on in silence a few minutes, and then I recommenced. "Have you ever travelled into Derbyshire, Miss Bennet?"

"No, I have not yet had that pleasure," she said with a smile.

I noticed she had said "yet." Did her smile mean she was thinking to the future, to a day when she hoped she might reside there herself? She then continued.

"I suppose now, knowing you have the advantage over me, you will tell me that the woods and groves of Pemberley are even finer than these," she said, gesturing to our surroundings with a wide sweep of her hand. "If so, I cannot disprove it."

"The shades of Pemberley are certainly very fine, but as to where they may rank compared to other places, I do not claim to know. *I* think Derbyshire the best place in England, but as it is my home, I cannot be objective."

"It is right that you should be loyal to your home county, I admit, and I might claim the same privilege for Hertfordshire."

I nodded. After another pause, I ventured, "Have you seen all of Rosings Park? The house, I mean. Clearly you have made yourself acquainted with much of the grounds."

"The house? No, I suppose not. Only the rooms where you yourself have seen me. Except for Lady Catherine's invitation for me to use the piano-forte in Mrs. Jenkinson's rooms…

I winced and interrupted, saying, "I am sorry, Miss Bennet, that my aunt should have insulted you with so ill-bred a remark."

"Yes, well, perhaps she meant it kindly, known as she is for her generous condescension. In any case, I have chosen not to avail myself of the invitation, and there has been no other opportunity for seeing more of the house."

"Of course. As you are the Collins's guest on this occasion, I suppose that is to be expected. Perhaps there may be more opportunity to properly explore the house on your *next* visit to Kent, Miss Bennet."

I left her to consider this idea a moment, wondering if her mind would travel the same path as mine had done unbidden. Then I said, "I hope your friend is not sorry to have given up her parental home in Hertfordshire. Do you think Mr. and Mrs. Collins's alliance is an amicable one?"

"That seems an odd question, Mr. Darcy, especially coming from you."

"Does it?"

"Besides, I have recently resolved against making judgements of that kind. One half of the world cannot understand the choices of the other. There is no point in attempting it."

"As you say, it is not always easy for outsiders to determine the success of a marriage, or indeed, what constitutes a desirable match in the first place."

"My ideas on the subject have suffered some revolutionary changes of late, I'm afraid."

"I am intrigued to hear it, Miss Bennet. May I know more?"

"Your curiosity today amazes me, Mr. Darcy! I have never known you to be willing to talk so much before. What do all these questions mean? I cannot make it out."

I thought for a moment. "Perhaps I am only following your suggestion."

"*My* suggestion?"

"Yes, that I practice more in order to improve my conversation. Are you not pleased?"

29
All My Struggles

It was nearly time for Fitzwilliam and I to conclude our stay at Rosings, and my mind still struggled with a major quandary. One minute I was fully decided to do my duty, to go away as planned and never see Elizabeth Bennet again. The next, however, feeling profoundly bereft at the idea, I believed it impossible that I should do so. One minute I clung to my old resolutions and my sensible intention of doing the 'right' thing and marrying Miss Lambright. The next, I had convinced myself that there would be no actual 'wrong' in throwing over everything I had planned, promised, and worked toward, that it would in fact be the most reasonable thing in the world.

If there had been a firm engagement between myself and Miss Lambright, there would have been no question as to right and wrong. In that case, I like to think I would not have wavered. I would have gone away at once, regardless of my aunt's inevitable objections, the moment I found myself slipping into danger. However, Amelia's equivocal answer to my proposal, her own wishes, had left the door ajar – for herself but also for me – and now matters had altered so far as to make walking through that open door a genuine temptation.

During the past week, I had been indulging in risky behavior. Against my own better judgement, I had begun envisioning a future with Elizabeth: Elizabeth working by my side as mistress of Pemberley, Elizabeth keeping me company with her sparkling eyes and conversation on our travels, Elizabeth sharing my life... and my bed. Dangerous imaginings which had proved impossible to put out of my head once they had found their way in.

And so, the battle within me over what I should do about my potent attraction to Miss Bennet raged on.

It was Thursday, and we were to leave on Saturday. That morning, as we all sat in the drawing room, Fitzwilliam yawned, clapped his hands together, and abruptly stood, saying, "I have clearly stayed sedentary too long. I believe this will be as good a time as any for me to take my annual tour of inspection round the park. The weather is fine. Darcy, will you come?"

I excused myself by saying I wanted to read the newspaper in my hand, when really I hoped to return to my rooms to be alone with my thoughts. Once Fitzwilliam had gone out, I prepared to make my escape as well. My aunt had other ideas, however.

"Wait a minute," Lady Catherine told me, and there was no question but what it was a direct order, not a suggestion. After sending Anne and Mrs. Jenkinson upstairs on some pretense or other, she turned back to me and continued. "Now then, Darcy, I know your stay is soon coming to an end, and I must have some assurance from you for how things stand before you go."

I sat down heavily. I knew where this was leading, but I pretended ignorance nonetheless. "I cannot imagine what you mean, Aunt. Assurance of what?"

"How can you be so obtuse, Darcy? You must know that I am thinking of your intentions toward Anne. I have been *extremely* patient, you must admit, and so has she been. But we grow weary of this waiting game you seem to be playing."

I was concerned then. "Has Anne complained? Is she vexed with me?"

"Anne? Why, you should know that she is the mildest creature in the world. She would never dream of saying a word against you to me or anybody else. But even she cannot help but be distressed by this perpetual delay. It is not a flattering thing for a young lady to be kept waiting. I am very fond of you, Nephew. You are the only son of my dear departed sister, and for her sake I am loath to criticize you. However, this has gone on long enough. You have a duty to perform, and you had best get to it."

"I am perfectly aware of your wishes in the matter," I said.

"And of your mother's? Remember, it was her earnest desire as well as my own that our children be united in marriage."

"I have not forgotten. You may believe that I shall always endeavor to do my true duty and also to please my family wherever possible. In that, I know we shall never disagree. However..." I paused to choose my next words carefully. "However, I am not a child. I am a grown man, and I reserve for myself the responsibility of deciding what is right for me to do, including when and how to do it.

"As for my cousin, what I can assure you is this. Anne possesses my true affection and highest respect. My coming to Rosings this time has been of great benefit, for I believe she and I now clearly understand each other as we did not before. That will have to be enough for you, Madam. I have nothing more to say on this subject and no apology to offer."

So saying, I left the room over my aunt's vociferous objections, seeking sanctuary out of doors, where I felt relatively certain I would not be pursued. Since I wished to be alone, I did not set off for Elizabeth's usual pathway but strode towards the stables instead. I intended that a hard ride should relieve my agitation and clear my head, the better to reason out my dilemma. It may not have done all that, but I did feel somewhat better by the time I returned my horse to the groom.

Encountering Fitzwilliam upon leaving the stables, we walked together back towards the house.

"You may be sorry you did not join me in my tour of the park, Darcy," he said teasingly, "for I had a lovely companion to share a portion of my walk."

"Elizabeth, I suppose you mean."

"Indeed, and some fine conversation passed between us, in which *you* featured prominently, by the way. I hate to flatter your vanity, but so it was."

I waited for him to continue, but he would not until I asked. "Tell me, then, for I can see that is your design."

"Ah, it is, but now that I reconsider, perhaps I should not. It was a *private* conversation, after all, and the lady may have

179

intended that it should remain that way. I will just give you this one hint – the most interesting bit. She asked me why you did not marry, saying she thought you should find having a wife a great convenience to yourself."

I shot him a sharp look.

He held up his hands to fend it off. "Her words, my dear fellow. What do you make of them? Do you take it as a suggestion? The way is clear for you now, if you should choose to take it. For I did find an opening in our conversation to drop my own hint – that younger sons may not marry where they like, even the younger sons of earls."

"I hope you were discreet about it, Fitzwilliam," I said sternly. "There was no need to embarrass her."

"Have no fear, friend. Have no fear. Nothing could have been more diplomatic; I was subtlety itself. The words blended in so gracefully that I daresay she hardly noticed them. But the point was made."

~~*~~

I knew that the inhabitants of the parsonage were engaged to drink tea with us that same day, so I would have to see Elizabeth at least that once more. But then the other three turned up without her.

"A severe headache," Mr. Collins explained. "I questioned her myself, your ladyship, and I am convinced she really is quite ill. Indeed, nothing less could keep any person of sense from partaking of the pleasures of Rosings and of your gracious presence…"

I could not properly attend after that, for I was truly concerned. Much as I might have liked to avoid Elizabeth, especially since I had all but decided it would be best if I should leave Rosings without doing something rash, I would not have wished illness to be the cause of it.

In the drawing room, Anne sat companionably beside me, neither of us joining much in the main conversation. Having early on put the question of the supposed engagement between us aside, we had become far more comfortable in each other's presence in all the days since. I had even wondered if her keen powers of observation might have given her to suspect that Miss Bennet had captured my especial attention. So I was not surprised when she quietly asked me, "Is anything the matter, Cousin? You seem uneasy."

I hesitated only for a minute, deciding she had earned my confidence. "I am concerned about Miss Bennet," I answered in a similarly low voice. "She has a vigorous constitution, and I have never known her to be the least bit unwell before."

"All the more reason not to worry, William. A headache can be a serious thing in someone of delicate health, but not to a person who is strong."

I thanked her and tried to take solace in her wise words. After all, Anne knew something about the difference between illness and health. But it was no good; I could not calm my worries for long. Anne was sensitive enough to notice.

"Perhaps you would be easier," she whispered, "if you were to call on her, to see for yourself that she is in no danger."

I warmed to the idea at once, but how was I to make my escape?

"Leave Mother to me," said Anne. "Just say you need some air and go."

And so I did. Nothing could have been easier. I slipped from the house quickly and set off for the parsonage by a path where I could be sure I would not be observed from the windows.

I hurried along, hardly knowing what I would do or say when I arrived. I only knew that I must see Elizabeth. I must be assured that she was well. Beyond that, I could not think.

If I had known what heavy mortification awaited me at the parsonage, perhaps I would not have rushed to meet it.

30
Declaration

How could I have been so dimwitted? How could I have been so blind? How could I have been so totally mistaken about *everything*?

When I arrived at the parsonage, I was quickly relieved of my first worry. Elizabeth was not so ill that she had retired to her bed. In fact she looked quite well when I came in, if a little subdued. I felt a bit foolish for barging in on her, for once again disturbing her privacy. I excused myself as best I could by relaying concern for her health and a desire to hear that she was better.

"Everybody was alarmed to learn you were unwell," I explained.

"Is that so? Well, I am in no immediate danger, as you see. In fact, I was feeling nearly recovered before you arrived."

"I am glad to hear it."

"It was only a headache, Mr. Darcy, and headaches generally pass… that is unless the cause of them persists," she added rather coldly.

"I suppose that is true," I agreed. I could have enquired after the cause of her illness, but that seemed intrusive; she did not volunteer it, and I did not ask. So there seemed nothing more to say on the subject.

In hindsight, I should probably have left it at that and gone away again. Instead, I sat down, which was in itself an admission that I had come for more than the purpose of ascertaining the lady's state of health. I had come to be alone with her. I had come so that I might have one more chance to discover her feelings and perhaps to inform her of my own. For I was a lost man. I was in love with Elizabeth Bennet, and I had come for the chance of proposing marriage to her. Deep down, I knew that was the truth of the matter. Unable to overcome my passionate regard, I was now prepared to surrender to it, come what may.

Although I longed to open my heart to her, Elizabeth was not making it easy for me. She sat straight backed and silent, her hands tightly folded in her lap. She would not smile or give me any other sign of encouragement. She only watched me, waiting to see what I would do, I suppose.

What I did was stand up again and walk about the room in agitation while one final battle raged in my head. Should I proceed or wait for a more propitious time, when Elizabeth might be in better spirits? Or should I give up the idea altogether?

No. I knew I could *not* give her up, even if I had wanted to, for she had already taken up residence in my mind, my heart, and my imagination. There was nothing to do but speak while I had the opportunity. And so finally I approached her and plunged ahead.

"In vain have I struggled. It will not do. My feelings will not be repressed. You must allow me to tell you how ardently I admire and love you."

I could see at once that I had surprised, even shocked her. She started, colored, opened her mouth, and then closed it again. To fill the unbearable silence that developed, I blathered on.

"I have surprised you, I think, my dear Elizabeth. Perhaps you might have preferred a different setting or expected that I had come to the point sooner. You cannot wonder at my regard for you, though; I am sure I have done a very poor job of disguising it. I was bewitched almost from the first moment, I think – bewitched by your beauty, your vivacity, your wit and intelligence. You are unlike any other woman I have ever known."

Oh, that I had stopped at this! The outcome would have been no different, but at least I might have minimized my guilt and mortification. However, I did *not* stop.

"To be completely honest, you are also unlike the sort of woman I always thought I would marry, and it has been this and only this that has held me back from speaking sooner. As you cannot help but acknowledge, there is a vast gap between us as to our situations in life. Society will no doubt consider it a degradation to my family to become allied with yours. And though I care little enough for the *ton*, I cannot entirely dispute the justice of such a charge. I should by rights have married a woman more my equal. That is what my father stipulated, what everybody expects of me, and what my own reason and character have demanded all along – that I would choose wisely.

"But my heart will not be denied, you see, dear Elizabeth. I am utterly undone. After my long struggle, I am now determined to put all these arguments aside in the hope that you will relieve my suffering and consent to be my wife."

There. I had at last spoken the words. I had humbled myself, divulged my feelings, and confessed the truth. But now that I had finally made my declaration, I thought surely my struggle with myself was over, for there was no going back. So I looked to the lady before me and, God forgive me, waited expectantly for my reward.

I record this much to be sure I never forget my arrogance and complacency, to punish myself for my sin of pride in thinking such a worthy woman would be honored to receive such an appalling proposal.

Elizabeth's response I will not delineate or criticize. Needless to say, it was not at all what I had hoped or expected. However, it was I suppose understandable, considering the circumstances, and hardly more severe than I deserved. I was told in no uncertain terms that she would not have me. None of the advantages I could offer her, least of all my love, could overcome the profound contempt in which she held me – primarily, she explained, for blighting Wickham's chances in life and for ruining her sister's hopes of happiness forever.

These accusations, as well as her general antipathy, came as so much of a shock to me that I was nowhere near calm enough at the time to answer the two charges – very different in nature and gravity – with any coherence. I had begun pacing the floor again as she spoke, hardly believing my ears.

"*This* is your opinion of me!" I then said, incredulous. "This is the estimation in which you hold me. I thank you for explaining it so fully. My faults, according to this calculation, are heavy indeed!" I stopped and faced her. "But perhaps these offences might have been overlooked, had not your pride been hurt by the honest confession of the scruples that had long prevented my forming any serious design on you. These bitter accusations might have been suppressed, had I with greater policy concealed my struggles, and flattered you into the belief of my being impelled by unqualified reason and inclination. But disguise of every sort is my abhorrence. Nor am I ashamed of the feelings I related. They were natural and just. Could you expect me to rejoice in the inferiority of your connections? To congratulate myself on the hope of relations, whose condition in life is so decidedly beneath my own?"

I am not proud of this speech. I can only say that extreme perturbation drove me to it. I was hurt, humiliated, and yes, even angry at being rejected, not to mention being blamed wrongly or at least my motives being misunderstood. But I would have done better to have held my tongue, for Elizabeth made me pay. Her reply I will never forget.

"You are mistaken, Mr. Darcy, if you suppose that the mode of your declaration affected me in any way except to spare me the concern I might have felt in refusing you, had you behaved in a more gentleman-like manner."

Her words cut me to the quick. I could bear any accusation – true or false – better than that the woman I loved should find I had behaved ungentlemanly towards her. I was staggered to the point I barely heard what followed, but this was the gist: she had always known me to be arrogant and selfish, and that I was the last man in the world she could ever imagine being prevailed upon to marry.

I could not get away fast enough. I believe I apologized for inconveniencing her with my presence and proposal, wished her well, and then hastily departed.

It had been an unmitigated disaster, one of my own making, I later came to admit. I had been wrong about everything – everything I had thought and how I had accordingly acted. Elizabeth had never warmed to me. She had certainly never intended to flirt with me, as I had imagined. All the time, her hostility had been barely concealed, veiled beneath her pleasant smiles. All the time she had been laughing at me, her teasing civilities a clever disguise to cover her contempt. How was it possible I had so misread the situation as to think she might be desiring my addresses?

I had made myself ridiculous and absurd, and all hope was at an end. She had undeceived me on every point where I had been found to have erred, and now there was no excuse to deceive myself any longer. I must bind up my wounds and get on. And yet, I knew I could not without first making some attempt at setting the record straight, for I was not the only one who had been deceived. Elizabeth should know, for her own safely as well as in the name of truth, what sort of man Wickham really was.

When I arrived back at Rosings, I did not join the others but went straight to my rooms, for I was in no fit humor to talk to anybody or to conceal my present perturbation. Fitzwilliam knocked minutes later, apparently having been dispatched by our aunt to fetch me, but I sent him away again on the pretense of having just remembered urgent business requiring my immediate attention. It was no lie, however, for I knew what I must do.

Imagining I was perfectly calm but in truth driven on by all the energy of strong emotion roused to activity, I took pen and paper from the desk and wrote.

> *To Miss Elizabeth Bennet,*
>
> *Be not alarmed, Madam, on receiving this letter, by the apprehension of its containing any repetition of those sentiments, or renewal of those offers which were last night so disgusting to you...*

I apologized for the liberty I took in demanding her attention, but demand it I did in the name of justice. Then I went on to address the two charges she had laid at my feet.

I did not equivocate. I was candid about my observations of her sister and my objections to Mr. Bingley's marrying her – the same objections that I had endeavored to put aside in my own case – not merely the want of connection but the want of propriety frequently displayed by some of her closest relations. I knew these ideas must give Elizabeth some pain; that was unavoidable. And I had little confidence that she would then credit my motives as sufficient justification for the part I had played in separating the young lovers. Her superior knowledge of her sister would indicate I had been in some error there as well.

Although I could only guess what lies Wickham had told her, I trusted Elizabeth would find nothing to censure in my dealings with *him*, once she knew the story in full, including his treachery to Georgiana. Though Elizabeth hated me, I knew I could rely on her discretion where my innocent sister was concerned. And if she did not believe my assertions, which I foresaw as a distinct possibility, I recommended she seek Colonel Fitzwilliam out to confirm the facts.

In the end, I was calmer for the long exercise, for the chance to explain and defend myself where possible. I had written, read, scratched out, torn what I had written, and begun again more times than I could count. It took me all night, but by morning I had something with which I had to be satisfied, for there was no more time and I had exhausted myself with the process. I folded and sealed the pages, written all over on both sides in a tight hand, and then trusted to Elizabeth's habit of solitary walks for the opportunity of putting the letter into her grasp.

31
Taking Leave

I went out into the Park early, for the best chance of intercepting Elizabeth, should she venture out as well. My first inclination was to wait where we had met three times before – along the wooded pathway on the ridge. But upon reflection, I reasoned that might be the very last place she would go, for she would now be highly motivated to avoid me, even more so than before. Instead I took up a post in the grove that forms part of the park's perimeter, from which I could observe several aspects at once.

For more than two hours, I stood still or paced by turns, my letter at the ready, until finally I glimpsed her not far off, pausing at one of the gates of the park paling. She had not yet seen me, which gave me time to quickly advance enough to prevent her retreat.

"Miss Bennet!" I called out to her, requiring her to acknowledge my presence. No doubt unwillingly, she came back to the gate to meet me. I held out the letter, which she instinctively took. "I have been walking in the grove some time in the hope of meeting you," I said coolly. "Will you do me the honor of reading that letter?" Not waiting for a reply, I bowed slightly, turned, and walked off.

The question – for so I had phrased it – remained with me, however. Would Elizabeth read the letter I had so painstakingly prepared? I had succeeded so far as to place it into her hand, and yet it might still be for naught. Considering how much she apparently despised me, she was as likely to throw it straight into the fire as to open it. I could only hope her curiosity would overcome her unwillingness to be directed by me in anything.

I would probably never know, but I had done all that I could and must leave it at that.

My letter delivered, I briefly called at the parsonage to take leave of the Collinses while Elizabeth was still out. Then at last I returned to Rosings, weary of spirit and dreadfully tired. I was fortunate, then, that only Anne saw me come in.

"Did you find Miss Bennet well when you saw her yesterday," she innocently inquired.

It seemed a lifetime ago that I had set forth to the parsonage by Anne's encouragement; so much had changed since that moment. I shook my head and answered more bitterly than I intended. "I found her well but left her vexed and agitated."

I saw confusion and concern in Anne's knitted brow as she waited patiently for me to explain, if I would. Her kind forbearance crushed me. I sighed the sigh of a defeated man and lightly took her hand. "She will not have me, Anne," I confessed to her sympathetic ear. "God help me, but I have been a conceited fool, and she will not have me."

I regretted my confession to Anne almost at once, not because I minded so much Anne knowing of my unrequited attachment to Miss Bennet but because I minded anybody, especially anybody I respected, witnessing my weakness. Also, I should not have imposed my troubles on her. Accordingly, I apologized to her in private the following morning, shortly before Fitzwilliam and I drove away.

"It was no imposition," she assured me.

"Thank you. You are very kind, and I know I can depend on your secrecy as well. There can be no occasion for upsetting my aunt or dwelling on such vain wishes…" I required a moment to master myself before continuing. "These things bring no pleasure to anybody and cannot be too soon forgotten. Promise you will waste not another thought for it."

"I freely promise to say nothing to anyone, William. It is more difficult to promise I can forget something that has made you so unhappy."

"You are too good to me, my dear, and not just in this. You gave me the clear conscience to try for happiness. My gratitude is not diminished in the least for how it has turned out. You have been kinder to me than I have been to myself. Why do you suppose it is that one wants those things one is not meant to have and not..." I stopped myself just in time. Hopefully Anne did not complete the thought and find an insult in it. "Never mind," I said. "If I am to conquer this foolish inclination, I must stop asking questions with no sensible answers."

We closed the lamentable subject, wished each other well, and parted as better friends than we had been before.

~~*~~

For days, wild emotions had threatened to toss me about like a small boat on a stormy sea: at first love, passion, and hope, later giving way to despair, mortification, indignation, and even fury. They had not only muddled my mind but driven my actions. This was nearly the worst part for a man who had made a study of governing his life by reason. Consequently, my peace of mind was badly cut up, and my very identity as a man of sense, compromised.

Therefore, until I could entirely rid myself of the turmoil excited by Elizabeth's rejection, I consciously chose the less debilitating emotions. Rather than linger any longer in the incapacitation profound sadness over lost love would have occasioned, unable to move or breathe, I soon chose anger, which when properly directed could at least drown out the rest for a time and fortify a man to powerful action. It could also dull the pain.

So I allowed anger (and the accompanying bitterness) to prevail. I even cultivated it where Elizabeth was concerned. I dwelt on the injustice of her accusations, for a long time scarcely allowing her to have spoken a true word against me. She was smallminded and shortsighted, and she would live to rue the day she had insulted me, letting such an exalted opportunity as I had offered slip through her fingers. I, on the other hand, though I had been foolish to ever think of her, was otherwise blameless. My every questionable action and judgement were summarily dismissed, and I was fully acquitted in my own mind.

This façade could not hold forever, for the very rationality I so assiduously clung to would not allow me to deny the truth indefinitely. But it seemed my best strategy of self-defense in those early days.

I reminded myself of this newly adopted mindset that morning when I joined Fitzwilliam in the carriage to depart Rosings. Clearly, I would no longer be able to evade him – his questions, his inquisitive looks – since we would now be trapped together for the length of time required to travel back to London. His questions would be asked, and I would be required to give the right answers to them this time. He knew me too well to be fooled into accepting anything less.

This being the case, I chose to start with my own question as soon as we were down the lane and onto the turnpike road. "Fitzwilliam," I said, "did Miss Bennet seek you out for a private conversation on a particular topic yesterday?"

"Yesterday? Should she have?"

"Not necessarily."

"No, not one word, for I did not see her at all, despite waiting at the parsonage for more than an hour in the hope of it. This is all very intriguing, though, Darcy, and you have behaved strangely too. What have you been about, and why should Miss Bennet have wished to speak to me? I should have been glad to be sought out by her, you understand, although I suppose after I made it clear I could not marry her, some of my charm had gone off!" he finished jestingly.

I was entirely sober, however. "An advantageous marriage may not be her primary object after all. But perhaps she would have preferred your suit to the one I laid before her."

"Good God! So you *did* offer for her! This is momentous news. Why did not you tell me, man? Oh, but wait. Surely she could not have rejected you, not with all *your* property and wealth!"

"She could and she did."

"Foolish girl!"

"Indeed, conventional wisdom would say so. But it seems the idea was so repugnant that no amount of money could tempt her," I said sardonically. "Apparently I am the last man in the world she could consider worth marrying."

"Do be serious, Darcy. What did she really say? What reason did she give to justify herself in doing something so contrary to the established mode?"

"I am perfectly serious, Fitzwilliam. She claimed, and I admit not without some justification, that I made a shambles of the proposal. But I do not suppose it signified in the end, for she has long held grievances against me that no quantity of fine words could have dispelled. The most serious charge is that I treated with blatant disregard the rights accorded by my father to *poor Mr. Wickham*, in whose welfare she takes an unaccountable interest. I placed a letter into her hand yesterday morning, explaining the truth of my dealings with the man and inviting her to confirm with you anything upon which she doubted my word. That is why I asked."

"No, she did not come to me. The last time I saw her was the day before, when, as I told you, I met her whilst I was taking my tour of the Park."

"Well, it is of little matter."

"Dear me, I *am* sorry, Darcy. What will you do now? Do you have any hopes of changing Miss Bennet's mind, perhaps by your letter?"

"No, none at all. The letter was only meant to set the record straight. I certainly will not renew my addresses to her, nor would she desire me to do so." I paused, then firmly shook my head. "No, it was a preposterous idea from the start, acted on in a moment of weakness. I have come away unscathed, however, and it shall soon be as if it never occurred. You are, of course, sworn to secrecy,

Fitzwilliam. Bad enough that you should know of the nonsense. Let it go no further, though."

"My lips are sealed, my dear fellow. You have my word on it." He then directed his attention out of the window.

I looked sharply at Fitzwilliam, suddenly apprehending that *he* was the likely source of Elizabeth's information about my part in separating her sister from my friend. Though I had never mentioned any names, if the story I told Fitzwilliam had been repeated to her, Elizabeth would have been at no great difficulty to fill in those blanks. Already thinking ill of me, she would have easily seen me in the roll of a villain there too.

Fitzwilliam, who was as close to me as a brother, would never intentionally have betrayed me. I knew that. And I would not now be such a brute as to reproach him for something that was my own fault. I should have kept my mouth shut about the business entirely or sworn him to secrecy, as I had done today. So I said nothing about it to him. In any case, the report, unfortunate though it was that it should have come to Elizabeth's ears, was essentially true. And as I had written in her letter, I had not yet learnt to condemn my motives for what I had done.

A few minutes later, Fitzwilliam said, "*As if it never happened?* Does that mean you will still marry Miss Lambright if you can?"

"Can you doubt it? I have just made a lucky escape from a most inappropriate connection; I should be a fortunate man indeed if such a superior woman as Miss Lambright accepts me in the end."

32

Damage Control

I was glad to return to my sister in London. It was pleasant to spend time in company with a female who did not find my presence and my attentions disgusting to her, a lady who instead thought me everything fine and agreeable. To be certain that my sister was not taught to believe otherwise, I now knew I must take great care that she never speak to Elizabeth Bennet, who had made such a thorough cataloguing of my faults.

Georgiana wished to hear all about my time in Kent, which, according to my abbreviated report, was "quite unremarkable." I naturally omitted any mention of the one person who had made my visit anything but that. There was no reason to raise awkward questions for which I had no answers. Nor did I wish to excite my sister's pity... or her contempt for my foolish behavior. Fitzwilliam knew, but we would never speak of it again.

"It was just what you would expect from a visit to Rosings," I told her, "and what you have experienced for yourself many times before. Our aunt likes to have people about to pay her court and to receive benefit of her copious opinions. I have now done my duty for another six months."

Georgiana nodded. "How did you find Anne?"

"She is much the same, I suppose – still not particularly strong, and shy as always. I must say that I gained a new appreciation for her, though. She was very kind to me."

"Perhaps I should have gone to Rosings with you, for her sake."

"Next time. For now, write her a long letter," I suggested. "Considering her situation, she must be in serious want of meaningful communication with a sympathetic soul like yours, somebody beyond her own household. I do not believe she ever gets out into society or has many true friends."

"Very well, I shall. It is the least I can do."

"Speaking of friends, had you any callers while I was away?"

"Franklin Lambright came again. I did not see him alone, of course. Mrs. Annesley stayed by my side the entire time."

An interesting piece of news. "Of course. His coming a second time is a very kind attention," I observed.

"No doubt he was hoping to find *you* here when he came. He asked me to greet you on his behalf."

"Have you warmed to him at all?"

Georgiana gave a noncommittal shrug. "He is pleasant enough, I suppose," she said. "He asked me to play for him, and I did." Then she seemed glad to move on to something else. "Another day, Mrs. Heywood and Andrea called," she said of these long-standing friends.

"Ah, I hope that they are well, and the rest of the family too."

"Perfectly well, I believe. They wished to be sure of us for their annual gala in July. I said we would make every effort to be there."

"Of course. While I am eager for the country, to spend the majority of the summer at Pemberley, business will no doubt carry me to town at least once. When we receive the Heywoods' invitation, we will make our travel plans accordingly."

After being away for nearly three weeks, I had much to keep me occupied for that first fortnight back in town, which was fortunate. The last thing I wanted was leisure to sit meditating on my recent folly, to have time to dwell on what I had desired, done, and lost. Work was the best therapeutic, work to keep my mind if not my body engaged.

When there was no legitimate business to occupy me, I invented something rather than sitting idle. I bothered my solicitor at his offices on more than one occasion, using the most insubstantial of excuses. I saw my tailor and was measured for a new suit of clothes that I did not really need. I visited my club more often than I had any true inclination for. And I haunted Fitzwilliam, Bingley, and every other one of my close friends to save me being alone with my thoughts.

Correspondence demanded a share of my time as well, as was always the case when I was away from Pemberley. I had found a letter from Mr. Adams waiting for me when I returned to London, apprising me of how things stood on the estate and asking my direction on a number of matters. That was the first letter to be answered. Then my second most pressing letter would be to Miss Lambright through Lord Harcourt, not because it was expected of me but because I required it of myself.

Although according to Amelia's own stipulations I had technically been at liberty to change my plans, I still felt some guilt on her account for my behavior in Kent. I had certainly been inconstant – to her and to my stated intentions – and yet it felt much worse than that. My conscience accused me of being positively duplicitous, of betraying Amelia and my own honor. I should certainly have been loath for either Harcourt or his daughter to learn that while I was out of their sight, I had been imagining myself in love with and proposing marriage to another woman.

Now, I wished to atone. At the same time, I wished to solidly close the door on that whole dismal affair with Elizabeth, to put it behind me once and for all, to return to the straight and narrow, to the sensible path I had originally set for myself. This letter within a letter was intended to do all that.

Had Amelia and I been officially engaged, I could have claimed the right to correspond directly with her, but with the situation between us settled so awkwardly, I did not feel free to take that liberty. So I began with the outer layer, the cover letter to her father.

Lord Harcourt,
  I hope this finds you very well, sir – you and your daughter. I am well and just back from three weeks in

Kent, where I visited my aunt, Lady Catherine de Bourgh, and my cousin Anne. I am sure you will remember that I have spoken of them before. Now my intention is to remain some weeks here in town with my sister, and then in June we will both return to Pemberley for most of the summer. I would be much obliged if you would deliver the enclosed note into your daughter's hand on my behalf.

Yours, etc.

Darcy

Now for the more delicate business...

Dear Amelia,

Do not be afraid that I am writing to press you for an early answer to my suit, for that is not at all the case. While you are still completely free to choose for yourself, one way or the other, I assure you that my own wishes in the matter are unchanged. In truth, however, the uncertainty of the situation has proved...

Here I paused in search of the correct word, coming up with nothing better than...

...challenging for me. So it will ease my mind considerably to have the question firmly settled on my side. Therefore, I desire to renew my offer of marriage to you in writing and make it obligatory for myself alone. Know that I now consider myself honor bound to you unless or until you definitely decide against me. I hope that is clear and agreeable. Your respectful servant,

Fitzwilliam Darcy

Perhaps Amelia would consider this a little odd, but as I told her, it was mostly for my own peace of mind that it needed to be done. I hoped it would indeed serve as an effective protection against any further vacillation on my part, a strong deterrent against unwise and unlicensed wavering of purpose.

~~*~~

In May, I learnt through Fitzwilliam's connections that Wickham's regiment of militia had moved on to Brighton. This was welcome intelligence, as it meant that he was safely away from Meryton and could no longer threaten harm to anybody in that neighborhood whose interest still concerned me.

In June, Georgiana and I left the harsh pavements of the metropolis behind for the verdure of the Derbyshire countryside and our home. There, I continued in my campaign to stay meaningfully occupied in an effort to conquer all inappropriate ideas and feelings, more particularly, any lingering thoughts of Elizabeth.

I believed myself to be somewhat more successful in these new surroundings, for at Pemberley there was always some exertion I could make in the name of duty. There was variety of work and diversion, especially of a physical nature. When dark thoughts threatened, I might immediately head to the stables, from whence a hard ride – driven on as if my life depended on it – would go far towards clearing my head and relieving my distress. Another time, a precipitous plunge in the cold waters of the lake might serve as well.

My protective coat of anger that I had deliberately donned and fiercely clung to after Elizabeth's rejection of me had eventually grown threadbare. Holes soon developed here and there, revealing a painful glimpse of the true state of affairs underneath. And finally the remaining rags fell away, exposing what remained: a heart still full of longing, and the injuries done by Elizabeth's sound reproofs.

"...had you behaved in a more gentleman-like manner... Your arrogance, your conceit, and your selfish disdain of the feelings of others..."

More than two months later, her words still rang in my ears, cutting me afresh each time. I could still clearly see the disdain written on her countenance, the flashing scorn in her eyes as she told me I was the last man in the world she could ever be prevailed upon to marry.

Much as I had at first denied the justice in her accusations, with the benefit of time, distance, and a cooler head, I had since owned there to be some truth in them after all. Her words had humbled me, teaching me how insufficient were my claims to please a woman so worthy of being pleased. They had also caused me to reflect, to attempt to view myself and my ways with an impartial eye for the first time in my life. When I did so, I could not approve of what I saw.

I saw a proud young man with nearly every worldly endowment – health, wealth, property, position, a tolerable person – and yet possessing little of the one essential: the milk of human kindness. I was good to my sister, I believed, and acted honorably according to the standards and expectations of my peers, including gifts to the poor. And yet I had little *true* regard for anybody much beyond my own household. I was used to thinking well of myself and meanly of others. My principles may have been correct, but my practice of them was faulty. I knew that in God's sight we are all equal, but I did not behave that way myself. I made distinctions, not by quality of character but according to birth and situation. I made allowances for some and judged others more harshly.

Moreover, I lacked the sort of unselfish love and charity praised in the thirteen chapter of First Corinthians. According to that high authority, then, I was no more useful than a clanging brass cymbal. Or to paraphrase Macbeth, my life was comprised of sound and fury without signifying much of anything of lasting value.

I vowed I would do better. Although it was too late to change Elizabeth's opinion of me, I could at least allow her reproofs to take their proper course. I could at least try to become more worthy of the respect of such a woman – not for her but for myself… and perhaps for Amelia.

33

One Day Early

As June melted into July, I began to every day expect some word from Miss Lambright. The full six months she had asked for were nearly gone, and yet she was silent still. But I resolved to wait with patience – another of the laudable virtues I had vowed to cultivate more of. Finally, however, I had to give up the idea of knowing my fate before we should return from our temporary foray to town to take in the Heywoods' gala, amongst other things.

When we repaired to the north once again, Georgiana and I would not be alone. With her blessing, I had extended what had become an almost yearly invitation to the Bingley clan to while away the hottest weeks of the summer at Pemberley. And so we prepared to set forth in caravan fashion just after the first of August.

At the last minute, however, I received a correspondence from my steward saying that my attention was required at home at the earliest possible moment. And so I altered my plans in order to arrive a day sooner than I had originally intended. Georgiana, I decided, could continue with the carriage at a more comfortable pace, under the protection of Mr. Bingley and Mr. Hurst, whilst I rode on ahead.

My secondary reason for doing so was in order that I might be sure that all was in readiness for Georgiana's surprise. It was a fine new instrument – a superior piano-forte. And although it was probably no more genuinely necessary than the new suit of clothes I had purchased for myself during my busy, contrived errands about town earlier that year, it was at least sure to give pleasure to one more deserving. Now that the instrument was finished – built to my specifications – it was being shipped from London to Pemberley ahead of us, to be in place and ready for my sister upon her arrival.

I was in fact thinking of the new instrument – that perhaps I would just step in to see it before meeting with Mr. Adams – as I walked the short distance from the stables to the house that day. But when I came out to where I could look over the lawn, all former thoughts deserted me. For there I saw – or did my eyes deceive me? – the last person I expected to find at Pemberley: Miss Elizabeth Bennet, mere yards in front of me.

I started, stopped, and stared. Elizabeth saw me at about the same moment and reacted in much the same manner. Then, recovering myself, I moved towards her and her party – a fashionable looking lady and gentleman standing a little aloof from her. Elizabeth and I must now not only meet; we must speak. What an uncomfortable event for us both, especially considering the words and sentiments of our last encounter. There was little time to think of what to do, though, only long enough for me to form the strong intention of demonstrating that I could be civil and gracious, not haughty, and that I was not so mean as to resent the past.

As I advanced, Elizabeth, her hands to her cheeks, turned away and then back again to meet me, red faced but affecting a weak smile.

"Miss Bennet, what an unexpected pleasure." I said with what I intended to be understood as warmth and sincerity.

"Mr. Darcy. I am surprised to see you as well. We were told you were away from home, or we should certainly not have imposed."

"Not at all. It is no imposition. You are very welcome here."

She inclined her head. "Thank you."

After a little silence, I tried again. "I hope you are well, you and all your family."

"Yes, very well, thank you… at least my family was so when I quitted Longbourn a fortnight past."

"And you and your friends have been travelling since, for the pleasure of it?"

"Yes, exactly so."

"Are you staying in Lambton?"

"We are, only for a few days."

"I hope you are pleased with Derbyshire, Miss Bennet."

"I could not be more pleased. It is beautiful country, just as I believe you once told me."

"Yes, but everybody has his own taste. I should not presume that others will think as I do."

"In this case, at least, sir, I agree with you, wholeheartedly."

"I am glad to hear it," I said. And then I repeated the same words again for good measure whilst groping for what to say next. Finally, I continued. "Travel can become very fatiguing, when the conditions are unfavorable – weather, roads, and so forth – or when one is gone from home too long."

"Indeed, but we have been lucky as to the weather and the roads. As for the length of our journey, I could have wished it to be longer, not shorter."

"How long have you been away from home now?"

She looked at me, bemused, and said, "A fortnight."

Stupid blunder! I was speaking too quickly, with a brain much distracted and discomposed. "Yes. Yes, of course, as you said. Forgive me." Then every idea failed me, except the thought of my disheveled appearance. With my hands spread and a downward glace at my dirty riding clothes, I said, "You must excuse me now, Miss Bennet. I have just this moment arrived, and I'm afraid I am not fit to be seen at present."

She nodded her comprehension. I gave a little bow and walked briskly away toward the house.

I frightened a host of servants into confusion as I burst through the door and flew up the stairs to my dressing room to tidy myself. I dispensed with my coat at once, letting it fall where it might. Then I furiously dragged my soiled cravat from my neck and threw clean water on my face. By this time my valet, who had come ahead of the main party with the luggage, appeared out of nowhere to assist me with the rest.

Meanwhile, my prior resolutions were all forgotten. Instead of putting Elizabeth from my head, I could think of nothing else. My mind raced with a thousand questions and recriminations. What did it mean that she should be here, of all places? Why had I been so dull and stupid in my conversation with her? And why had I left her so abruptly, saying nothing about returning? Had I only confirmed Elizabeth's prior bad opinion of me, or was there a chance she could have noticed a change for the better in only those few minutes? Perhaps Pemberley would sway her at least a little in my favor. Oh, where was she at that moment, and what was she thinking? I must see her again before she and her friends could get away.

Toward that end, I called for and sent a footman to stand by the visitors' carriage. "Detain them if you can," I told him. "Say that I will soon come to receive them properly. And invite them in for some refreshment. Now make haste!" As the footman turned to go, I added, "But be polite!"

These measures proved unnecessary, though, for when I emerged from the house again, freshly dressed and hurriedly groomed, I was told I would find the party I sought proceeding along the path by the river. And so I went in that direction in the hopes of intercepting them.

When I did overtake them, Elizabeth met me with what seemed a less embarrassed and more genuine smile than before. "Oh, Mr. Darcy," she began with enthusiasm, "I must tell you that the grounds are delightful and everything charming. I think I should like walking here even better than at Rosings!" Then she looked up at me, stopped abruptly, and colored again.

I could only imagine that she had suddenly become conscious that I might construe this praise of Pemberley as a sign that she now considered being its mistress as less odious than she had before. I hoped that might be, but I could not dwell on such ideas at that moment. I hastened to rescue her from her discomfiture, acknowledging the compliment with a nod and then moving on. "Will you kindly do me the honor of introducing me to your friends?" I asked.

"Of course," she said and proceeded to do so.

I was surprised to then learn that the gentleman and lady with Miss Bennet were Mr. and Mrs. Gardiner, her aunt and uncle from London. This was in fact the very uncle whom I already knew to be in trade. Though I was surprised, I was also immediately sensible of the opportunity before me. Here was my chance to show Elizabeth that I had mended my ways, that I had attended to her criticism. I would not treat her relations with the distain that she no doubt expected or that my former prejudices might have provoked. No, I would presume Mr. Gardiner the gentleman he appeared to be and treat him and his wife accordingly.

It was not difficult, I discovered, for as I entered into conversation with Mr. Gardiner, every sentence he uttered marked him as a man of intelligence and taste, a man with whom I would be happy to spend more time. Before I knew what I was doing, I had forgotten all else and invited him to come and fish on the premises whenever he liked.

"Do you see that spot, Mr. Gardiner," I continued, pointing, "just at the bend in the river? There is an eddy that forms on the downstream side where the trout like to hole up. I have had some tremendous sport while fishing there, I can tell you. You must try your hand at it, if you have the time."

"You are very kind, Mr. Darcy," he returned, "but I have not brought my tackle with me."

"That does not signify in the least. I would be happy to supply you with everything you need."

We had continued walking back towards the house as we talked, the two ladies ahead and myself and Mr. Gardiner behind. But after all stopping a moment to inspect a plant on the bank of the river that interested Mrs. Gardiner, that lady then took her husband's arm to resume our forward progress, leaving Elizabeth to my share – a circumstance which I could not regret in the least.

Elizabeth began the conversation. "I wish to say again, sir, how unexpected it was to meet with you here today. My aunt did so wish to see the place, though, and your housekeeper assured us that you would not be arriving until tomorrow."

"Indeed, so I had planned it. But when I found I had rather urgent business with my steward, I decided to ride ahead of the rest of my party. They will arrive tomorrow, and…" This would be awkward, but it needed to be said. "…and amongst them are some who claim a prior acquaintance with you: Mr. Bingley and his sisters."

We exchanged a brief look, which was enough to confirm to me that we were both reminded of the last time Bingley's name had been mentioned between us, and in what heated context. Nothing further needed to be said on that subject.

"There is also another person in the party," I ventured presently, "one who will particularly wish to know you. Will you allow me, or do I ask too much, to introduce my sister to your acquaintance during your stay at Lambton?"

This, I think, surprised her – surprised and pleased.

"I should be very happy to make her acquaintance," said she.

"Perhaps I might bring her to the inn where you are staying the morning after tomorrow?"

She nodded her assent to this proposal.

We had by this time reached the Gardiners' carriage, but they themselves having lagged far behind, Elizabeth and I were left standing there some minutes, mostly in awkward silence. Then, in an attempt to forestall their departure, I entreated all three that they might walk into the house to take some refreshment. Since they declined, there was nothing to do but for me to hand the ladies into the carriage and politely bid the party farewell. I watched them drive away with some regret, but also with the considerable consolation of knowing I would see Elizabeth at least once more. I would have at least one more opportunity to improve her opinion of me. That was all I wanted, I told myself. Nothing more.

34
Looking the Part

Georgiana's party arrived the next day in time to eat a late breakfast, after which I revealed the surprise awaiting her in the music room. My sister's reaction to the new instrument was everything I could have hoped, and she instantly sat down to play with as much spirit and enjoyment as I had ever seen her take in anything.

After that excitement, we settled in the south drawing room and became very dull indeed. Mr. Hurst reclined on a settee and promptly began to snore. Miss Bingley and Mrs. Hurst stared blankly ahead with nothing to say. Even Bingley was uncharacteristically silent.

I was restless, however, so I turned to my sister, who was beside me, with the only subject I had on my mind. Speaking in low tones for her ears only, I said nonchalantly, "An acquaintance of mine, whom I should very much like you to meet, is staying in Lambton. It is one of the Miss Bennets from Hertfordshire, of whom I remember telling you before. Miss Elizabeth Bennet is traveling with her aunt and uncle. They visited here yesterday, and I promised to return the call after you arrived. We had engaged for tomorrow, but no doubt today will do as well or better. Would you mind terribly, Georgiana, spending another hour in a carriage going with me to Lambton and back?"

She hesitated and then said, "Do you think it wise, coming in on people before they expect? They may not thank you for it. And neither may your guests here, for deserting them nearly as soon as they arrive."

"Look about you, my dear sister. The entire company, with the possible exception of Mr. Bingley, appears intent on sleeping the afternoon away. If we were to slip out and back quietly, I daresay not one of them will know we have ever been gone." It was an exaggeration, but it carried my point home.

Georgiana thus agreed, and a whisper in Bingley's ear easily persuaded him to join us. Miss Bingley did look up then, wondering where we were off to. "A drive into Lambton," I said. "Did you wish to come?"

"More time sitting in a carriage? Heavens, no! I cannot countenance any such thing. Charles, you must be mad."

"Perhaps I am," he said cheerfully, "but there is no need for you to join us in the scheme. Stay here and rest yourself."

"I intend to," Caroline replied.

Once in the carriage and away, Georgiana asked, "Can you tell me something more about this Miss Bennet, so that I many know what I am to expect?"

I heard in her question her typical nervousness at meeting somebody new. But when I thought of Elizabeth, pictured her face... I drifted. Then I called myself back to belatedly answer, "She is a gentleman's daughter, and therefore a perfectly respectable person for you to have amongst your acquaintance."

"I do not doubt it. Indeed, it never occurred to me she could be otherwise. But how well do you know her?"

How to explain? I looked to Bingley for assistance.

"We were very often thrown together with the Bennet family while we were staying in Hertfordshire," he said. "Meryton is a small community, so we saw them at nearly every assembly – public or private. And then, of course, Miss Elizabeth Bennet was several days at Netherfield, nursing her sister, who had become ill while visiting us there."

"Several days?" Georgiana repeated with a lift of her brows. "You must have formed some opinion of the lady in that time, Brother. Did you not?"

"I suppose I did, yes."

"And what *was* that opinion?" she prodded.

"I concluded that she was a person I should not object to knowing better, and one whom I hoped someday to introduce to my sister's notice. Really, Georgiana, I think that will do. You shall judge for yourself in a few minutes when you meet the lady."

"Only one question more. Is this Miss Bennet musical?"

I smiled slightly at this. "You will find her very modest of her own claims, but I certainly found nothing wanting in her performance. In fact, I have rarely heard anything that gave me more pleasure."

We were fortunate enough to find our party in when we arrived, and they graciously received us. I made the necessary introductions and all the standard pleasantries were duly exchanged. Georgiana's shyness was apparent, but Elizabeth kindly encouraged her. And I saw no hint of lingering resentment at all in Miss Bennet when she spoke to Mr. Bingley.

We stayed half an hour, and all passed off as smoothly as I could have hoped. Most importantly, though, before leaving we received the Gardiners' promise that their party would dine with us at Pemberley two days later. So once again, I had managed to secure the next meeting with Elizabeth before the last expired.

As it happened, we saw them sooner.

~~*~~

Mr. Gardiner I expected to welcome to Pemberley that next morning, since that was the agreed upon time for him to come for the fishing. But only after he had been with us (Bingley, Mr. Hurst, and myself) at the river some time, did he mention that the ladies of his party intended to wait upon my sister that same morning, returning her kind call of the day before.

At this, I told Mr. Gardiner that although he might remain at the river as long as he liked, I felt I must return to the house to assist my sister with her guests.

"I have done very well for myself already!" said Mr. Gardiner, chuckling. "Perhaps it is only fair that I quit before I have depleted your stock of trout too severely."

And so he accompanied me back to the house, where we found all the ladies in the saloon partaking of some refreshments. In addition to my sister, Elizabeth, and Mrs. Gardiner, there were three others: Mrs. Annesley, Miss Bingley, and Mrs. Hurst.

I was glad to see that Georgiana seemed to be managing her duties as hostess tolerably well. In fact, when we came in, she so far exerted herself as to say, "Had you good fishing, Mr. Gardiner?"

"We had! Thank you, Miss Darcy," he replied with a little bow and an affable smile.

"It is true," I said, directing my comment to Elizabeth, who sat across the room. "Miss Bennet, your uncle's presence at the stream seems to have brought us all luck. I hope you have been getting on just as well here."

Perhaps I should not have shown her this marked attention, for I at once perceived that every eye – and not all of them friendly – turned in anticipation of seeing how she would respond.

Elizabeth did not quail under this scrutiny, however. Rather, she raised her chin and answered with apparent ease. "Very well indeed, sir. As you see, Miss Darcy has received us in this delightful room and provided for our every comfort. I could not be more pleased."

It was not only her words that gratified me; it was also her command of the situation… and especially the way she steadfastly held my gaze for several long seconds afterward. It seemed as if volumes were silently spoken between us in that one look.

"Excellent," I murmured.

I suppose we had looked at each other too long for Miss Bingley's liking, for that lady then stepped in front of me with a swish of skirts and a flutter of eyelashes, demanding my attention against my will and saying, "But then your sister is always such a gracious hostess, no matter *who* comes calling. She does everything the best in the world, and I am forever boasting over her. 'Miss Darcy, though she is only sixteen, is by far the most accomplished young lady of my acquaintance,' I always say. I care not if my friends grow weary of hearing it."

Georgiana's discomfort was obvious to me. Dropping her eyes to her lap, she said with diffidence, "You flatter me, Miss Bingley, but this is much more credit than I deserve."

"No, no," Miss Bingley declared resolutely, "I will not be talked out of my opinion on the subject. I am quite immovable, you see."

"Yes, I do see," I told her with a measured glare. "But you have been much at Pemberley before, Miss Bingley, and have become accustomed to treating it as your own. I do not, therefore, fear for *your* comfort. It is for Miss Bennet and her friends…" Here I bowed in Mrs. Gardiner's direction. "…who are new amongst us, that we must endeavor to make an effort."

"It is just as you say, Mr. Darcy," Miss Bingley eagerly agreed, "they being so far from home too!" Facing about, she continued. "Miss Bennet, you must be missing Hertfordshire dreadfully and impatient to return to your family."

"Not at all, Miss Bingley," Elizabeth answered, and I thought I saw that familiar spark in her eye. "I find the glories of Derbyshire quite surpass my expectations, and I should not object to remaining here a good deal longer. I certainly could not hope to be half so well entertained at home."

"Poor Miss Eliza," returned Miss Bingley. "I see what you are feeling, and I daresay it is true. Are not the regiment of militia now removed from Meryton? That must be a great loss to *your* family indeed."

Elizabeth's momentary discomposure I attributed to the same cause as mine at that moment – concern for my sister's feelings. Miss Bingley had already ventured too near the forbidden topic of Wickham, and she must go no nearer. Before I could think what to do to prevent her blundering ahead, Elizabeth had recovered and soon adeptly managed the situation.

"As to the removal of the militia, your information is correct, Miss Bingley. But I consider it no loss at all. We shall go on very quietly and very happily without them, I assure you."

This put an end to the topic, and the visitors shortly departed, to return the following day for dinner. But their absence merely spurred the vindictive Miss Bingley on to more direct attacks against Elizabeth, particularly regarding her appearance, finally throwing my own regrettable words back in my face.

"*She a beauty!*" Caroline parroted, "*I should as soon call her mother a wit.* But later she seemed to improve on you, and I believe you even thought her rather pretty at one time."

I could contain myself no longer. Because I was completely powerless to expunge my own past remarks from the record, it seemed all the more incumbent on me to defend Elizabeth now, to set the record straight.

"Yes," I said decisively, "but that was only when I first knew her, for it is many months since I have considered her as one of the handsomest women of my acquaintance." So saying, I left the room, not caring what anybody might think.

While it gave me tremendous satisfaction to put Caroline Bingley in her place, Elizabeth's performance that day had given me still more pleasure. To have witnessed her dignity under fire, her competency in taking control of the difficult situations thrust upon her. To have basked those several seconds in the warmth – and dare I hope, the burgeoning affection? – of the look that had held between us, a look which had seemed to tether us together as tangibly as a sturdy cord might have done. And all this within the walls of my own house! It no longer required any stretch of my imagination to picture Elizabeth presiding as mistress of Pemberley.

I had taken myself out of doors to drink in fresh air and to revel in my pleasant musings alone. As I gazed down the road, where Elizabeth's carriage had so recently travelled, my heart swelled within me. Perhaps… just perhaps, there was a chance for us yet. When the heavy clouds overhead released their pent-up load, I laughed, turned my face heavenward, and let the summer rain soak me through. And yet I felt light as a feather.

All this gives evidence for how very far I had slipped off the sensible path I had prescribed for myself for so long, for how completely bewitched I had become by Elizabeth Bennet. All my efforts to extinguish my earlier ardor had been for naught. One long look, one encouraging word, one spark from her eye: that had been enough to cause the latent embers to burst aflame once again, blazing even brighter than before.

But reality brought me crashing back to earth when I returned to the house and was presented with a brief message, which had arrived earlier from Lord Harcourt.

35
Commitment Calls

Lord Harcourt's message read as follows.

Come to Ravenshaw at once, Darcy. My trying daughter has at last made up her mind to something definite. She must tell you the news herself, of course, but I will just give you this hint. I think you will be very pleased with her decision. I know that I am. Harcourt

My sodden clothes turned to lead.

Miss Lambright. How could I have forgotten her… again? How could I for one minute have allowed myself to be carried off in another fantasy about Elizabeth, when I already had a binding commitment to another woman? – a commitment that was now become permanent, for Amelia had decided to accept me. That was clear even from what little Harcourt had written.

Thrusting the unhappy note into my pocket, I dragged myself upstairs to change.

After he had attired me in dry clothing, I dismissed my valet. But I could not bear a return to the others downstairs – not in my present state. So I allowed myself time to work through my overpowering disappointment and become reasonable again.

Vigorously pacing the length and breadth of my bedchamber, I railed to the four walls about the perversity of my fate. Why was I always out of step with time and opportunity? When I was being sensible and wanted Miss Lambright for my wife, she was not ready to accept me. Now that I had – God, help me – given in to my passion for Elizabeth, I must have the sensible Miss Lambright instead!

So went my lament.

I would be ashamed to admit how long I carried on in this deplorable manner, bent on self-pity. At last, however, I exhausted the preponderance of my frustration. "You are behaving like an infant!" I reprimanded myself aloud. "Only a spoilt child continues to pine for what he cannot have."

After one final sigh, I threw back my shoulders and called myself to attention. I was not the first man to suffer disappointment... even more than once. I was not the first who must set aside personal desires to do his duty. I would certainly not be the last. And after all, it was a duty of my own designing. So I would go to Miss Lambright and stand by my commitment, not betraying to her anything of my changed sentiments. She had been my first choice once, and she deserved to continue thinking she was still. For all the reasons I had originally proposed to her, perhaps it would turn out well in the end.

But to walk away from Elizabeth without a word of explanation? No, not if there was the slightest chance she had begun to reciprocate my regard. If I had by my behavior over the last two days given her any idea that I might renew my addresses, I could not leave her wondering in suspense. I owed her some resolution, some clear sign of my current intentions – a clarification I could not very well give over the dinner table the next day with others looking on.

Before I rejoined Georgiana and our guests that evening, I had made a plan. I would ride to Lambton in the morning, hoping for a private word with Elizabeth. It would be not only absurd but highly indecorous to declare all I felt when it could go nowhere. No, I would simply say that I was grateful circumstances had brought us together again so that we could now part on better terms than before. I would thank her for her timely reproofs last April, to which I continued to attend. I would be a better man for their instruction. Then I would wish her very well and very happy in such a way as to make it clear we would not see each other again. Perhaps she would soon hear of my marriage and understand the rest. That was the best I could do. God forgive me if it were not enough.

These good objectives were immediately overturned when I arrived in Lambton the following morning. I found Elizabeth alone, as I had hoped, but flushed and in such a state of agitation that nothing else mattered but that I should do what I could to alleviate her distress. After some gentle urging on my part, she told me her trouble.

A letter had come from her sister Jane containing the dreadful news that Lydia Bennet had run off from Brighton with Mr. Wickham. And what at first appeared to be an elopement was now feared to be worse, since the pair had been traced travelling towards London, not Gretna Green.

Elizabeth was naturally distraught. Not only was her youngest sister lost, but the whole family would surely partake of her ruin and disgrace.

"My father is gone to London," she said tearfully, "and Jane has written to beg my uncle's immediate assistance. I hope we shall be off in half an hour, but nothing can be done. I know nothing can be done. How is such a man to be worked on? How are they even to be discovered? I have not the smallest hope."

I could say nothing; as yet I had no answers for her.

With renewed passion, Elizabeth continued. "When my eyes were opened to Wickham's real character, oh, that I had done what I ought! If I had but told some part of the story to my own family… But I was afraid of doing too much, of revealing too much. Wretched, wretched mistake!"

Elizabeth was not to blame, though; *I* was. Had I made Wickham's true character known in Hertfordshire, this could not have happened to a girl from a respectable family. The fault was my own, and now so must the remedy be.

I'm afraid I could not properly attend to what Elizabeth was saying, much less to respond with appropriate consideration, because my mind had already begun to apply itself to the problem, divining what action within my power might limit the damage done and alleviate Elizabeth's pain. I could do nothing for her while I remained in that place however, and I already felt myself an unwanted intruder upon her sorrow.

"I am afraid you have long been desiring my absence," I said then, "nor have I anything to plead in excuse of my stay but real, though unavailing, concern."

Feeble. Words were useless in such a situation. With as few of them as possible, and with only one serious backward look, I took my leave of Elizabeth Bennet, perhaps for the last time.

~~*~~

Since I could hardly be in three places at once – with my friends at Pemberley, with Miss Lambright at Ravenshaw, and about my necessary mission for Elizabeth – I was hard pressed to order these important concerns.

My friends at Pemberley could get along without me and must be left to their own devices, I quickly concluded. So I hired a boy from the inn to take a message to apprise them of the new situation. First, that the Gardiners and Elizabeth, having been called home on urgent business, would be obliged to forego dinner at Pemberley that day. Second, I myself would not be returning until the evening. The rest – that I was bound for London on the morrow – I would tell them later.

Meanwhile, I rode for Ravenshaw.

~~*~~

Since I had been sent for, Lord Harcourt was not the least bit surprised to see me, and his face was wreathed in smiles when he received me in the drawing room, his daughter with him.

"Oh, this is a happy day, friend, to finally have you back at Ravenshaw again," he said, heartily shaking my hand and embarking on a flood of questions, giving me no time to answer in between. "Were the roads in good condition? Did you come all this way on horseback? Are you in health, and how does your enchanting sister get on? Are matters going forward tolerably well at Pemberley? How long are you staying with us this time?"

Meanwhile, the two of us remained standing, and only a glance and a slight bow had been exchanged between Amelia and myself. This was soon remedied, however.

"Well, now," Harcourt continued after I had satisfied each of his opening queries. "Your time is short, you tell me, and you are not come all this way to talk to me, are you, sir? No, I daresay you are not! You have important business to conduct with my daughter, from which I do not wish to detain you another moment. I will now leave you to it!"

He sent the footman away with a flick of his hand, followed him out of the door, and before closing it behind him, gave me a conspiratorial wink.

The room fell ominously silent. I turned toward Amelia, who gave me a tremulous smile. Securing my own pleasant expression in place, I crossed to take a seat with her on the sofa and enquire, "Are you quite well, Miss Lambright? You in fact look rather pale."

"Do I? I suppose I am a bit nervous; that must account for it."

"Of course." I sat a little straighter, took a deep breath, and forced myself to go forward. "Miss Lambright, your father wrote that you have some news for me. Are you ready to tell me what it is?"

"Indeed, Mr. Darcy. That is what you have been brought to Ravenshaw to hear, is it not? And since Papa is particularly bad at keeping secrets, I'm quite sure you have already guessed that I have decided to accept your proposal. We may be married just as soon as you say."

I nodded solemnly. "You do me great honor, Miss Lambright."

"Amelia. You must call me Amelia. You already had my permission to do so, and it is particularly proper now we are engaged."

"Yes, of course, Amelia. As to when the rites will take place, though, that is for you to judge."

"But I remember you wanted to be married in the summer, and it is August now."

"Believe me when I tell you that idea is no longer of any consequence. You must take all the time you like. I am quite ignorant of such matters, but no doubt many preparations are required for a proper wedding. And perhaps you will even want the banns published."

"Oh, no! I could not bear it."

Taken aback by this uncharacteristic outburst, I asked, "What do you mean, Miss Lambright? Amelia, that is."

She took a moment to compose herself. "Forgive me. I only meant that I want no notoriety, no fuss made at all. No announcement in the papers, no engagement party, no banns, no hundred guests attending, and no grand wedding breakfast afterwards. Could we not be married by a special license with only close family present?"

"Certainly, if that is what you wish. What you describe will suit my own preferences very well."

She looked much relieved. "Oh, thank you! And may we be married at once?"

"At once? Is there a reason you are suddenly so... so eager?"

"You have been exceedingly patient with me – both you and Papa. Besides, delay is of all things detestable to me. Once a decision is made, it is time to move forward. Would not you agree?"

"Yes, ordinarily I would. And ordinarily I would be pleased to gratify this and every other wish of yours, Amelia. Unfortunately, there must be at least a little delay. Urgent business requires my immediate attention in town. That is why I may not stay tonight. I am for London early tomorrow."

She frowned. "How long will you be away?"

"I wish I could tell you, but the uncertain nature of the business makes it difficult to predict. It may be brought to a conclusion in a week, or it may very well take a good deal longer." She was still frowning. "If I could put it off, I assure you I would, but it is an issue of the most vital importance to... to a dear friend, and I am honor bound to attend to it myself. It is clearly my responsibility, and I am the person in the best position to help. There is no one else, you see."

"Well then, of course you must go," she said dolefully. "I would not have you neglect your clear duty on my account. It is very disappointing; that is all."

"Yes, it is. I will return as soon as possible, though. I promise you that. And I will see to the special license. What about your brother? You will want Franklin with you, I daresay."

"Certainly! I will write to tell him the news and that his presence will be required at home whenever your business in town is concluded. I suppose I must be content with that. Oh, but Mr. Darcy?"

"Yes?"

"What should I call you now?"

"Well, I suppose you might just call me Darcy. Or if you think that too impersonal, my given name is Fitzwilliam, of course. That creates some confusion, however, since I have a whole family of cousins also named Fitzwilliam. So some, including Georgiana, call me William. You may too, if you like it."

"William. Yes, that sounds very well. And so, William, return to marry me as soon as you are able."

36
A Parting Gift

I told nobody at Pemberley that evening about my engagement to Miss Lambright or of the true nature of my mission to London. And it occurred to me that I was becoming quite adept at keeping secrets – my own as well as other people's.

As with Amelia, I blamed the same undisclosed "urgent business" for taking me away so abruptly. "Unforgivably rude," I confessed to the Bingley clan, "but it simply cannot be helped, I assure you. You all know your way about Pemberley and may treat it as your own as long as you choose to stay."

"I hope your leaving is in no way a compliment to Miss Eliza Bennet," said Miss Bingley teasingly.

"What?" I asked, startled by the question.

"First we hear that she and the Gardiners are called home to Hertfordshire on 'urgent business,' and now you claim the same yourself, Mr. Darcy. It is enough to make one wonder."

"Nonsense," I returned. "A mere coincidence. Besides, my business is in London, not Hertfordshire. A letter from my solicitor I found awaiting me in Lambton informed me of the need to come at once." Another lie. What had become of my proud claim of being above disguise of every sort? One more lesson in humility.

"I trust you shall not mind my absence so very much," I told my sister privately. "The Bingleys are easy guests. You need not feel constrained to put yourself out overly for them. And I will return as soon as possible... Perhaps I will have a surprise for you when I come," I added, thinking of my impending marriage.

"Of what nature is this surprise?" Georgiana asked.

"Not another piano-forte, but hopefully something you will like just as well. That is all I shall tell you. Now, be a good girl and mind Mrs. Annesley while I am gone."

I kissed the top of her head and bid her good-night as well as good-bye, since I intended to be off before the others would be down in the morning. And so I was.

Once again, long hours in the carriage gave me time to think. But the important and active cause before me proved an excellent defense against relapsing into bouts of self-pity. I had a job to do, a service to render to Elizabeth. If I could rescue her sister and retrieve her family from the brink of ruin, it would be a greater kindness than anything else I might do for her. It would be my parting gift.

But where to begin; that was the question. When I considered it, there was one and only one answer that came forward: Mrs. Younge. Wickham had no relations in London; I was sure of that. And I believed many of his former friends might have thrown him off after discovering his true character or being left with the embarrassment of his unpaid debts on their hands. But Mrs. Younge, to my certain knowledge, was a recent friend and co-conspirator. Although I had foiled their previous scheme, my instincts told me that Wickham would go to her again.

Consequently, when I arrived in town, I went immediately to the place she lived more than a year before, when my sister had been in her charge. The unfamiliar butler who came to the door, however, told me that the house had new owners. Mrs. Younge had removed to Edward Street, he understood. A drive down Edward Street revealed nothing useful, however. So, considering the lateness of the hour and my own weariness, I was forced to leave off the search for the night.

The next day, I had better luck. Discreet enquiries and a little coin offered here and there brought me to the correct house; cunning and patience did the rest. The first day I presented myself at her door, the manservant who let me in and took up my card, returned with the news that Mrs. Younge was "not at home."

"Very well. I will wait," I told him. Setting my hat on a table and beginning to remove my gloves, I prepared to make myself comfortable in the vestibule.

The man, obviously disconcerted, looked over his shoulder nervously. "You do not understand, sir," he said. "I beg your pardon, but it will do you no good. The lady will not see you."

"Yes, she will, if I have to sit here all day every day for the next week. I am quite determined."

The servant went away again, and soon Mrs. Younge herself came down to me. "Mr. Darcy, this is quite irregular," she said in a hushed but scolding voice. "What do you mean by coming here and making threats? This is a respectable house where respectable people let lodgings from me. I will not have you upsetting my paying guests."

"I quite understand your situation, Mrs. Younge, so I will state my business and go away as soon as you tell me what I want to know. Where can I find your old friend Mr. Wickham?"

"Mr. Wickham? How should I know? I have neither seen nor heard from him these many months. He might be in China, for all I care."

"That cannot be the case, Mrs. Young, as I am quite certain you are aware. I think it is much more likely that he is here in this very house than in China. Have you let him a room?"

"No, I have not. The house is full. If he had come to me for lodgings, I should have had to turn him away. But as I told you before, I have neither seen nor heard from him, and I do not know his whereabouts."

"I see. Then I suggest you discover his whereabouts as soon as possible, for I will return to this house every day until you tell me the truth. Believe me when I say that I can make things quite uncomfortable for you if you do not."

I repeated this performance on the next day. Then on the third day, with a small bribe to overcome the irritation to her conscience of betraying her friend, Mrs. Younge told me what I needed to know. Then it was the work of another hour (and another coin or two) to reach the place where the man and his stolen lady lodged and be assured that they were in.

Upstairs in the passageway of the second-rate rooming house, I drew a deep breath before making my presence known. The active exertion of the pursuit had kept me occupied and had seen me through the unpleasantness of dealing with Mrs. Younge. However, now that I had run my principle quarry to ground, I would have to confront the foul scoundrel face to face. I would have to behave with restraint instead of the violence his actions deserved. And if I could not persuade Lydia Bennet to quit her disgraceful situation and return to her friends, I might be obliged to reward Wickham's villainous behavior by offering quite a large sum of money to coerce him into marrying her. Revulsion at the prospect gave me pause, but then I reminded myself why I had come. This was for Elizabeth.

I rapped soundly on the door. There was no answer except the scrape of a chair and a few whispers from within. I rapped again. "Wickham!" I called out. "I know that you are there. You may as well admit me, for I certainly shall not go away until I have seen you."

At last the door opened a few inches, and I immediately shoved it the rest of the way. But that was the only act of force I permitted myself.

There stood Wickham with Lydia a little behind him in a less than respectable state of dress. "Darcy," said Wickham with the smallest of bows, "to what do we owe the pleasure of such an unexpected visit?" The slight tremor in his voice belied his affected ease of manner.

Showing no shame, Lydia then came forward, slipped her arm through Wickham's, and added, "Yes, Mr. Darcy, this is a surprise. We did not expect to receive any callers today."

I closed the door behind me and got down to the distasteful negotiations.

Lydia would not hear of leaving her paramour, as I first proposed, hoping that if she could be got away from her seducer, she might eventually return to her family. "I shall surely not come away, Mr. Darcy," she declared obstinately, "no matter what you or my father might say about it! Wickham and I are in love, and we will be married some time or other. I cannot understand what all the fuss is about."

"Yes, what business is this of yours, Darcy?" Wickham asked. "Why should you involve yourself in our affairs? Do you imagine yourself the hero, come to rescue the fair damsel in distress? Well, as you see, she is *not* in distress; she is perfectly happy here with me. Or perhaps you are sent by the Bennets?"

"Nobody has sent me," I said calmly. "I have come in the interest of seeing justice done. You have despoiled this girl and now it is only right that you should marry her. It is as simple as that."

"But that is where you are wrong, old friend. The situation is very far from simple. I cannot afford to marry, you see. I have the most shocking debts; you have no idea. And then there is the matter of what on earth we should live on. Regrettably, I am currently without any paid employment, since I was obliged to leave my regiment due to my... pressing embarrassments. And a wife can be terribly expensive, I understand. Lydia is accustomed to the comforts of a gentleman's house. It would be unfair to ask her to live in poverty for me. You do see what I mean, don't you, Darcy?"

Yes, I saw. I saw the unpleasant brightness in his eye. I saw that he was aware of his momentary power over me. I saw that he intended to take full advantage of it too.

We could not come to terms at once, but I was no longer concerned that he would flee, for the tempting lure of money was before him. I knew he would not be able to resist the opportunity for some immediate relief from his distress of circumstances, perhaps even a handsome profit. And so he stayed.

Several meetings were required before his demands could be brought within reason, but at last the deal between us was struck.

My subsequent visits to Mr. Gardiner were a great pleasure by comparison. Elizabeth's uncle, who had so favorably impressed me when I first knew him at Pemberley, proved his worth again as he became my willing and able partner in seeing that the marriage would take place as quickly and quietly as possible. And under his auspices too, for I wanted no undeserved praise for the inferior remedy necessitated by my own mistake of pride.

Lydia went to her uncle and aunt in Gracechurch Street for a fortnight until they could be married at St. Clement's, the church of the parish in which Wickham's lodging house was situated. When the appointed day – August 31st – arrived, I was there to ensure Wickham's capitulation and to conclude the accompanying financial transactions. Then at last the sad business was finished.

Other than the time spent with the Gardiners, it had been an onerous affair, only made supportable by the thought that it must bring some solace to Elizabeth and her family. There was no time to dwell on that gain, however. I had other obligations awaiting me, most particularly, my commitment to return as soon as possible to marry Miss Lambright.

37
Returning to Amelia

A special license for our marriage did not prove difficult to obtain. And then there was no more reason to delay my return to the north, to Ravenshaw, and to Amelia.

Accordingly, I sent off a message by express to Lord Harcourt of when I could be expected. Then I dispatched another to Franklin Lambright advising him of my plans, in case he should like to travel with me, although I hardly knew if I wished him to accept the invitation or not. His company would help distract my mind and occupy the time, but I wondered if I could so long keep up the pretense that I was delighted to be marrying his sister. In the end, an excellent compromise developed. Since Franklin desired to have his own equipage at his disposal, we travelled in tandem. I had his amiable company each time we stopped or stayed, but I could enjoy the unrestraint of privacy during most of the hours of travel.

By this time, I had had nearly a month to adjust my thinking to the idea that Amelia would indeed soon be my wife. I had therefore done my best to consign Elizabeth to the past, to that place every responsible adult keeps for storing away outgrown and abandoned dreams. One might from time to time take them out, turn them over in one's mind, and remember them fondly. But then they must be put back and the door locked once again. There never could be any question of reviving them.

I was concerned, however, that the conversation I had intended to introduce with Elizabeth that morning, weeks before at the Lambton inn, had never transpired. The news of Lydia's elopement had swept all before it, and things that should have been said between us never were. I had no chance to thank her for her reproofs, to which I had endeavored to attend. I had not been able to say how grateful I was that we had been brought together again at Pemberley, so that we might part on better terms than before. I had no opportunity to say a proper good-bye and to sincerely wish her health and happiness as we went our separate ways. It was a matter of regret, for which I could foresee no possible remedy...

"You are very quiet tonight, Darcy," Franklin said midway through our supper at the inn where we broke our journey. "Something on your mind?"

"Oh, yes, I suppose so. A bit of unfinished business. That is all."

"Ah, I can well imagine. Is it a lady?"

"What? No, of course not! Why on earth should you have thought so?"

"Easy on, friend. I only imagined that, were I on my way to be married as you are, I should be thinking of all the women I have known and left behind, wondering if I were doing the right thing."

Recovering my composure, I declared, "That is a sign you are not ready to be married."

"I daresay you are right about that."

"Your time will come, Lambright. When you meet with a young lady who completely captures your imagination, who makes you forget all the others, then you will have no such doubts to think of."

"Ha! Is that what my sister has done to you, Darcy? Remarkable. I never suspected her of being a woman of such capabilities. But then she is only my sister. I cannot be expected to see what *you* see in her."

Muttering my agreement, I then dropped my head to earnestly address the hearty meat pie before me. I could not look at Franklin, lest I should give myself away. For I had not, in fact, been thinking of Amelia when I said those things.

That final day of the journey, I realized I had only deceived myself into thinking that I was calmly resigned to my fate, for the closer we drew to Ravenshaw, the more tormented I became. How glad I was to be alone in my carriage those last few hours! No, I did not yell or tear my hair out. No actual tears were shed. Most of my struggle remained internal. Still, I could ill have born being closely observed by another creature while settling one final contest of will versus inclination, of duty versus desire.

Then suddenly the long miles had slipped away, and I recognized from the landmarks that Ravenshaw was only a few minutes ahead. Exertion became absolutely necessary then. It was time to order my thoughts and my countenance. Time to put away my regrets and move forward to embrace my future wife and the rest of my life.

~~*~~

The house itself came into view, and we made the final sweeping approach along the gravel drive. When the carriage rocked to a stop, I took one more deep breath to prepare myself. Then leaving our carriages to the care of others, Franklin and I approach the door.

The butler admitted and greeted us formally.

"Good to see you again, Wilson," said Franklin. "Is my father in the drawing room?"

"No, sir. I am afraid his lordship is out."

"Out? What kind of a trick is this, Wilson? He knew to expect us today, did he not?"

"Yes, sir," Wilson answered evenly. "He said I should apologize to you and especially to Mr. Darcy, and that unforeseen events took him away. He will return as soon as possible and explain all then. That is as much as I know, sir."

"Ah, very well, Wilson," Franklin said with a sigh. "I suppose we must be content with Amelia, then. Has she been told of our arrival? She will be eager to see Mr. Darcy." The butler grimaced slightly. "Well, what is it, Wilson?"

"I regret to say that Miss Lambright is… She is also away from home at present."

"Away from home? This is a rum affair, I must say. No one here to greet us? Come, Darcy. It appears we shall have to entertain ourselves until the wanderers return. I cannot think what has taken them both away, today especially."

I could not either, but I held my peace.

The house seemed preternaturally silent with the ebullient Lord Harcourt and his daughter both away, and even the servants seem to move about more noiselessly than usual. Franklin and I amused ourselves in the billiard room until a late supper was served, with still just the two of us to eat it. Then, over several hands of cards, we settled down to wait some more.

I kept my thoughts mostly to myself, but I could not help agreeing with my friend that this was a very strange turn. As the clock in the hall ticked the minutes and then the hours away, my eyes were often drawn to the window, where I watched the last of the early September light fading from the sky. Darkness fell, and still Amelia and her father did not come.

"I cannot imagine what is keeping them," Franklin said yet again. Flinging his cards on the table, he jumped to his feet, raked his hand through his flaxen hair – so like his sister's – and strode across the room. "I'm sorry, Darcy. It must have been some sort of sudden emergency, else they would surely have been here to receive you properly, even if they did not feel such courtesy necessary for me."

"Pray, do not make yourself uncomfortable on my account, Franklin," I said, likewise laying my cards aside. "I am not in the least affronted, although, like you, I cannot help but be concerned. As you say, no ordinary day-to-day occurrence can be responsible."

Franklin went to the window. "It is all but black out there. Not much of a moon to travel by."

"Perhaps now they will not come until morning," I suggested. "Your father is a sensible man and would not risk the safety of all, even to keep an important appointment."

"Perhaps," Franklin agreed, but he remained where he was, peering out of the window into the darkness.

It was a terrible kind of suspense, for, though I did not say so aloud, it seemed to me that only the direst sort of emergency could be responsible for it. Had illness or injury to either Amelia or her father taken them away? That did not seem likely; surely a doctor would have been summoned to attend the patient at Ravenshaw instead. And why would Wilson have scrupled to say so? Or perhaps something else – something of a confidential nature – had occasioned their absence, and now that had been compounded by an accident, preventing their timely return. The longer the situation carried on, the less likely it appeared that the cause could be anything trivial or entirely harmless.

When I could sit still no longer, I got to my feet as well, methodically patrolling the room and periodically joining Franklin at the window that overlooked the sweeping arc of the drive.

Hearing the clock chime one in the morning, I laid my hand on his shoulder. "Depend on it; they have decided to spend the night wherever they are, rather than risk travelling in the dark. We may as well retire, for we shall surely not learn anything more until morning."

"No, no, wait!" he said with renewed animation. "I am sure that I see a light coming."

I looked and waited, and soon I was sure of it as well. "Yes, it is as you say."

We both moved through the front hall and out onto the steps to meet what could be nothing else than a carriage, its lanterns bobbing up and down. It was slow moving, no doubt due to the hazardous conditions, and yet it was definitely drawing closer, minute by minute. More agonizing waiting, but at least now we had the promise of the answers we sought, especially when the carriage was close enough to be recognized as belonging to Lord Harcourt.

Finally, it pulled abreast of us, the footman jumped down and opened the door, and Lord Harcourt was helped out. As he came towards us, I waited to see Amelia alight as well. But she did not.

Franklin voiced my own question. "Where is Amelia, Father?"

Harcourt looked very weary – weary and grim. "Let us go in," he said. "I have much to tell you both, and none of it good news."

38

Missing

Franklin and I followed Harcourt in.

"To the library, I think," he said, which sent a servant scurrying ahead of us to light some candles. When we were alone and the door was closed behind us, Harcourt came to me, shook my hand, and with a look of pure misery said, "Darcy, I cannot begin to tell you how sorry I am. Here you are, a friend and a gentleman. You do not deserve to be treated so shamefully."

"Nonsense, Harcourt," I returned, benignly. "Think nothing of it. I am not the least put out for being kept waiting."

"Oh, if only that were all!" he wailed.

"My dear sir," I said, taking his arm. "Do sit down here and calm yourself. Franklin, a drink for your father."

Harcourt allowed me to take him to a chair, where he all but collapsed, his head dropping at once into his hands.

"Here, Father," said Franklin presently, offering him a glass. "Take some of this, and then tell us what has happened. Where is Amelia? Is she well? Do not leave us in this awful suspense."

Harcourt downed the drink, set the glass aside, and then looked up, first at his son to say, "Amelia is well. You need not have any more fear on that head." Then he turned to me. "Darcy, I am so terribly sorry, but she is… She is gone."

"Gone?" I repeated, mystified.

Harcourt was overcome, however, and took several seconds to master himself enough to continue. "She has flown off… in the middle of the night, no less… with John Fairhaven, Lord Avery's second son. I went after them, of course, hoping to intervene before it was too late, but…" He trailed off.

"Fairhaven!" cried Franklin in outrage. "Carrying my sister off? Oh, wait until I get my hands on him; I shall wring his neck, the scoundrel!"

"Now, now, Franklin," said Harcourt, wearily. "He has not abducted your sister; he is not such a scoundrel as that. She went with him willingly, and I've no doubt Fairhaven means to act honorably by her. It is Amelia – my own dear, sensible Amelia – whose behavior grieves me to my soul. It seems the whole scheme was her idea! Darcy, she means to marry Fairhaven and not you, I'm afraid."

"So I gather."

Pulling a paper from his pocket, Harcourt handed it to me. It was a note. I sat down near the light to read it.

Dearest Papa,

I am so desperately sorry for how distressed you are sure to be when you discover I am gone. I hope you can in time forgive me, but I am off with John Fairhaven to Gretna Green to be married. Pray, do not be angry with him, for I gave him little choice in the matter. Eloping was all my own idea, you see.

I have long harbored amorous feelings for John. But since I believed they would never be returned, I endeavored to set them aside in order to marry Mr. Darcy, as you desired me to do. I know he would have been very good to me.

In the end, however, I simply could not go through with it, especially after John made his own declaration. And then we had to act in haste, for I could not face Mr. Darcy and see his disappointment in me. Please convey my most sincere apologies to him for how badly I have behaved. He is better off without me, I daresay.

Amelia

Amelia! I could hardly imagine the sensible woman I knew doing something as reckless and impetuous as to elope to Gretna Green! And in the name of love, too. Ha!

"Say something, Darcy," pleaded Lord Harcourt when I had finished reading. "Are you *very* angry?"

Angry? I was having the devil of a time stopping a wide grin from breaking across my face. Handing Amelia's note back to her father, I adopted a deliberately serious tone and expression.

"No, sir. Do not be dismayed. I take no umbrage with you or your daughter over this affair. Naturally, I am disappointed, but ours was not a love match, as you are no doubt aware, so my heart will not suffer. And even my pride has been mostly spared. Since nobody was aware of our private engagement, nobody will be aware that I have been thrown over. I only wish Amelia had told me. I would have gladly released her from our engagement, and then there would have been no need for running off to Gretna Green in the middle of the night."

"Most unfortunate," said Harcourt, shaking his head. "Most unfortunate indeed. You are uncommonly generous to overlook such a slight, Darcy. Very good of you. So very good."

"Not at all. But how has this come about? When I was here a month ago, your daughter wanted us to be married as soon as possible. She even made me promise to bring a special license when I returned."

"I wish I could tell you, sir, but at present it is a mystery to me as well. She appeared perfectly calm, even after Mr. Fairhaven had been here to call on us a fortnight ago. And then, when we received your express telling us that you were on your way, Amelia began to shake – just a little tremble at first, which I put down to natural excitement, but then violently enough that I thought she might come to pieces. I could get no word of ex-planation out of her, however, and after an hour or two of rest, she seemed herself again. So I had no warning at all that something of this sort was in the air! As you say, I wish she would have told somebody how she felt."

We were all silent a moment, and then Franklin spoke. "She did."

"What?" ejaculated Harcourt.

"She *did* tell somebody; she told me." He looked from his father to me and back again before continuing. "When I was at home last, she told me she was in love with John Fairhaven. But she despaired of him returning her affection, at least in sufficient strength to do anything about it. And then there was the difficulty of his situation: a good family, but a second son with little fortune of his own. Amelia was sure you would not consider the match eligible, especially when compared to Darcy's suit."

"Well, there is some truth to that. Still, I wish she had given me a chance. Did you know about this elopement, though?"

"Not a bit of it. I had a letter from her about a month ago, saying that she had given up all hope of Fairhaven and decided to marry Darcy, which seemed the right and sensible thing to do. Fairhaven must have stepped up at the last minute."

"It is of course none of my business, Harcourt," I said, "but I hope you will forgive Amelia and welcome her and her husband when they return."

"If you can forgive her, Darcy, I suppose I can as well. I must, in fact, to salvage the situation. If she is received by her family, it will go a long way towards hushing up any hint of scandal. And I know I can depend on you to keep what you know to yourself."

"Absolutely."

"Besides, Father," added Franklin, "John Fairhaven is not really such a bad fellow. And now that I have got over the shock, it occurs to me that except for the dashed peculiar way it came about, there is nothing essentially disgraceful in the match."

"As you say. Let us hope Lord Avery is of the same opinion. He may do something for them, and of course Amelia has some money of her own from her mother. In any case, it is done now, and I suppose we must be ready to make the best of it. Still, I cannot help but feel it is a disagreeable business. Ah, well, I am for bed," Harcourt said, rising with difficulty. "It has been a most trying day, and my strength is at an end."

I likewise retired – to rest and to ponder all that had transpired. I was still staggered by Amelia's actions, although, as I told Harcourt, not angry in the least. What an astonishing turn of events! Why, I no more expected when I rose that morning that such a thing should occur than that I should witness an eclipse of the sun!

However, Amelia's actions were not what my thoughts most dwelt on, not in the least. For the direct implications to myself had not escaped my grasp from the very first moment. I was free, honorably free.

I drew from my pocket the special license I had acquired at Amelia's insistence, now of no use whatsoever. Without hesitation, I happily consigned it to the past, dropped it in the empty fireplace grate, and struck a spark to it. The flame caught and flared as it consumed the paper. At the same time, I felt a faint hope rekindling in my heart. Now that I was free again, might I stand a chance with Elizabeth?

I left Ravenshaw and my friends there the following morning, for I was distinctly an outsider at that point, and my continued presence would have served no purpose but as an awkward reminder of their troubles. I could only hope that their distress would be of short duration and the family amicably reunited soon.

As I retraced the route I had so often travelled in recent months – from Pemberley to Ravenshaw and back again – I could not help remembering the day I had first come that way in search of a wife. Oh, what twists and turns for all concerned might have been avoided if I had never taken the notion to do so! And yet, it had been a sound plan in the beginning, as to a logical solution to my situation; I still believed it so. But I had now learnt that logic alone might not always be the best guide in such matters. Amelia had defied the logical course to follow her heart instead. I wished her well. I wondered if I might do the same.

The optimistic thoughts of the night before – thoughts of Elizabeth – had since been somewhat tempered in the clear light of day, however. First and foremost, despite what had transpired at Pemberley, I did not know for certain that Elizabeth cared for me – enough, or indeed at all. If I asked her again, I might receive the same answer as before.

And then, those other seemingly insuperable barriers to our marrying still existed; only the specifics had changed. Amelia no longer stood between us, it was true, and the Gardiners had proved themselves no disadvantage at all. But by recent events, the failings of Elizabeth's immediate family members had been confirmed beyond a doubt. And one more thing. If Elizabeth's connections had held me back before, they were far more odious to me now. For it occurred to me that, partly thanks to my own actions, the man who subsequently married Elizabeth Bennet would make himself forever brother to George Wickham.

39
Rethinking the Situation

"Where is my surprise?" my sister asked after we had shared an embrace upon my arrival at Pemberley.

"Your surprise? Oh, yes, I forgot. I do have news, but not quite what I had expected to bring you. Let us make ourselves comfortable in the saloon, and I will tell you."

We walked in that direction.

"Yes, of course," said Georgiana. "You must be tired from your travels. Shall I call for some refreshments to be brought in?"

"Thank you, no." A moment later, I asked, "The Bingleys have gone, then?"

"A week ago. When the weather took a turn, they decided to move along to Scarborough. Mr. Bingley has left you a letter – of thanks, I suppose. You will find it with your correspondence."

"Very good. Have you been well while I was away? The duties of playing hostess were not too taxing, I hope."

"I have been very well. And little exertion was required of me by our guests. As you said, they made free to act as if this were their own house. Miss Bingley even took upon herself the chore of making the menus. I do not think Cook liked it much above half, though."

"I can imagine." We had arrived in the saloon: one of my sister's favorite rooms, because of the tall windows and generous light. She seated herself, but I remained standing for the time being. "Well, Georgiana," I said evenly, "the surprise I expected to be bringing you was news that Miss Lambright and I were soon to be married. Instead, the news is that Miss Lambright has definitely decided *not* to marry me. In fact, she is marrying somebody else." Seeing a frown forming on my sister's face, I hurried on. "No, you must not suppose that I mind it. Not in the least. It is for the best, I am convinced."

"But after waiting so long for her answer? Now you will have to start all over with somebody new."

I hesitated. "Perhaps not somebody *completely* new."

"What do you mean? Is there a lady of your acquaintance you think of?"

I nodded slowly and sat down beside her. "Georgiana, can I ask… That is, would you mind telling me… I cannot decide if it would be at all eligible, but what would you say to Miss Elizabeth Bennet?"

Her face lit and she actually clapped her hands. "Oh, yes, William! Do ask her. I like her so very much!"

I was astonished at her enthusiasm. "Truly? You never said so before."

"When did I have the chance? You were gone as soon as she was."

"Yes, well, about that, there is something I should explain. As it happens, Miss Bennet, if she should ever agree to marry me, would come to our family with some unpleasant baggage – unpleasant to you as well as to myself." I then explained the reason for my recent mission to London and what was the result.

"You would be brother to Wickham?"

"Yes, and so you see one of the reasons for my reluctance. He would never be allowed on the premises, either here at Pemberley or at our house in town. But still, I could never be entirely rid of him either. And you might be confronted with hearing his name mentioned more than you would like. Should you be able to bear it, do you think?"

She dropped her eyes. "I can never think of him without embarrassment, but it has been more than a year, and I certainly do not feel any fondness for him anymore. I see now that he is not at all the kind of man I should admire, and I surely can bear the mention of his name, if it should happen in my hearing. I am sorry for Elizabeth's sister, though, married to him forever. It might have been me but for you."

"And Fitzwilliam. He deserves as much or more of the credit. Since I have been loath to mention the topic, I never told you that it was Fitzwilliam who first perceived the danger. He saw Wickham coming away from Mrs. Younge's house and wrote to me. That is the only reason I knew to follow you to Ramsgate."

"Oh, how much I owe to him! And never to have thanked him? He must think me very ungrateful."

"Nonsense. He does not desire or require your thanks, Georgiana. His reward, like mine, will be to one day see you happily settled, married to somebody worthy.

"Now, what would you advise me about Miss Bennet? She is nothing like the sort of lady I thought I should marry. She is not high born or rich and so will not at all suit the family's elevated expectations. She can be maddeningly contrary too, I should warn you, and vastly impertinent. I daresay she will never learn to hold her tongue when she has a strong opinion or if she believes I am in the wrong about something. And then there are her unfortunate family connections, as I told you."

"William, do you realize you have just given me all the reasons you should *not* marry Miss Bennet? The fact that you are still considering it can mean only one thing."

"Oh?"

"You must be in love with her, of course. It is useless to deny it, for I have seen that certain look in your eye – when Elizabeth was with us and when you were speaking of her just now."

"Well, yes. As much as I struggled against it, especially when I thought I must marry Miss Lambright, I have to admit it is true; I am in love with Elizabeth. How did you become so perceptive all of a sudden? But perhaps she will not have me. She used to despise me, you know, and I am by no means certain that she returns my regard even now."

"I believe she does. I observed a certain look in *her* eye as well."

"Did you, now?" I felt the meager hope in my heart swell a little larger.

"Oh, yes. And as you have said yourself, I am very perceptive about such things. If you truly love her, William, you should marry her if you can and sort the rest out together. That is my opinion."

"Thank you, Georgiana," I said, embracing her, "you are a dear."

My conversation with my sister had been encouraging, not only because of her decided approbation of Elizabeth, but because she confirmed what I thought I had recognized myself: that Elizabeth's sentiments towards me were more favorable now. But were they favorable enough to actually consent to marriage? I would require some way to ascertain the truth of the matter if I wished to avoid embarrassing us both with another unwanted proposal, which I did. Some plausible excuse to spend more time in her company first was needed. But what? I could hardly appear at her door out of nowhere; that would imply too much too soon.

Seeing no immediate answer to that question, I went to the library to deal with whatever correspondence had accumulated during my latest absence. There I found Bingley's letter and opened it.

> *Darcy,*
>
> *I hope your urgent business has been concluded to your satisfaction. How surprised we all were – surprised and dismayed – at your abrupt departure. And yet we carried on very well without you, as you foresaw that we would. Dear Georgiana made everything fine for us. Our whole party is very much obliged to you both.*
>
> *Would you allow me to return the hospitality? I have a mind to go to Netherfield about the middle of this month, for the shooting. It is my home, after all, legally rented, and I have a perfect right to take in the sport afforded by whatever game birds abound. I may invite Mr. Hurst as well, although I expect him to decline, as he is quite*

partial to Scarborough. Either way, there can be no occasion for bringing the ladies this time. Do write to advise me if you will come.

Bingley

My instant reaction upon reading this was that I must stop my friend from going, just as before, that his affection for Miss Jane Bennet was not sufficiently cooled yet as to make it safe for him to see her again, which he must certainly do if he went to Netherfield. But then the next moment I remembered Elizabeth's strictures on the subject.

Do you think that any consideration would tempt me to accept the man, who has been the means of ruining, perhaps forever, the happiness of a most beloved sister? ...the unjust and ungenerous part you acted there. ...your arrogance, your conceit, and your selfish disdain of the feelings of others...

Had I learnt nothing after all? Had I failed to benefit from Elizabeth's reproofs as I had determined to do? No, I knew better. I had seen where I had been wrong before, and now only needed to think and act accordingly.

It was arrogance indeed to suppose I had the right to judge for my friend whether or not he might go to his own house and if he might be allowed to see Miss Bennet again. She herself was kind and perfectly respectable. If they would make each other happy, who was I to interfere? It would be the height of hypocrisy to do so while at the same time contemplating making *myself* happy by the very same means – marrying into the Bennet family, despite their supposed inferiority.

Then I nearly laughed aloud at my own absurdity as another irony presented itself. I had been used to thinking of Lord Harcourt's family as entirely superior, and yet his daughter had just committed nearly the same crime as Mr. Bennet's. And had not my own sister contemplated an elopement as well? Were two – two young ladies and their families – to be pardoned and the other condemned? When it came to that, my own behavior over the past year was hardly above reproach.

Judge not, lest ye be judged. Hearing these well-known words repeating in my mind, my thinking became clear and a weight lifted from my shoulders.

I had thought myself free when released from my engagement, and yet it was not true, for I was still bound by my false prejudices – still deeming one family my equal and the other beneath me. These were the tenets taught me by my father and his father before him. These were the imperatives by which society and most of my relations still functioned. But if at their heart, these conventions were wrong, I need not feel bound to follow them any longer.

On the contrary. My highest responsibility was to act according to God's laws, not any man's, not even my father's. I would break no divine commandments by marrying Elizabeth. Therefore, I was perfectly free to pursue happiness with her, and free to permit my friend to take his chance as well.

No, I would not attempt to prevent Mr. Bingley from going to Netherfield and seeing Jane Bennet if he wished. In fact, I would accept the invitation to go with him.

40

Return to Netherfield

Georgiana was not happy that I would be leaving again so soon, at least not until I explained where I was going and why. Then she smiled, sent me off with a kiss, and told me not to come home again without an accepted proposal from Elizabeth Bennet.

An exchange of letters informed me what day Mr. Bingley intended to go to Netherfield, and consequently when I should come myself. I thought it very sly of him that in neither of his letters did he allude to my earlier advice to stay away from that place. I likewise said nothing about it, either in writing or to his face when I arrived. We both behaved as if such an exchange between us had never occurred – or at least if it had, that the circumstances were now entirely altered – when in truth, the only thing that had altered was my way of thinking.

I waited to see if or when my friend would open the subject. Not a word about his neighbors, the Bennets, did he utter that first day at Netherfield, however, or indeed the second. But on the morning of the third, he could evidently restrain himself no longer.

"The shooting has been good so far," he began as the two of us breakfasted together. "But I fancy a change for today. What do you say?"

"I am entirely at your disposal, Charles. What is it that you have in mind?"

"Perhaps we might make a few calls of courtesy," he said nonchalantly. "It must be done at some time or other, and no doubt word has got about by now that I am in the neighborhood again. If I delay too long, my former acquaintances may feel slighted."

"What is right to do may as well be done without delay," I agreed.

"Shall we begin…" He hesitated a moment and then said more decidedly, "I think we should begin with the Bennets."

"Just as you please," I said mildly, as if it was of no particular interest to me which neighbors we saw.

Perhaps Bingley had expected an argument, but now his countenance relaxed. He suddenly pushed his plate away, stood, and asked if I were finished as well.

"By the time the horses are ready, I will be," said I, remaining where I was. The kippers were excellent, and I saw no point in letting them go to waste.

As we rode the short distance to Longbourn, I carefully counseled my mind and my features to be composed, but all the same, I could not help wondering if I were doing as poor a job of concealing my excitement as my friend was. In a few more minutes, I would see Elizabeth, and yet I knew I must remain calm.

My intention on this first reunion was to observe, not to act. For better or for worse, Mrs. Bennet's presence and her penchant for talking would serve as a natural restraint between Elizabeth and myself, preventing such easiness of manner as we had enjoyed at Pemberley.

That was indeed the case. I said very little and tried to content myself with fairly brief glances at Elizabeth. Oh, but it did my eyes and my heart good to see her again! She sat quietly, keeping her attention mostly on the needlework before her. But there was high color in her cheeks. Was it for me? Or perhaps it was due to her own mortification. I believed that I knew her well enough to see in her blushes embarrassment over her mother's behavior.

Mrs. Bennet's manners were just what they had been before: cold civility to me and overly officious attentions to Bingley. Her style of conversation had undergone no revolution for the better either. If I had expected that the tragic loss and then fortunate restoration of her youngest daughter would work some profound change in her – made her forever sensible and gracious – I would have been very much mistaken. Since I had not, however, I suffered no shock of disappointment. Besides, it gave me the opportunity to practice the improvement in my own character in the form of forbearance.

We went away after half an hour, but not before being compelled by Mrs. Bennet to dine at Longbourn that Tuesday. I had made very little progress in determining Elizabeth's sentiments. She had spoken to me only once, to ask after Georgiana's health, and though our eyes had briefly met, she had withdrawn then again much too quickly. It was a sad regression after our previous congenial meetings at Pemberley, and yet I believed I had attributed the change to the proper cause: the difference in circumstances.

I achieved more in looking to the benefit of my friend. Though he was obliged to speak primarily to Mrs. Bennet, Bingley's eye was drawn, I noticed, so frequently to Miss Bennet that there could be no doubt of his interest in her being fully rekindled, if indeed it had ever flagged under their separation. Miss Bennet I also observed, now through the improved lens of her sister's information to me. Although her behavior in Bingley's presence was as calm and her countenance as serene as before, my interpretation now was vastly different. I decided that what I had taken as indifference could indeed be attributed to something else: a natural modesty and reserve, to being too shy to wear her emotions where all the world could see them. This was something I could understand and respect.

I hoped for some progress in my own case on our subsequent visit to Longbourn on Tuesday. The fates, however, seemed determined to thwart me at every turn. It was a large party, and I was forced to take a place at the table as far from Elizabeth as well might be found, and next to Mrs. Bennet besides. After dinner, as Elizabeth poured the coffee in the drawing room, she was surrounded by such a close confederacy of women as to leave no avenue of approach for me. I perceived that her eye was often upon me, though, as mine was upon her. And then, when I returned my cup to her, we at last had a few words together.

"Is your sister at Pemberley still?" Elizabeth asked.

"Yes, she will remain there till Christmas."

"And quite alone? Have all her friends left her?"

"Mrs. Annesley is with her," I explained. "The others have been gone on to Scarborough these three weeks."

The chief benefits of this brief exchange – the freedom to gaze upon Elizabeth for a minute or two and to hear her voice – was as much pleasure as the evening afforded.

Bingley had continued his earnest attentions to Jane, Jane receiving them with apparent pleasure. And so, even without his saying one word to plead his case to me, I knew what I must do. It would be a difficult task – a humbling one – but best done without further delay.

~~*~~

I was obliged to leave Netherfield temporarily, to go to town to see to my affairs there. Before I went away, I wanted this thing off my conscience. I had carried it long enough; it was time I was free of it. So the evening before my going to London, I prepared to make my confession.

"Bingley," I began soon after supper, "I owe you an apology."

He looked quite surprised by this. "You do?" he said. "Darcy, what can you mean?"

"I have wronged you, though I did not mean to. I have wronged you... and Miss Bennet."

I allowed that much to make its weighty impression before continuing. Bingley remained silent, his expression fully alert now and guarded, peering at me in what seemed like disbelief or at least confusion. I hated to go forward, knowing the pain I must inflict – pain that would soon turn to pleasure, I hoped.

"Although I honestly believed what I said to you at the time – that it would be for the best – I should never have attempted to come between you and Miss Bennet. It was a gross impertinence, which I have come to regret."

Bingley sat forward and opened his mouth, but I held up my hand to stop him. "No, you must allow me to finish, friend. There is more I must say to you; my conscience demands it."

Bingley resumed his former attitude and waited.

"It was arrogant and absurd of me," I continued, "to set myself up as judge and jury over you, to suppose I had the right to direct in what manner you were to be happy. I even betrayed my own principles by employing the art of disguise, which you know I abhor. When I learnt that Miss Bennet was in town earlier this year, in Gracechurch Street for three months with her aunt and uncle, I concealed it from you."

At this, Bingley shot to his feet and burst forth at last. "She was in town! For all those weeks! And you concealed it from me?"

"Yes. It was very wrong of me, and I apologize. I should never have interfered."

Bingley strode across the room in agitation, dragging his hands through his hair. Then he turned back to face me, saying, "Wait. Did my sisters know of this too? Did they know of Miss Bennet's being in town?"

I hesitated and then said, "I take full responsibility for my own actions. I am not here to accuse others."

"In other words, they did. Of course they did! As their acquaintance, Miss Bennet would have written of her arrival in town, called on them, and probably received them in Gracechurch Street in return!"

I dropped my eyes but said nothing.

Bingley strode back to where I sat. Looking down on me he nearly shouted, "How was it that I never knew any of this? I never had the slightest suspicion that I was being lied to!"

I attempted no defense. "You have every right to be angry. Indeed you do. But may I tell you one thing more?"

"There is yet *more*?"

"Yes, but this part I think you will find entirely agreeable. I am now convinced that I was also mistaken in my belief of Miss Bennet's indifference to you last autumn."

Bingley interrupted when I did not continue quickly enough. "What are you saying, man? Tell me at once!"

"That I now have every reason to believe she was in fact quite partial to you – was and is."

He looked almost dazed. "Are you saying that... that she might... that she might still care for me? I had not dared to hope."

"Who can know for certain? But I have good authority for what I am telling you."

Bingley's anger had apparently dissolved, and he now stood before me looking lost in pleasant daydreams instead. Presently, he said, "So you think she might accept me – from her heart, not in obligation, that is. And you no longer have any objection?"

"None whatsoever. I only hope that we can remain friends, Bingley, and that your angelic wife shall not think too ill of me either." That sent him into another private reverie that lasted some minutes.

The next morning, he shook my hand warmly before I departed Netherfield, no trace of resentment against me in evidence. What an excellent fellow he is! When I drove away, I expected that matters between Miss Bennet and my friend would be favorably settled ere I returned to Netherfield.

41
Taught to Hope

I was in London above a week and was nearly on the point of leaving it again when I received unexpected visitors: my cousin and aunt, Anne and Lady Catherine. Supposing at first that it was an ordinary call, occasioned by nothing more than our all happening to be in town at the same time, I welcomed them with an equanimity that very shortly passed away.

"Lady Catherine, Cousin Anne," I said upon receiving them. "Please do sit down. To what do I owe this pleasure?"

"Anne may sit," my aunt said imperiously, and Anne did so. "I will remain standing, for I am far too provoked at present to be comfortable."

I was thus obliged to remain on my feet as well, watching Lady Catherine's pacing and her other demonstrations of displeasure. I still had no clue as to the purpose of her visit, only that it would obviously be unpleasant. Presently I said, "I am sorry to hear it, Aunt. How may I be of assistance?"

"You may be of assistance by giving me the assurances I require. I have just returned from Hertfordshire where I had some serious words with Miss Elizabeth Bennet, who, I am sorry to tell you, was as perverse and contrary as any person I have ever encountered. I am not accustomed to such language as she inflicted upon me."

I could not have been more astonished. "Miss Bennet?" I asked. "What business could you possibly have with her?"

"If you do not know, perhaps you are indeed ignorant and innocent in this contemptible affair. Very well, then, allow me to inform you. I received a report of an *alarming* nature two days ago, and it concerns you, sir. I was told that the whole countryside surrounding Longbourn is waiting in confident expectation of soon hearing the announcement of your engagement to Miss Bennet! There, now you see what has me in such a state. I naturally took the report as a scandalous falsehood and went straight to the source to silence any further gossip."

I required a moment to take this in, but when I had done so, I was very far from joining my aunt in her outrage. In fact, this news suggested interesting possibilities. My only immediate concern was to know more about it. Keeping my tone impassive, I replied, "I take it your efforts were somehow frustrated."

"Darcy, how can you be so calm while the family name is being dragged through the dirt?"

"I have heard no evidence of that as yet, Lady Catherine, but I am ready to listen to whatever else you have to say. Miss Bennet failed to give you satisfaction?"

"Yes, in the extreme! I rue the day I distinguished her with my notice and condescension, receiving her at Rosings as I did. I surely would *not* have, had I suspected her true character. She has presumed upon my kindness and yours. And when I questioned her, she refused to oblige me at every turn. She not only denied she had originated and circulated the rumor herself – when common sense clearly shows that to be the obvious explanation – she even claimed to have never heard such a rumor before."

"Perhaps that is true; I have never heard it myself."

"If that were the case, then why would she make such a point of defending the idea?"

I looked up sharply. "Miss Bennet defended the rumor?"

"Not the rumor itself. I did finally force her to admit that no engagement currently existed, but she argued against its being an impossible match and flatly refused to promise never to accept you. And *this* after I informed her of your understanding with Anne! Can you imagine?"

"Yes, I believe I can," I said slowly, picturing the scene. Since I could not suppress a sly smile, I turned away from my aunt and towards my cousin instead. Giving her a conspiratorial wink, I asked her, "What about you, Anne? You have seen enough of Miss Bennet to form an opinion. Can you imagine her behaving in such a disobliging way?"

"Miss Bennet is a spirited young lady," said Anne, her eyes twinkling at me. "I believe she is not one to be easily intimidated when she feels herself to be in the right."

"Exactly," I said.

"But she is most definitely *not* in the right in this case," countered Lady Catherine, "and her failure to admit it shows a very unbecoming obstinacy, a dangerous degree of willfulness, and a total disregard for the claims of duty, honor, and gratitude. And so I told her. The idea of such a girl having pretensions to marry into a noble family is... Well, I refuse to lower myself by using such language. You must have nothing more to do with her, Darcy. She has shown herself to be an unprincipled person; that should be reason enough to shun her. Beyond that, visiting Longbourn or even Netherfield again will only fuel these noxious rumors."

"I think you overestimate their power, Aunt," I said calmly. "If there is no foundation, rumors of this sort die away soon enough."

"I wish I could agree with you, Nephew, but I will not have the honor of the family subjected to such a test. I will not have my daughter's name or yours sullied by the gossip of the lower orders. No, the only solution is a clean break. Promise me you will never see that young woman or any of her relations again. Since she refused to give me satisfaction, sir, you must!"

Now it was my turn to pace, conscious that what I said next would affect more than myself. I could walk away from my aunt's outrage, forever if necessary, but Anne... When I glanced at her, I could see she understood my hesitation on her account. Nevertheless, she gave me a nod, authorizing me to proceed. There would be unpleasantness whenever the truth came out; she was just as aware of that fact as I was.

"Come now, Darcy," Lady Catherine prompted. "This is not a difficult thing I ask of you, only what you owe to yourself and all the family. Not long ago you acknowledged the careful designs set in place for your future and assured me of your good understanding with Anne. This is simply the necessary extension of that commitment."

I came still, drew a deep breath, and spoke respectfully but firmly. "Lady Catherine, in that conversation to which you refer, I told you I would always endeavor to do my duty and also to please my family whenever possible. I stand by that statement."

"There, now," she said with a decisive nod.

"But that does not mean I concur with all the rest you have said. I will on no account allow you or anybody else to dictate to me where my duty lies and how I must perform it. Nor will I allow any person to tell me whom I may see and whom I may not. In fact, I agree with Miss Bennet in standing up to this kind of interference, whether it comes from a stranger or a near relation."

Lady Catherine opened her mouth, but I gave no opportunity for her to interrupt. "You have had your say, Aunt, and now it is my turn. I am truly sorry if it pains you, but it seems there is no avoiding it now. Since you press the issue, it is time you became aware of the nature of my understanding with your daughter. It is something other than what you have presumed. Out of our mutual respect, Anne and I have agreed to each free the other from any perceived obligation to what our parents once planned for us. Therefore, Anne is not to consider herself bound to me, and I am also at liberty to make a different choice if I like. I hope I shall choose wisely. What constitutes a wise choice in a mate, however, may depend on factors beyond what you can comprehend.

"Miss Bennet has been truthful with you; we are not engaged. I agree with something else she told you, however. There would be nothing impossible or disreputable in such a match. She is the daughter of a respectable gentleman, and I have never seen anything in her own conduct to censure. That is all that I require. Anything more speaks of avarice and unbecoming ambition."

Lady Catherine could be held at bay no longer. "But her nearest relations – low connections everywhere, a mother totally in want of decorum, and a sister whose marriage came too late and only at the behest of others. Heaven and earth, Darcy! Are the very shades of Pemberley to be soiled by such as these? Are these people to henceforth make up the chief part of your innocent sister's society?"

"These are things for me to decide, Aunt, not you. Perhaps I shall marry Miss Bennet and perhaps I shall not. That is really none of your affair. It is just possible, you know, that she would refuse me. Same as you, she may be put off the match for fear of acquiring unpleasant family connections."

After an exclamation of disgust, Lady Catherine turned to her daughter in desperation. "Say something, Anne! It is your future being thrown away here. Everything I have planned, everything I have hoped and strived for... I have done it all for you and your happiness. Think carefully before casting it aside like so much rubbish."

There was a suspenseful pause, during which I silently acknowledged that Anne could make things difficult for me if she gave in to her mother's pressure, as she usually did. When she answered, however, it was with more firmness than I had hitherto known her capable of.

"I appreciate your solicitude on my behalf, Mama, but I will not be made happy by my cousin marrying me against his will. If he chooses to wed Miss Bennet or somebody else, I shall be the first to wish them both joy."

Brimming with admiration and gratitude – and relief – I took Anne's hand and kissed it.

My relations very shortly went away, and immediately thereafter, I began preparations for my own departure on the morrow.

Lady Catherine's vociferous arguments against a connection to Elizabeth Bennet had been so repugnant as to leave me not caring if I should ever see my aunt again. Worse than this, however, was the knowledge of how closely her sentiments had echoed my own prior prejudices, and thus, how closely my current disgust of them must enlighten me to the offense Elizabeth herself had felt at my ungracious proposal. No wonder, then, that she had hated me.

And yet these sober reflections were soon set aside, for I could not help smiling. Thanks to my aunt's information, I now had more reason to hope than ever before. I knew that if Elizabeth still hated me, if she had absolutely decided against me, she would not have hesitated to say so when confronted by my officious relative. But that she had vehemently refused to promise she would never marry me, seemed like the most positive sign I could have asked for.

42

An Auspicious Opening

I could not get myself back to Netherfield quickly enough, and there I was met with the agreeable news that Bingley was indeed now engaged to Jane Bennet. He need not have told me so; his wide grin would have revealed the truth without any further explanation. I had never seen my friend so happy.

"My hearty congratulations," I said at the news, vigorously shaking his hand.

"Darcy, you cannot imagine how famously happy she has made me. She is an absolute angel."

"As you said from the beginning."

"Yes, and she has forgiven me everything, including my inconstancy in going away for so long."

"My fault."

"I did not say so. I did not tell *her* so either. I only explained that I had become convinced – not how it had happened – that she was indifferent to me; that I was completely ignorant of her being in town in the winter, which is true; but that I had not been able to overcome my tender regard for her. As to the last, she said it was just the same for her. Now it is settled that we are to be the happiest couple that ever was married."

"I am sincerely pleased for you both. Your engagement was well received by the whole family, I make no doubt."

"Oh, yes, Mr. and Mrs. Bennet could not have been more kind to me, welcoming me to the family."

"Of course. And Elizabeth?"

"I do believe she was especially delighted at the prospect, mostly on her sister's behalf, I suspect. Otherwise, having me for a brother could not have put such a smile on her face." He laughed.

"I am glad to hear it." Should I say more? I had brought Colonel Fitzwilliam up to date on my romantic pursuits when I was lately in town, but I had not planned to say anything to Bingley just yet, not unless or until the matter was decided in my favor. Then I could not seem to help myself. "You know," I continued, "I take a very particular interest in Elizabeth Bennet's happiness." I looked at my friend sidelong to see if he understood me.

"What? Can you mean it? I thought of it once, but Jane was sure it could never be. Do you really have a strong regard for Elizabeth, then?"

"Every bit as passionate a regard for her as you have for her sister, I would wager."

"Darcy, you have astounded me again! How long have you felt like this? For I never suspected it."

"No, I took great care that you should not, nor anybody else. I denied it to myself for a long time. And even now, I probably should not have told you. But I *must* try for her, Bingley. I must indeed."

"How marvelous! What a fine thing it would be for our friendship if you succeed. Then we should be brothers as well as friends! Although Caroline will be disappointed, I suppose."

"We should not have suited, Bingley."

"No. I admit I never thought that you should. This is better, and we shall be brothers just the same."

I agreed. In the past, I had spent so much time worrying about acquiring disadvantageous family connections that I had over-looked the reverse: the very great advantage of a nearer con-nection to Bingley, without the necessity of my marrying his sister or of his marrying mine. If I succeeded with Elizabeth, instead of drifting apart like friends often do after marrying, our continued connection would be forever secured. Our holidays would be spent together. Our children would be cousins and playfellows to each other. What a charming picture that made. If only...

It seemed that Bingley was now in the habit of spending the greater share of each day with the Bennets. So he said they would be expecting him the following morning and could not possibly take it amiss if I were to join him on his visit there. I hoped it was true, or at least that one particular member of the family would not take it amiss.

We made an early start of it. Already secure of his object, Bingley was relaxed and ebullient. Contrariwise, I rode beside him mute, my nerves on edge, knowing that this could be the day that decided my entire future.

After the unintended encouragement I had received from my aunt, I was eager to try for Elizabeth again. I had decided, however, that I would not allow my impatience to force the question on her too precipitously. There was no need to rush. I had time to wait for an appropriate situation, a propitious opening in the conversation. But any progress at all was dependent on getting Elizabeth where I could talk to her undisturbed, unmolested by her disapproving mama.

"Since the weather is fair," Bingley said as we progressed towards Longbourn, "I shall propose a walk to get us away from the house and any... any unwanted interference. Once we are on our way, I will draw back with Jane, so that we can be alone, and the rest will be up to you, friend. Here," he said, reaching awkwardly across the gap between us. "Shake my hand again, and perhaps some of my great good fortune will rub off on you."

I prayed that would be the case.

Another ten minutes, and we had arrived. I quieted my nerves as best I could and prepared to see Elizabeth again. As we entered the drawing room, where the ladies received us, my eyes fixed earnestly on her at once. She returned my gaze with what seemed like a question in her eye. I wondered what it could be. We had had so little time to talk in our previous two encounters that perhaps as much remained unsaid for her as for me.

We no more than sat down when Bingley popped up again with his suggestion of a walk. His ease in arranging the matter impressed me. He exuded a new confidence, I noticed. And it was clear that in Mrs. Bennet's eyes, he could do no wrong. He was even more her darling than before, and she could deny him nothing.

Mary declined the exercise, but the other five of us presently set forth, our direction determined by Kitty's wish to call at Lucas Lodge. As Bingley had promised, he and Jane soon lagged behind. That left Kitty still walking with Elizabeth and myself, none of us speaking much at all.

I was wondering how to achieve the desired privacy when Elizabeth said, "Kitty, I see no occasion for all of us to call at Lucas Lodge again so soon, when everybody but Mr. Darcy was there only yesterday. You run along and see Maria, though. I think the rest of us will carry on with our walk." Then she turned to me. "Will that suit you, Mr. Darcy."

"Admirably," I answered.

So again, the matter had been easily and expertly handled by another. I began to think this might be an auspicious day for me after all.

When Kitty had left us, Elizabeth and I walked on together, and before I could think of what to say, Elizabeth began a little breathlessly. "Mr. Darcy, I am a very selfish creature; and, for the sake of giving relief to my own feelings, care not how much I may be wounding yours."

Looking at her and seeing her perturbation, I grew concerned. "What is it?" I asked.

"Only that I can no longer help thanking you for your unexampled kindness to my poor sister. Ever since I have known it, I have been most anxious to acknowledge to you how gratefully I feel it."

I had not expected this, and my surprise was accompanied by a certain degree of distress. "I am sorry, exceedingly sorry," I replied, "that you have ever been informed of what may, in a mistaken light, have given you uneasiness. I did not think Mrs. Gardiner was so little to be trusted."

"You must not blame my aunt. Lydia's carelessness first betrayed to me that you had been concerned in the matter; and then, of course, I could not rest till I knew every particular. Let me thank you again and again, in the name of all my family, who are yet in ignorance of their debt to you, for that generous compassion which induced you to take so much trouble and bear so many mortifications on our behalf. You have been a true friend."

Was this the opening I had been hoping for? After a moment of deliberation, I pressed ahead. "If you *will* thank me, let it be for yourself alone. I confess that the wish of giving happiness to you directed me. Your family owe me nothing. Much as I respect them, I believe I thought only of you."

Elizabeth smiled, colored, and looked away, remaining silent.

I had already come this far. Turning back now no longer seemed reasonable or fair to either one of us. Besides, I could wait no longer; I had to know my fate. I therefore stopped and turned to her, taking her gloved hands in mine.

"Miss Bennet, you are too generous to trifle with me. If your feelings are still what they were last April, tell me so at once. *My* affections and wishes are unchanged. I still love you; I still, more than anything, desire to marry you. But with one word, you can silence me on this subject forever."

She did not speak, not for two seconds... three... and then four. I could see some kind of distress in her expression. Was she grieved that she must reject me again, only this time it would give her more pain to do so than the last?

"I am sorry, Mr. Darcy," she said, shaking her head to indicate a negative.

My heart sank within me. I sighed and asked, just to be certain, "Then your answer is no, the same as before?"

"No, I mean yes. Dear me! Last time you made a muddle of the question, and this time I have spoilt the answer! Let me try again." She took a breath and then hurried on. "I am sorry for your anxiety, Mr. Darcy, and for how I abused you in the past. But know this without further delay. I can hardly tell you how the change occurred or when, but my sentiments are now quite the reverse of what they were before."

"Then, do you mean that… that you are prepared to accept me?"

"More than that. I mean that I now freely return your affection and regard, I am very grateful for your renewed proposal, and I am tremendously pleased to accept it."

I held her gaze for a long moment, staring in disbelief, I am afraid, before I could entirely trust that I had heard correctly, that Elizabeth Bennet had just agreed to marry me. Her sunny smile and the corresponding crinkles at her eyes seemed to confirm it, and yet I had to ask, "Dearest Elizabeth, can this be true?"

She nodded merrily.

A rush of pure joy welled up inside me, and my heart seemed to expand to where my body could hardly contain it anymore. "You have no idea how happy this has made me," I said.

"Perhaps I do," she responded, her eyes twinkling. "If you are one tenth as happy as I am at this moment, it would be enough."

When Elizabeth started forward again, I took her hand, now even more precious to me than before, and threaded it through to rest on my arm. And so we carried on, not knowing where we were going or what had become of Bingley and Jane. We were in a world of our own, apart from everyday life, and treading on air.

I was quite overcome with emotion and for a few minutes could not speak. Finally Elizabeth said, "I am sorry to trouble you, Mr. Darcy, but I'm afraid the situation requires that we have *some* conversation. It would look very odd to be entirely silent for half an hour together. Do not you agree?"

I quickly saw her mischievous expression. She was alluding to the past. "Your words to me as we danced at Netherfield," I said. "I remember."

"How little we understood one another then. I was so determined to dislike you and thought myself uncommonly clever in doing so. Once I had made up my mind to it, everything I saw and heard was easily interpreted to your discredit."

"Let us not argue who should have the larger share of blame for our early mistakes. Let us simply count it a miracle that, despite our rocky beginning and the many circumstances which conspired to keep us apart, we have come safely through." I was thinking about my acquaintance with Amelia, of which Elizabeth was yet in total ignorance, but I judged it too soon to mention anything about that. So I just said, "Another day we shall add up all the ways our paths to this moment have been protected. Darling Elizabeth," I continued, "my heart is so full and I have so much to tell you. Will there ever be time for all of it, do you suppose?"

"My love, we have years and years."

43
Becoming Widely Known

The dam, once breached, could not easily be stopped up again. As long as Elizabeth and I were alone together that day, our conversation flowed nearly uninterrupted, in spite of my normally taciturn ways. I am sure Elizabeth was amazed – but pleased, I think – to discover I was capable of holding up my part.

We talked of our regrets for the past and our hopes for the future. We answered each other's lingering questions, demystifying some of our former actions and misunderstandings. We professed our love over and over again. I would never before have believed it could be like this with anybody – that *I* could be like this – and I reveled in the thought that the sweet intercourse passing between us was merely a foretaste of what was to come in our married life.

Finally, however, we could no longer avoid returning to the house, where we were required to explain our long absence with the excuse of having accidentally wandered farther afield than we had intended. We then resumed our former roles. While the acknowledged lovers, Jane and Bingley, talked and laughed, Elizabeth and I remained nearly silent, as we had been so often in the past. It would not always be so, but there were certain formalities to be performed before our new situation could become widely known.

I did not mind. In fact, I was relieved that so little conversation was expected of me, for my mind was too preoccupied with more important things to speak of such trifles as generally made up the fare in Mrs. Bennet's drawing room. I was therefore free to indulge myself in pleasant reveries about my beautiful betrothed and our future together, with long, meaningful looks at her, which nobody else except perhaps Bingley seemed to notice.

Bingley had the secret out of me before we had left the grounds of Longbourn. "I knew it!" he cried. "You did a good job hiding it, you sly creatures, but there was something different in you both, and I knew at once what had happened!"

I smiled benignly at his effusions. "Your luck must have rubbed off on me after all, and your scheme of a walk worked to perfection. I am in your debt, Bingley."

"You owe me nothing; I could not be more pleased. For all of us! But I was hard pressed to hold back from whispering something of what I knew to Jane."

"Elizabeth will tell her tonight, and then you may speak freely between yourselves. How soon the subject can be canvassed beyond, I know not. Perhaps I will have the opportunity to speak to Mr. Bennet tomorrow."

Mr. Bingley proved himself of infinite use during this brief period. The next day, as guardian and self-appointed forwarder of our happiness, he again contrived a chance for me to be alone with Elizabeth. As soon as he and I arrived at Longbourn, he inquired, "Mr. Bennet, have you no more lanes hereabouts in which Lizzy may lose her way again?"

"I advise Mr. Darcy and Lizzy and Kitty to walk to Oakham Mount this morning," answered, Mr. Bennet. "It is a nice long walk, and I daresay Mr. Darcy has never seen the view."

Bingley frowned a little. "I know the walk you mean, and it may do for the others, but I am sure it will be too much for Kitty. Won't it Kitty?"

Kitty obligingly confessed she would rather stay at home.

"*I* am quite intrigued, however, Mr. Bennet," I said. "If your elder daughter will consent to show me the way, I should very much like to see this view you speak of." I looked at Elizabeth, who smiled furtively at me and indicated to her father her willingness to do so.

After we were well away from the house, I asked Elizabeth, "How did your sister bear the news?"

Elizabeth laughed. "For the longest time she refused to believe me! And then when I had finally convinced her that we were truly engaged, she questioned whether we knew what we were about. *You*, she has always valued, but she made me swear I loved you quite enough to deserve you."

"You must be joking," I said.

"Well, it was not precisely so, perhaps. But now that Jane is convinced that we both feel what we ought, she is *very* pleased. In fact, we were kept awake half the night making plans and debating which of us is to be happiest." Then becoming more serious, she added, "Darcy, Jane and I decided we should like to be married together, in a double wedding. Should you mind it?"

I thought a moment. "When two men, who are the best of friends, marry two sisters, who are as close as you and Jane, clearly nothing else would do."

She squeezed my arm. "You are too good to me, Mr. Darcy!"

"That is," I added, "so long as it will not cause any delay, for I am quite impatient to make you my wife at last. I have been waiting a long time for it, as you know."

She ignored the allusion to the past and answered my primary concern. "A double wedding will mean just the reverse, I assure you! Jane and Mr. Bingley, since they were first engaged, would have the right to marry before us. This way, we will not have to wait until afterward. I am impatient as well, you see," she said, looking up at me through her dark lashes.

I could not help imagining the joyous day… and the pleasures of the night following. My voice came out in a throaty rumble. "The sooner the better."

"Yes, the sooner the better," she said before at last turning away and resuming our walk. "Next month, then. We must at least allow time for your sister and our other friends to arrive."

My thoughts were redirected at the mention of my sister. "Georgiana will be so delighted. I shall write to her tonight with the news. And to Fitzwilliam."

"But first, you must speak to my father."

"Of course." An awkward but necessary measure. "What can I expect from him, do you think?"

"Utter surprise, I should imagine."

That evening, Mr. Bennet, as was his habit, withdrew to his library at his earliest opportunity. With a glance at Elizabeth and a nod between us, I soon discreetly followed him. In answer to my knock, I heard a weary, "Come in, if you must." Mr. Bennet did not look up from his book when I opened the door. Instead, he said in the same tired tone, "Mrs. Bennet, I am in no humor to listen to your complaints. For the sake of our guests, I have made myself agreeable for as long as I could. Now I expect..." At last he had caught sight of me. "Oh! It is you, Mr. Darcy. You must forgive me. Is there something I can do for you?"

I closed the door behind me and took a chair across from him. "You can, sir, if you will. For I have a serious matter to discuss with you."

"A serious matter, you say?"

"Yes, one of the highest importance."

"I suppose I must take you at your word. Although I cannot imagine what your business with me could be, please do proceed."

"Gladly, sir. It is simply this. I desire your blessing to marry your daughter."

"My daughter?" He looked bemused. "Which one?"

"Why, Elizabeth, of course. I have known her now for a considerable time, and I love her most sincerely. Shall we have your consent to marry? I can assure you that she will want for nothing."

His mouth was agape. "I would never refuse you, Mr. Darcy. *My* consent you may have and gladly. I doubt you will be as successful with my daughter, however. I have known her some-what longer than you. And in case you have not noticed, she has a lively mind and an independent heart that I think will not easily be won."

"There seems to be some mistake, Mr. Bennet. She has already accepted me, you see."

"She has what?"

"She has accepted me, sir. Yesterday, in fact."

"Will wonders never cease?" He took a moment to digest these facts before continuing. "Once again, I find you must forgive me, Mr. Darcy. I meant no insult, and as I said, you have the permission you seek."

"Thank you."

"In my defense, I had it on very good authority that such a thing as this could never take place."

"I understand, sir, believe me. I did as well, but the situation is happily altered."

"It seems so, only you must allow me to speak to Lizzy next, so that she may set my mind at ease about this surprising news."

"Of course. I will send her to you now, shall I?"

"If you would be so kind."

I bowed and left him, returning to the drawing room. Elizabeth looked up at once. There was anxiety in her countenance, which I attempted to alleviate with a swift but brief smile. After a minute, I went to where she was sitting by her sister Kitty. Leaning over as if to admire the needlework Elizabeth had in hand, I whispered, "Go to your father. He wants you in the library." Then I walked away again.

Elizabeth was absent much longer than I had been, and every minute that passed seemed an age. At last, though, she returned, saying and looking enough to assure me that all was well. Before Bingley and I went away that evening, she told me, "I will explain it all to Mama tonight, and then perhaps she will be tolerably calm again when you come tomorrow. At least I hope she will."

"Your mother may not be pleased, for she has always hated me."

"Like mother, like daughter, do you mean? That thought should be enough to make me quite ashamed of myself! But I expect Mama's sentiments towards you will be converted far more quickly than mine were, once she learns you are to take me off her hands."

~~*~~

The news of our engagement was known to all the family by the following morning (and no doubt to the rest of the neighborhood by the afternoon). Mr. Bennet, to his credit, took immediate pains to further our acquaintance. Mrs. Bennet seemed to lose her courage around me, but what she did say was of a character markedly different from before, signifying deference rather than disgust.

I tolerated the unwanted attentions our engagement created, telling myself that it would not be for long. In a few short weeks, Elizabeth and I would be married and away. In the meantime, we were allowed to be alone together much more than before. Carrying on with our new habit of taking long walks whenever the weather permitted, our understanding of each other increased day by day. There seemed to be no end of new avenues of conversation to explore, and even some old questions to answer.

In a playful spirit one afternoon, Elizabeth began, "I did my best the other day to explain how my violent dislike turned into violent admiration. Now it is your turn. How do you account for ever having fallen in love with me? Oh, I can comprehend your going on charmingly when you had once made a beginning; but what could have set you off in the first place?"

"I cannot fix on the hour, or the spot, or the look, or the words which laid the foundation. It is too long ago, and I was in the middle before I knew that I had begun."

"My beauty you had early withstood, and as for my manners… My behavior to you was at least always bordering on the uncivil, and I never spoke to you without rather wishing to give you pain than not. Now be sincere; did you admire me for my impertinence?"

"For the liveliness of your mind, I did."

"You may as well call it impertinence at once. It was very little less. The fact is, you were sick of civility, of deference, of officious attention. You were disgusted with the women who were always speaking and looking and thinking only for your approbation. No doubt I roused an interest in you, because I was so unlike them. There! I have saved you the trouble of accounting for it. And really, all things considered, I begin to think it perfectly reasonable. To be sure, you knew no actual good of me, but nobody thinks of that when they fall in love."

"Was there no good in your affectionate behavior to Jane, while she was ill at Netherfield?"

"Dearest Jane! Who could have done less for her? But make a virtue of it by all means." We walked on a little. "So then what was it that caused you to come to the point at last? For the second time, I mean," she added with a look of chagrin.

"The groundwork was laid at Pemberley."

"I am almost afraid of asking what you thought of me when we met there. Did you blame me for coming?"

"No, indeed; I felt nothing but surprise. And then at once I resolved to show you, by every civility in my power, that I was not so mean as to resent the past. I hoped to obtain your forgiveness, or at least to lessen your ill opinion by letting you see that your reproofs had been attended to. I could not be sure, but your manner seemed to indicate some success in this. I was so hopeful then, but there was one more impediment to clear up first."

I looked about and spotted a fallen log. "Here, let us sit down, for there is something I must relate to you before we go any further."

And so I told Elizabeth the story of all my dealings with Amelia Lambright. She listened, looking thoughtful but unalarmed.

"So when you came to Lambton that morning," she said after I had finished, "you came to tell me goodbye."

"Exactly. I was miserable but resigned. I thought it would be the last time I would ever see you."

"As did I, but for different reasons. Oh! What a near thing it was! What a narrow escape! No, I do not mean that as it sounded. No doubt Miss Lambright is a lovely girl, and perhaps you might have been happy with her. But how glad I am that she ran off with somebody else instead!"

"As am I. And so I came to Netherfield to see if I would be encouraged enough to try you again. Then Lady Catherine's report gave me the final push, as I have told you before."

"Poor Lady Catherine. Shall you ever have courage enough to tell her what is to befall her?"

"It shall be done and done directly, as soon as we return to the house."

"Very well. And if I had not an aunt of my own also deserving of a letter, I might sit by you and admire the evenness of your writing, as another young lady once did. But we may compare the results when we are both finished, shall we?"

So while Elizabeth wrote to her aunt, Mrs. Gardiner...

Dearest Aunt,

I would have thanked you before, as I ought to have done, for your long, kind, and very satisfactory letter. But to say the truth, I was too cross to write. You supposed more than really existed at the time. But now suppose as much as you choose. Give a loose to your fancy. Indulge your imagination in every possible flight which the subject will afford, and unless you believe me actually married, you cannot greatly err.

You must write again very soon, and praise him a great deal more than you did in your last. I thank you again and again for not going to the Lakes. How could I be so silly as to wish it! Your idea of the ponies is delightful. We will go round the Park every day.

I am the happiest creature in the world. I am happier even than Jane. She only smiles; I laugh. Mr. Darcy sends you all the love in the world that he can spare from me. You are all to come to Pemberley at Christmas...

...I wrote to mine in a very different style.

Dear Aunt,

I am a most fortunate man. Miss Elizabeth Bennet has done me the great honor of accepting my proposal, and we are to be married in November. I do not delude myself into thinking you will receive this news gladly. However, now that everything is definitely settled, I pray you will endeavor to adjust your mind toward accepting my decision, that you will determine to put aside your former prejudices and welcome into the family the lady who is soon to be my wife. All further intercourse between Pemberley and Rosings depends on it, for my sister and I will by no means continue to associate with any person who persists in insulting someone we both care for so deeply. The matter is entirely in your hands, Madam.

"Yours is very well done," I said after we had each read the other's. I am sure it will give your aunt much enjoyment."

"Certainly much more than *your* aunt can expect. I do not know but what I would give your letter my preference, for I like hearing myself praised, especially by you." A moment later, she continued. "I said 'Poor Lady Catherine,' but now that I consider, it is Caroline Bingley who deserves our sympathy whenever this news should overtake her. To be losing both you and her brother to the unworthy Bennet sisters! To learn that all her ideas of felicity and consequence are to be overthrown in one day, she is much to be pitied."

"Fortunately, that is not *my* letter to write," I said.

44
Two Shall Become One

I stayed at Netherfield for more than a week after Elizabeth and I formed our engagement, spending most of each day in her delightful company. Then it was time for me to go home to Pemberley for a short interval before returning with Georgiana for the wedding.

What can I say about the day that formed the culmination of the hopes and dreams of so many months duration? It marked the single most significant day of my life, upon which depended every day that has followed since.

The wedding itself was a small affair at the Bennets' parish church, with only family members and a few close friends attending. Mr. Bingley had his sisters and Mr. Hurst. I had only Georgiana and Fitzwilliam. Jane and Elizabeth were better represented. With them were their parents, Mary, Kitty, their Aunt and Uncle Phillips, and their Aunt and Uncle Gardiner.

Mr. and Mrs. Collins came from Hunsford but nobody else. Not surprisingly, Lady Catherine declined to be present, writing in part… *As for your suggestion that I meekly accept your decision and your intended bride, this can never be! My character, which has been ever celebrated for its frankness, will not permit it…* and so forth. I believe Anne would have come to celebrate with us had she not been prevented by her mother.

The ceremony, read from The Book of Common Prayer, was most remarkable for the fact that there were two couples taking their vows at once. A fine breakfast followed – extravagant by Longbourn standards – and then at last Elizabeth and I could be off on our own, man and wife, driving by carriage into town to spend the wedding night at Darcy House. It was a long drive, but there were small friendly compensations along the way. Plus I considered the situation at Darcy House as much to be preferred to an inn for comfort and privacy.

I was proud and pleased to introduce my new wife to what would henceforth be her home whenever we were in town. I knew Elizabeth was nervous, but we got through the arrival ceremonies without incident, she behaving before the assembled servants as if she were perfectly accustomed to being the mistress of a great house. Then I insisted on giving her a tour of the principle rooms myself, the public rooms on the main level and then the bedrooms above.

"This chamber," I said as I opened a door on the bedroom level, "I had newly furnished especially for your arrival, my love. I hope you will find it to your liking."

Looking about herself, Elizabeth got no more than two steps inside before stopping, her eye arrested by the well-appointed bed, it seemed.

At her hesitation, I went on. "You can, of course, make any alterations you like… if it does not suit you… in any way at all."

"No!" she said at last, recovering her voice. "No, I would not change a thing. It is a very handsome room. Everything is just as I would have wished. Thank you," she said, briefly laying a hand on my arm.

"I am glad you approve," I said, much relieved. "Your dressing room is there to the left and this…" I moved to the right and opened a door. "This leads to the master's bedchamber."

"*Your* room? And this one is mine?" Elizabeth asked in some confusion.

"Exactly."

"But… but I had thought… That is…"

Understanding her then, I said, "Oh, no, never fear. We may arrange things between ourselves as we like. Just because there *are* two rooms… and two beds, that does not obligate us to use them both… separately, that is. In fact, I hope…" I stopped and tried again. "What I mean is, everything will be managed for your comfort, Elizabeth. I promise."

"That is very good of you. However," She gave me an arch smile. "I trust, Husband, that we, both of us, will find sharing the *same* bed is the most convenient." She moved through the doorway into my bedchamber, where she added, "… and the most rewarding."

After such an agreeable suggestion, it would have been difficult to pull myself from the room. But as I moved to kiss my tempting wife, a servant appeared to say that the dinner I had ordered was ready to be served. Elizabeth and I exchanged a longing look and then retreated to the dining room.

No doubt it was a very fine supper, well prepared, but neither of us could do it justice. The delicately roasted quail went nearly untouched. The parsley potatoes failed to hold our interest. We drank our wine without tasting it. The cook was not the least to blame; our appetites were simply engaged elsewhere.

Finally giving up all pretense of interest, we abandoned our dinner. Taking my bride's hand, I kissed it and led her towards the stairs.

"You are, perhaps, a little uneasy," I whispered in her ear as we ascended. "That would only be natural."

"Perhaps, but only a very little bit."

"Your mother has prepared you well, then."

She laughed. "Hardly! I owe to my Aunt Gardiner whatever useful education on the subject I have acquired."

I could not help smiling at this. "I have always liked your aunt; now I have one more reason to appreciate and admire her."

We paused at the door to Elizabeth's bedchamber. After looking right and left to be sure we were alone, I raised her chin and kissed her, softly first and then more deeply. Then I forced myself to break away. "Call your maid to assist you undressing," I said in a low voice. "I will come to you shortly."

After one more kiss, I remained stationary while my new wife opened the door and slowly passed through it, our eyes, hands, and then just our fingers tips maintaining contact until the last possible instant.

The door closed, parting us, but only temporarily. God had joined *this man and this woman* together in holy matrimony, and soon the two would become one flesh.

Those words repeated themselves in my mind and imagination as I made my own preparations and then waited. Hearing faint murmurings from the adjoining room, I could not help picturing what must be taking place on the other side of the wall. Elizabeth's maid would be helping her to shed her gown and don her night clothes, letting down her long, dark hair. Yes, I could well imagine, and it was near torture to remain where I was. Next time, I would suggest that *I* do those things for her myself.

When it was quiet again and I believed she was alone, I lightly knocked. "Elizabeth?" I called softly.

A delicious thrill ran through me when the door slowly opened. For a moment, we both stood there motionless, gazing at each other, the glow of candlelight revealing the outline of Elizabeth's form through her sheer nightdress, her hair down about her shoulders. I had never in my life seen a more beautiful sight. I was completely transfixed, filled with awe and wonder – at her nearness and at my tremendous good fortune. Then suddenly we were in each other's arms.

45
Epilogue

Our marriage was the starting point for the rest of my life. It is a marriage in which I have been supremely happy, and I pray Elizabeth and I are so fortunate as to have many, many more years together, our friends and our children gathered about us.

I can barely remember the time when I believed a loveless marriage acceptable, even preferable. Yes, to love potentially puts one at peril, and there will no doubt be pain ahead at some point. But to live without love would be the greater risk, for that would be no life at all.

We were home to Pemberley by the first day of December, Georgiana with us, and the house was filled with company and laughter at Christmastime, as it had not been for years and years.

Elizabeth, with Mrs. Reynolds to guide her, quickly mastered what she did not already know about managing a household like Pemberley. Her courageous spirit and native intelligence more than made up for whatever might have been lacking in her up-bringing. I need not have worried about my father's caution that such a task would be beyond any woman who had not been born to it.

The attachment between my wife and my sister soon grew to be everything I could have wished for. They were able to love each other quite as well as they had expected to from the beginning. I often found them closeted together, deep in talk upon subjects to which I was not admitted. Ah, the mysteries of the female mind...

The two soon began to collaborate with their music as well. Georgiana was undoubtedly the more accomplished at the piano-forte but Elizabeth at singing. The result of their combined efforts proved superior to what either could produce alone, and I was the chief beneficiary nearly every evening.

One more advantage appeared. With a new sisterly presence at Pemberley, Georgiana no longer felt the need of a permanent establishment in London. She was content to be where we were, whether town or country, which is just how Elizabeth and I liked it. It was the same with Mrs. Annesley, who continued with us as Georgiana's companion and tutor for a little while longer. When she did leave us to care for her ailing mother, there seemed no need to replace her. The void had already been filled by Elizabeth.

Considering how things had transpired – the fact that Amelia and I went our separate ways – intercourse between Pemberley and Ravenshaw very naturally subsided again. But then one day in April, unexpected visitors arrived.

A quality carriage drew up in front of the house, and from it alighted Mr. and Mrs. John Fairhaven. I had not seen Amelia since the summer; I had only heard that Lord Harcourt and Lord Avery had both recognized their marriage and received them. All was forgiven, and soon it would be forgotten that the way the couple had wed was not quite the thing.

Since I happened to be returning from the stables, I met them when they arrived.

"Are we welcome here, William?" Amelia asked hesitantly, without taking even a step toward the front door.

"Yes, of course you are!" I exclaimed. "I am very glad to see you, Amelia, Mr. Fairhaven. And so shall Elizabeth be. Do come in."

"Thank you, sir," said Fairhaven.

"Elizabeth is your wife, I think," said Amelia as I escorted them in. "I heard that you had married as well. I am glad for you."

"Thank you," I said, feeling my cheeks warm slightly. Then seeing the butler, I continued to him, "Oh, Henderson, do tell Mrs.

Darcy that we have guests. Ask her to join us in the drawing room."

I led the way, and we traded a few basic civilities until Elizabeth arrived. When I made the introductions, Elizabeth's face lit with interest upon hearing Amelia's name.

"Do sit beside me, Mrs. Fairhaven," she said. "My husband has mentioned you, and I am delighted to make your acquaintance."

Mr. Fairhaven sat nearer to me, saying, "I cannot suppose that you remember meeting me before, Mr. Darcy. It had been so long ago."

"Of course I do, Mr. Fairhaven, at the Ravenshaw ball. We were engaged in some rivalry for Amelia's attentions, as I recall."

"It was just as you say. I believe you had the upper hand at the time. No one could have guessed that *I* would be the one who would come away with the prize in the end," he said, looking adoringly at Amelia.

"You are to be congratulated, sir," I remarked.

I attended as best I could as Fairhaven related to me where they were living and the improvements they planned. I answered his questions about Pemberley and whether or not there was much sport to be had. However, I admit that I was much distracted by the surreal sight of Elizabeth and Amelia – both of whom I had proposed marriage to more than once – sitting side by side across from us, chattering away like the best of friends.

"Would you like to see the garden?" I heard Elizabeth ask. "It is just waking up from its winter sleep, of course, but I adore this time of year: new growth everywhere."

"Oh, yes," answered Amelia. "My mother taught me a love of gardening. She was quite partial to roses."

The ladies stood to go and compelled us to accompany them out of doors, which we did without complaint, our own conversation having begun to lag.

After our guest had admired the carefully manicured gardens close to the house, Elizabeth said, "Mr. Fairhaven, do you care for fishing?"

"I do indeed!"

"Then perhaps you would like to acquire a better view of the lake. I would be glad to show you. This way."

She led off with an eager Mr. Fairhaven beside her.

"Shall we?" I said to Amelia, suggesting that we follow.

She smiled and fell into step beside me. Presently, she nodded towards Elizabeth, saying, "She is lovely, William. I am very happy for you."

"As am I for you. Your husband seems entirely devoted to you."

"Yes, John is a darling," she said, smiling and blushing a little. "You are no longer the least bit angry with me, then?"

"I never was. I trust everything has worked out as it should have, for the best of all concerned."

"Doubtless I would have done better to have not accepted your proposal in the first place. But John and I had quarreled, and I was certain that hope was at an end. I just wanted the matter settled as quickly and quietly as possible. That is why I was so insistent that you marry me at once."

"We both made very similar errors along the way. In trying to distinguish what is right, it seems ideas of duty inevitably compete with the heart's desire."

She nodded, and we walked on a little.

"William, I must know," she presently inquired in some agitation. "If I had not flown off at the last moment, would you indeed have married me?"

"Of course, if you still desired it. I had the special license in my pocket."

"Even though you were by then in love with another woman?"

I looked at her in surprise. "How did you know?"

"Because your marriage to Elizabeth is so obviously a love match – anybody spending more than a few minutes in your company must see that – and also because of how soon your own marriage followed mine."

I felt my cheeks heat. "Yes, well, it is true that by the time you accepted me, I had begun forming other ideas for my future. I should have been pleased to release you from our engagement, but

279

I was prepared to put those ideas aside to do my duty. And perhaps we might have got on tolerably well."

"Perhaps. I am glad we did not put it to the test, however."

I nodded. "Affection often grows in a marriage founded on mutual respect, such as the one we originally contemplated. Where one of the parties holds a passionate regard for the other, there is even a better chance of success, I believe, for love can be learned. But I would not wager on the prospects of a union where *both* parties are each in love with somebody else from the start. As you say, it is well that we did not attempt it."

"You and I were meant to be friends, William, not a wedded couple, despite all my girlhood fancies. Did you never guess?"

"Never. Well, perhaps a little. You always seemed inordinately pleased to see me. And then there was the issue of my height."

Amelia laughed. "Yes. Well, my girlish wish finally came true; the tall and handsome Mr. Fitzwilliam Darcy proposed to me. But inexplicably, I ran away and married a different man in the end."

"Yes, quite inexplicable. But seriously, Amelia, I am grateful to you for taking a stand for what you really wanted before it had become too late for all of us. It was a brave thing to do, and I trust you will never be sorry for it."

Gazing at Elizabeth, the sun on her hair and the lake at her back, I knew *I* never would be.

Later, Elizabeth and I stood on the porch to see the Fairhavens on their way. "They seem very worthy sort of people," she said. "Amelia especially perhaps. You certainly need not be ashamed of ever wishing to marry her."

I could tell she was teasing me. "I am *not* ashamed of it. Amelia is indeed a very good sort of woman. I could have done much worse."

"Yes, it merely goes to show that you have sound judgement and admirable, if somewhat changeable, taste. First you preferred her, then me, then her, and then me again. Hmm. By this accounting, I see some sign of inconstancy. I believe that is your true crime after all, Mr. Darcy."

"If it be a crime, I have already been thoroughly punished for it, I assure you. In fact, I might suspect the two of you of conspiring to humble me. To be refused by one worthy woman is a considerable blow to any man's pride. To have a second go so far as to run away to avoid the horrible fate of becoming his wife is too bad indeed. I can only bear it because my humiliation is not widely known."

Elizabeth laughed. "Poor Mr. Darcy. I almost begin to feel sorry for my part in the business. How can I make it up to you? Would you accept a kiss perhaps?"

When she looked up at me, I saw that the teasing had gone, replaced by something speaking more of love merged with desire. I needed no further encouragement. Cupping her face with my hands, I lowered my lips to hers, the kiss progressing from tender to passionate and back again.

"I approve of your way of apologizing," I told her when we at last relaxed our embrace.

She smiled. "I am so glad. But I fear I have not yet fully paid my debt. Perhaps I might finish apologizing to you tonight?" she suggested with a spark in her eye.

"I shall look forward to it."

~~*~~

Since those heady early days, Elizabeth and I have carried on very well together, our love only growing richer and more deeply layered with time. Although there have been both delights and griefs of the sort that are common to all mankind, the blessing of the right helpmeet seems to double every joy and halve every sorrow. Moreover, I have never – not even in the worst of times – regretted making Elizabeth my wife. A day never goes by, in fact, that I do not thank the Lord in heaven for guiding us through our difficulties to form this happy union.

I often marvel over it, reviewing in my mind how it so easily could have been otherwise, how at any one of a dozen turning points we might have been carried in different directions. We might have kept missing each other, the timing always off.

Were it not for the necessity of intervening in Wickham's designs on Georgiana, I would have proposed to Amelia at a time she was disposed to accept me. No doubt we should soon have been married, and I would never have met Elizabeth. Or if I had, it would have been too late.

Instead, fortuitous delays – including Amelia's own hesitation – prevented me from moving forward with my early plans, thus giving me time to encounter Elizabeth in Meryton, Hunsford, and finally at Pemberley, until we at last understood each other. Even then, we might have missed our chance. Had not Wickham's actions again required an immediate response from me, Amelia would have had no time to reconsider her decision that I should marry her at once.

And so, were it not for providence, Elizabeth and I might never have come together at all. But now we are two ships, not silently passing in the night or meeting on hostile terms, but peaceably berthed together, side by side in a safe harbor.

The sublime wonder of the happy resolution to these events, now well in the past, occupies my thoughts again upon waking this morning. I yawn and open my eyes. Sunlight is winking through a narrow gap in the draperies, casting the vanguard rays about the room. Yet there is enough illumination for me to distinguish my surroundings.

I am at home, at Pemberley. And when I glance down, I see Elizabeth, just where she should be. Her head is resting on my shoulder, her dark lashes fanned across her cheeks and her tousled hair spilling over my arm in silken waves. Seeing her there is no hallucination or trick of the light. It is a glorious dream, one still coming true.

The End

About the Author

Shannon Winslow specializes in writing for the fans of Jane Austen. Her best-selling debut novel, *The Darcys of Pemberley* (2011), immediately established her place in the genre, being particularly praised for the author's authentic Austenesque style and faithfulness to the original characters. Since that auspicious beginning, Winslow has steadily added to her body of work – several more novels and one nonfiction piece – to make a total of eleven books published so far:

- *The Darcys of Pemberley*
- *Return to Longbourn*
- *Miss Georgiana Darcy of Pemberley*
- *The Ladies of Rosings Park*
- *Fitzwilliam Darcy in His Own Words*
- *For Myself Alone*
- *The Persuasion of Miss Jane Austen*
- *Murder at Northanger Abbey*
- *Leap of Faith: Second Chance at the Dream*
- *Leap of Hope: Chance at an Austen Kind of Life*
- *Prayer & Praise: a Jane Austen Devotional*

Her two sons grown, Ms. Winslow lives with her husband in the log home they built in the countryside south of Seattle, where she writes and paints in her studio facing Mt. Rainier.

Learn more about the author and her work at her website/blog: www.shannonwinslow.com.